"A rough-and-tumble ent_____ and plots twists a-plenty."

—*Kirkus Reviews* on *Breakthrough*

"Fast-paced, suspenseful."

—*Publishers Weekly* on *Breakthrough*

"*Exposure*, Pineiro's fifth book, is suspenseful and exciting."

—*The Baton Rouge Morning Advocate*

"Grisham fans will enjoy this well-written version of *The Pelican Brief* meets *The Net*."

—*Austin American Statesman* on *Exposure*

"As frighteningly real as tomorrow's headlines."

—Richard Henrick, author of *Crimson Tide*, on *Retribution*

"A scary scenario. . . . First rate."

—*Texas Monthly* on *Retribution*

"The action has a dramatic, urgent flair that has entertained readers and audiences since the days of Errol Flynn. All in all, if you like books that you almost can't put down and that keep you on the edge of your seat, you won't regret reading *Ultimatum*."

—*Austin Chronicle*

Books by R. J. Pineiro

*forthcoming

R. J. PINEIRO

Y2K

TOR®

A TOM DOHERTY ASSOCIATES BOOK
NEW YORK

This is a work of fiction. All the characters and events portrayed in this book are either products of the author's imagination or are used fictitiously.

Y2K

A Tor Book
Published by Tom Doherty Associates, LLC
175 Fifth Avenue
New York, NY 10010

www.tor.com

Tor® is a registered trademark of Tom Doherty Associates, LLC.

ISBN: 0-812-56867-2

First edition: October 1999

Printed in the United States of America

0 9 8 7 6 5 4 3 2 1

For all the children:

Cameron, Michael, Bobby, Kevin, Paola, Julio Cesar, Eddie, Rogelito, Juan Pablo, and Lorenzito.

In your hands you carry our families' hopes and dreams into the new millennium.

And

For Saint Jude, with my eternal gratitude.

ACKNOWLEDGMENTS

As always, there are many wonderful people to thank for their help throughout the process. All mistakes, of course, are mine and only mine. Thanks go to:

My wife Lory, "the best thing that's ever happened to me," for all your patience, understanding, and encouragement during the many nights and weekends I spent writing and rewriting this story.

Tom Doherty for taking a chance with me way back when, for your personal attention during my trips to New York, for treating me like one of the family, and for publishing the finest books in the industry.

Bob Gleason, my editor and friend, for your tireless and professional work. Your insightful feedback has made *Y2K* a better story.

The rest of the staff at Tor, in particular Linda Quinton, Jennifer Marcus, Karen Lovell, Steve de las Heras, and Ed Cooper.

Matt Bialer, my agent at William Morris, for all your help and confidence through the years.

My good friend Dave, for your technical support on weapons, tactics, and related subjects.

My parents, Rogelio and Dora, my sisters, Irene and Dora, and also my wonderful in-laws, Mike, Linda, Bill, and Maureen, for always being a source of support and inspiration.

Thank You,

R.J. Pineiro
Austin, Texas
June, 1999

Book One

■

The Profession

■

"The fox knows many tricks, but the hedgehog's trick is the best of all."

—Pigres

1

London, England. February, 1999.

Kate Donaldson breathed in the chilled air while running
a hand inside her leather jacket, reassurance filling her at
the touch of the cold stainless-steel slide of the Beretta
92FS pistol safely tucked in a chest holster. The high-
capacity clip of her semiautomatic held fifteen 9mm
rounds plus one in the chamber, giving her ample firepower which Kate hoped she would not need on this cold
and overcast morning in the British capital.

She zipped up her jacket and freed up her hands, letting
them hang from her sides as she strode up Newton Street.

Never compromise your hands.

Kate abided by this professional habit in the same manner in which she now surveyed her surroundings, checking
for tails without staring at anything in particular, looking
for the telltale signs of someone displaying an unusual
level of interest in her, albeit subtle. Two black cabs

cruised down the tree-lined street. Four teenagers sporting multiple body piercings and colorful hairstyles that defied gravity hung out at the corner, their dark clothing contrasting sharply with the light-colored jogging suits of an elderly couple walking a white poodle. A dozen businessmen marched hastily in both directions, gloved hands clutching attaché cases, folded newspapers tucked under their armpits.

Nothing.

Kate's trained senses, operating in what she called "Yellow Mode," perceived nothing unusual. The CIA operative had long assigned colors to her level of alertness. White was equated with a relaxed state, such as working behind her desk within the protective walls of the CIA headquarters at Langley, Virginia. Yellow constituted the next level up, the lowest in which she operated in the field. In Yellow Mode Kate remained ever-vigilant, always paranoid of someone after her, always concerned about a trap or an assassin or any other danger lurking nearby. Her state of readiness climbed to Orange Mode on visual contact with the enemy. Red Mode meant the discharge of a firearm anywhere outside of a firing range, either to attack or to defend. Her training called for different rules according to her current mode of operation. In Yellow Mode she could never relax, regardless of how safe her environment appeared.

In spite of feeling certain that she had not been followed, Kate continued surveying her surroundings. The shades of gray dominating the local scenery depressed her beyond the fact that today was her fortieth birthday, not that anyone knew it. Her personal records had been classified since the day she signed up to become a CIA officer twenty years ago. Perhaps she should have passed on this assignment and gone to the Caribbean as she had originally planned. Maybe the warm sand and clear waters would have lifted her spirits, compensating for the lack of a personal life. But her superior had insisted that she come here immediately to evaluate a situation.

Evaluate a situation.

The female operative sighed. Working for Counterterrorism within the Directorate of Operations, Kate Donaldson had been evaluating situations for many years. This particular job, however, required more than her standard assessment. Kate had been personally responsible for getting it started six months ago, when the CIA got word of a series of Year 2000 conferences to be held in the British capital in the month of February, sponsored by the European Economic Community to increase awareness of this very real problem as well as to improve communications among the nations forming the EEC. One such conference, where participants included guest speakers from lead software developers and industrialists from the United States and Japan, was scheduled to take place this week. The CIA, charged with the gathering of intelligence on the Year 2000 preparations by other nations, had set up a special surveillance operation under Kate's supervision. This week, however, Langley had stepped up the mission's objective from one of observing to one of *protecting*. The American speakers were executives from Fortune 500 companies leading the way on Y2K preparations.

Kate turned right at the corner of Newton and Oxford, walked two blocks, and went into the underground at Holborn Station, where she caught a random train, exiting at the next stop and returning to the street. Strolling several blocks, Kate reached another underground station. This time she stepped inside the train but jumped back to the platform just as the doors began to close. No one followed her.

She returned to the street and hailed a cab.

"Royal Opera House," she told the driver, gazing about

her before settling into the rear seat, feeling she had done her best at making certain she had not been followed. Her eyes, however, remained ever-vigilant as the taxi pulled off the curb.

2

Five minutes later the black taxi dropped her off at the steps of the historic Royal Opera House, across from the police court, eight blocks away from her destination: the Kingsley Hotel, adjacent to St. George Bloomsbury church.

Obeying another professional habit, Kate took a longer route to get to the hotel, all the while using tactics mastered long ago to lose anyone persistent enough to still have managed to followed her despite all the precautions taken thus far. She browsed through half a dozen department stores, changing floors often, and exiting through different doors. She backtracked several times, searching for brusque movements in the morning crowd.

Satisfied, she reached a pay phone a block from the church, dialing a number given to her twenty-four hours ago in Langley, Virginia, after she had shoved her Caribbean tickets into a desk drawer.

A deep male voice came on the line after the third ring. "Holland Florist. May I help you?"

Kate frowned at the accent, which sounded neither American nor British. She had set up this operation using CIA officers and a few local agents, British nationals on the CIA's payroll.

She tightened her grip on the phone. *Did Hollis deviate from my instructions?*

Hollis Carter was the youngest CIA officer to ever lead the London Station, mostly because of agency politics. He was the son of Randolph Carter, the former Director of Central Intelligence and current chief advisor to the president. The junior Carter actually wasn't a bad intelligence officer, if only he had been allowed time to gather some experience instead of being promoted before his time.

"Hello? May I help you?"

Definitely foreign, she thought. It actually sounded Slavic.

"How are your red roses today?" she asked.

"Not as good as our yellow."

"What about white?"

"We're expecting a shipment in ten minutes," replied the deep voice, completing the code.

The line went dead. The operation was still active and underway. Had red roses been available today, she was to go back and try again tomorrow, same time. Yellow indicated a temporary hold, a stand-by. White was a go. The brief conversation told Kate to report to the back of the church in ten minutes for a briefing.

She hung up, surveying the area around the large hotel and the church, killing time until she needed to report.

The rear of the seventeenth-century church faced a frozen pond surrounded by brown shrubbery, a few benches, and many trees, their jagged, leafless canopies adding to her depression. The hotel's charcoal facade rose beyond the small park.

A mother and two toddlers played in the snow around

the frozen pond, using peanuts to lure a pair of squirrels away from the safety of an oak.

Kate turned toward the church, strolling down a gravel path bordering the pond. One of the toddlers approached her, a girl dressed in a pink jacket and a furry hat. Her hazel eyes blinked at the CIA officer. She extended her little gloved hand and gave Kate a folded note, before running back to her mother, who took both kids by the hand, walked hastily to the street, and got in the rear of a white Mercedes, which drove off in a hurry. Kate glanced at the coded instructions before sliding the note in a pocket of her black jeans.

She creaked open a rusty, waist-high iron gate leading to a small fenced courtyard, her eyes landing on a wooden door opposite the weathered gate.

Kate opened the door and walked inside the sacristy, memories from her boarding-school days creeping out of long-forgotten corners of her mind. Three years of living with Catholic nuns had taught her more than she needed to know about the different sections of a church. The sacristy was the room in every church where the clergy's vestments and sacred vessels were kept. St. George Bloomsbury's sacristy also included a crucifix, a vestment case whose top served as a vesting table, a kneeler, a lavabo, and the sacrarium, a receptacle emptying directly into the ground for water used in washing the sacred linens.

Beyond the lavabo, a door led to the altar and the nave of the church. A second door, between the kneeler and the sacrarium, marked the only entrance to the bell tower.

Kate headed up the stairs, her left hand holding on to the handrail in the center of the tower. As if it were the church's breathing organ, a chilled downward draft whistled through the bell tower, mixing with the sounds of nesting birds and distant traffic. The crude pine stairs, whose creaky, unpainted steps Kate climbed to a height of about fifty feet, led to a murky corridor also floored in rustic planks of pine. Two men sat on plain chairs facing each other. One sipped from a mug. The second read a newspaper. The narrow hallway was built in the space between the church's vaulted ceiling and the roof. The stairs appeared to continue up to the bell room, the highest room of most churches.

The bulky figures, wearing dark clothing and military-style crew cuts, turned in her direction as she stepped away from the stairs. One of them stood. The other returned to his newspaper.

Kate slowly shook her head. *Amateur hour.*

"Donaldson?" asked the rookie, the mug still in his right hand, which Kate suspected was also his shooting hand.

"Are you gentlemen on break?"

The second rookie looked up from his paper, shooting her a puzzled glance. "Excuse me?"

She approached them, irritated at Carter for giving these young guns so much slack that they had forgotten what they should have been taught at The Farm, the CIA's training academy in Williamsburg, Virginia.

"Is this your idea of protecting the control center for this operation?"

The second rookie also stood, the paper still in his hands.

"Pitch the coffee, lose the paper, and try to *act* like the CIA officers you were trained to be." She walked past the startled duo and went inside.

Nine men crowded the rectangular room, roughly fifteen by thirty. Peeling white walls overlooked a discolored wooden floor. Two of Carter's technicians sat on stools while surveying the street in front of the hotel with bulky scopes mounted atop tripods. The London station chief sat behind them talking on a radio. Six operators wearing headphones and mouthpieces sat behind video and audio gear to the left of the trio. The glaring monitors, a dozen of them stacked three high, showed blinking images of the exterior and interior of the hotel.

Carter looked in her direction when she came in. "You're two minutes late."

"And your men out there are slacking off."

Carter approached her. He was as tall as Kate's five foot nine, with ash-blond hair and blue eyes that shot her an admonishing glare. "They've been on the job for eight straight hours."

"Then replace them with a fresh crew."

"The morning shift is due in another hour and—"

"Excuses are the sign of an amateur."

"Look, I know what I'm doing here. Everything is under control."

"Is it?"

"What does that mean?" he whispered out of earshot from the two spotters by the window and the technicians manning the video and audio gear.

"All right," she said in a low voice, deciding to keep this little chat private. "Let me start. The voice on the phone had a Slavic accent. This operation was to be conducted *exclusively* with our people and local agents—that means Brits, not Slavs. Second, a little girl, almost a toddler, handed me a note with instructions. Since when does the Agency recruit children to do its dirty job? And third, your cover out there is too relaxed. I could have taken them both out in a couple of seconds. And why isn't there anyone in the park to alert you if an enemy team is coming up to neutralize yours?"

Carter stared into the distance for a moment. "We already discussed the third one. As for the first one, his name is Viktor Popov, a Bosnian scientist who's lived in this country for the past five years, since Serbian troops leveled his hometown and killed his family. He's a British citizen now, married to a local. They have two kids. Popov's the software engineering director at Telecom, one of Britain's communications conglomerates. For the past three years he's led Telecom's efforts toward Y2K compliance. I personally recruited him four months ago. We've checked him out thoroughly. He's clean.''

"Why is he answering the classified number?"

"Popov's part of the planning committee for this Y2K convention. Thanks to him we have the itineraries of every person going in and out of that hotel, from speakers and janitors to British security. Problem is that last-minute schedule changes continue even as we speak, and security in the area is tight. We had to make sure that on our end the coast was clear for your arrival. That's why we set up Viktor to answer this number. We didn't want you getting old info and risk walking into British Intelligence, or someone else. We're supposed to be invisible, remember?''

"Why was I never informed of this recruit?"

Carter shrugged. "Guess I didn't want to bother you with it.''

"In the future, *please do,* because it's my ass on the line if something goes wrong. What about the mother and children?''

"Popov's family. He insisted on using them, arguing that it would look natural because his family's staying with him at the hotel during the convention. No one would suspect them playing at the park while daddy was busy working.''

"If they were supposed to be in the vicinity, why is it that they took off right after giving me the note?''

Carter shrugged. "Who knows. Maybe the kids got hungry. They did what they were supposed to. That was their only part. After that I don't care where they go.''

"And the lack of coverage by the church's entrances?''

"The spotters are covering the park and the rear of the

church. As for the front, it is locked at this time of the day.''

Bells were going off in her head. ''This is highly irregular . . . and dangerous. You're putting women and children in danger, and also letting a foreign national handle parts of an operation that should only involve CIA officers. Why is he so willing to help us? What's his motivation for spying for the CIA, committing treason against the country that gave him refuge from the Serbs?''

Carter rubbed a thumb over his index and middle fingers. ''He's in debt up to his eyeballs. Poor financial portfolio. We're helping him get solvent.''

''How much?''

Carter told her.

Kate let out the breath she had been holding and crossed her arms. ''*How* are you paying for this? That amount is well beyond the allowed budget.'' In spite of popular belief, the CIA normally kept a tight rein on expenses, and that included the budget allocated to pay off its agents, the foreign nationals recruited by officers like Carter and Kate.

''Got it approved by the director three months ago.''

Kate felt her blood pressure rising. ''And why wasn't I informed?''

The same shrug. ''I didn't want to—''

''Bother me with it?''

Hollis Carter nodded. ''Sorry. I—''

''Terrific. I take my eye off the ball and everything goes in the wrong direction.'' She turned around and paced the old room.

''You're being overly paranoid. I'm *telling* you,'' he hissed. ''It's under control. I've covered *all* of the bases. Look here.''

Kate shifted her gaze toward the electronic gear.

''I've got ten armed men outside the hotel and just as many inside, all linked to this control room. I've got surveillance cameras everywhere. Anyone going in or out of that place is being recorded.''

The seasoned officer tried to relax. Perhaps Carter was right. Maybe she was just being too apprehensive, but in her business it paid to be suspicious. On the surface, however, Hollis Carter did seem to have the situation under control, even if he had bent a few rules, including bypassing her on some calls.

''All right,'' she finally said. ''But from here on out we're sticking to the book.''

''You've got it.''

''Who else is down there aside from our people?'' she asked, pointing to the video monitors.

''Everyone. FBI, British Intelligence, the Japan Defense Agency, the BND, and also the DGSE.''

The JDA was Japan's version of the CIA. The BND was Germany's intelligence service. The DGSE was France's. ''What about the speakers?''

''The Americans are occupying the fourth floor, the Japanese delegation the third floor. Delegates from European nations are sprinkled in various—''

''Sir?''

Carter turned to one of the technicians manning the surveillance equipment, a kid in his early twenties.

''What is it?''

''Strange, sir. It's Popov. He's leaving the hotel.''

3

"What?" Carter raced to the monitors. The young technician pointed to a figure dressed in a dark suit stepping away from the hotel, briefcase in hand and climbing into a white Mercedes.

"Raise him on the radio!" the London station chief demanded. "The convention is about to start! He's supposed to stay inside to cover the presentations."

A second technician spoke on his headset for a few moments before turning to Carter. "No answer, sir."

Kate's throat felt constricted as she watched the Mercedes drive away from the five-story structure. "That's the same car used by his family at the park. What's going on, Hollis? Why is he rushing away from the building with his family?"

"I—I'm not sure where—"

A powerful explosion rocked the ancient church. Kate and Carter dove away from the windows, which shattered a moment later from the shock wave. The spotters screamed, their faces smeared in blood. Surveillance gear fell off the tables, crashing on the pine floors. The radio technicians jerked their heads back, away from their headphones, momentarily trembling, before falling on the floor unconscious.

The acrid stench of cordite assaulted Kate's nostrils as she raced toward the windows, her professional side forcing her to ignore the fallen men. There was little that she could do for them immediately. The spotters would likely be blind from the shards of glass crusting their faces, but their wounds were not lethal. The technicians, on the other hand, bleeding from their ears and noses, were already dead from the high-pitch sounds of the blast, amplified by their head gear, firing acoustic bullets into their brains.

Kate heard the young guns rush inside the room. "What happened?" one of them asked.

She ignored them. Inky smoke billowed past the jagged edges of the broken windows, engulfing most of the hotel. Tongues of fire flickered above the building, out of windows, projecting scorching debris onto the street. Cries and screams hung in the veiling haze. Figures staggered away from the wreck, through the boiling dust and smoke lifting skyward out of the rubble. Some coughed, others shouted for help, their trembling voices mixing with the concerted wailing of the building's fire alarms.

"Oh, my God!" Carter said, eyes flashing a mix of surprise and horror. "This is impossible!"

"Idiot!" she barked. "You imbecile!"

"I . . . I can't believe that he—"

"He *used* you! You never recruited him! *He* recruited *you!*"

"But—but I took precautions. I checked his background. It all checked out with—"

"You still don't get it, do you? It was all a scam. He knew you would be checking his background. He knew you would check his employment records, his personal life. Did you approach him or did he approach you?"

Flames shot from windows, blasting glass onto the street. Kate rubbed her aching forehead.

"Oh, God," Carter said. "He . . . he came to us."

"And he asked you about your plans to protect the convention?"

"Yes."

"And he offered his help after giving you his credentials?"

"Yes."

"And he put himself in the center of the operation, leaving you on the periphery looking in."

Carter didn't reply. He clutched the windowsill and gazed out at the commotion on the street.

"Was he the one who suggested the surveillance for the convention?"

He nodded. "He knew the place well. It seemed natural . . . *damn him.*"

Kate briefly inspected him before turning back to the chaos below, shoulders aching with anxiety, her stomach tightening. "What a mess. What a *fucking* mess." She turned to the rookie operatives and pointed at the two wounded surveillance men. "Pick them up. We're taking them with us."

"What about them?" asked Carter, pointing at the technicians on the floor.

Kate walked up to each one and checked for a pulse. As she had suspected, the acoustic energy had pierced their brains. Death had been instant. "There's nothing we can do for them. Were you following procedure on IDs?"

Hollis Carter, although visibly nervous, managed a slight nod, meaning that none of his operatives carried any identification that could link them to the Agency.

"All right, then. Let's get out of here."

Kate led the way, rushing down the creaky stairway,

followed by the rookies carrying the bleeding men. Carter went last. Their footsteps echoed up and down the bell tower, mixing with the muffled sound of the hotel's blaring alarms and also with the roaring sirens of nearing emergency vehicles.

Her heart hammering her chest, Kate reached the sacristy moments later and headed for the door leading to the courtyard. A tiny cloud of gravel abruptly formed by her feet, on the walkway connecting the entry way to the weathered gate of the courtyard. Frozen dirt suddenly erupted to her immediate right.

She sprung back into the sacristy, as if having stepped on a nest of scorpions. In the same motion, she reached for her Beretta 92FS and flipped the safety with her thumb, pointing the muzzle at the entry.

"Get back!"

"What—what's going on?" demanded the blond rookie, who was hauling one of the wounded operatives.

"Someone's got this door covered from a vantage point. We have to find another way out!"

"The front!" shouted Carter, heading out of the sacristy. "I hear the fire trucks and police cars! The commotion should cover us!"

"I thought you said it was locked!"

"I've got a key!"

They rushed into the altar, facing the ocean of pews crowding the long nave, under cathedral ceilings. At the other end, the vestibule led to the huge wooden doors dominating the front of the church. A massive pipe organ, surrounded by seats high above the vestibule, soared toward the cathedral ceiling, partially blocking the light shafting through the large, round stained-glass window behind it.

The smell of burning wood reached Kate. For a moment she thought it was the smoking incense next to the alabaster altar, or perhaps the candles surrounding the wooden statue of an unknown saint on the wall to her immediate right. But her nostrils told her it was the smell of a fire.

"It smells like . . ." began Carter, his weapon drawn. Both rookies also clutched pistols.

"I know," she said, scanning the empty church with her semiautomatic.

In the nearly hypnotic silence of the church, Kate heard several muffled spits. Carter collapsed behind a pew while clutching his shoulder, an agonizing scream echoing inside the nave. The blond rookie reached for his neck, blood jetting from a severed larynx as he dropped to his knees. Two more silent rounds struck the wounded operative he was carrying. Both men fell. In the same instant the second rookie also collapsed, victim to a fusillade of silent rounds, striking the floor like a sack of coal.

Kate immediately rolled toward the nearest pew. Dark floors, stained glass, towering columns, and cathedral ceilings blurred into a single image as she followed her trained instincts and kept the roll until her shoulder struck the oak pew. She inhaled once, twice, her chest swelling.

"Damn it!" hissed Carter, two pews away, trying to get back on his feet.

"Stay down," Kate said quietly. "I'm going to try to draw their fire to force them to show themselves."

On clambering hands and knees Kate crawled beneath the pew, wedging herself into the space between the floor and the bottom of the seat, her heartbeat throbbing behind her ears. She reached for the folded kneeling board of the pew behind her, lowering it, squeezing through the opening, reaching the same space in the pew in front, her face only an inch from the bottom of the seat.

Hastening footsteps over wooden planks overhead telegraphed the presence of two, perhaps three shooters. Breaking a sweat, Kate controlled her breathing and scrambled down to the end of the pew facing the center aisle. She crawled away from her improvised cover and rose to a deep crouch, her narrowed eyes searching for a target.

A near miss buzzed in her ear like an angered hornet, splintering the seat of the pew. A second round struck the Beretta just forward of the handle grip, nicking the skin between her thumb and index finger.

"Aghh!" She dropped the gun, clutching her bleeding right hand with her left, diving for the cover of a pew across the aisle. A brief glance at her hand told her the wound was superficial. She could still move all of her fingers, but she no longer had her weapon, which had skittered out of sight. It was at that moment that Kate Donaldson noticed the billowing smoke accumulating in the vaulted ceiling.

Ignoring her wounded hand, Kate lowered the kneeling board of the pew in front, squeezing through the opening, repeating the process several times, making her way back toward the altar.

Her ears tuned to footsteps clicking over the slate floor. It was just a matter of time before she would be found and also shot.

Create a distraction.

Kate needed something to distract the incoming assassin long enough for her to mount an attack.

She reached for the pew's built-in shelf, grabbing a burgundy prayer book, the size of a hardcover but almost two inches thick. Sweating profusely now from the commotion of the past few minutes and also from the rapidly rising temperature, she removed her belt, tying it around the tome to keep it from opening.

A pair of dark slacks slowly neared.

Wedged between the bottom of a seat and the cool slate floor, Kate felt the weight of her weapon, almost as heavy as a brick. She remembered using bricks as weapons during her gang years in San Antonio, Texas, before a near-death experience reformed her. She recalled holding them by one end and throwing them as she would a knife, improving range and accuracy.

Holding her breath, the *whoosh* of the glaring flames growing to an ear-piercing crescendo, Kate Donaldson pressed a corner of the book against her bloody palm, holding it in place with her thumb and forefinger, tight against her torn skin. The heat grew unbearable. She had to get out quickly or risk perishing in the rapidly spreading fire.

The assassin, now two pews away, stopped the moment hastening footsteps from across the nave became discernible through the roar of the fire. She saw the feet point away, meaning the assassin was looking away from her.

Briefly closing her eyes and swallowing the lump in her throat, Kate Donaldson rolled out from under the seat, surging from the floor in one fluid motion, her right hand already above and behind her head, vise-like fingers clamping the heavy tome.

The figure turned his weapon toward her just as Kate, mustering strength, flung the book at him with all her might.

The red tome streaked across the fifteen feet separating them, striking the assassin right above the sternum, the momentum pushing him back and forcing him to point the weapon at the ceiling.

As if a spring had snapped within her, Kate charged, hands tucked in mid-chest, elbows extended, the right one aimed at the disoriented assassin's head.

The assassin abruptly stepped sideways, and Kate ran past him without connecting, a paralyzing pain seizing her as the assassin drove the weapon's stock into her back. She crashed against a brick wall, bounced, and collapsed on the slate floor. The descending smoke partially obscured her executioner, who turned the weapon in her direction.

4

Two shots cracked above the blaring inferno, and the assassin's silhouette collapsed by Kate's feet, his weapon clattering across the slate floor.

Confused, Kate saw another figure, a weapon in his right hand, left hand clutching his wounded shoulder.

"Come," Carter said, his face darkened by the smoke, his free hand reaching behind him and producing Kate's Beretta. He had secured a white piece of cloth around his shoulder, slowing the blood loss.

"Are you okay?" she asked, rapidly getting up.

"I'll live."

Kate grabbed her weapon and used it to scan the church, detecting motion by the vestibule. The nave became enshrouded in darkness as the smoke expanded across the vaulted ceilings, like an angered storm cloud, descending over the pipe organ above the vestibule, enveloping it, obscuring Kate's target as she took aim at the figure rushing past the huge organ, toward the side staircase.

Kate fired once, twice, the reports roaring inside the church, stinging her ears. The spent cartridges were flung to the side by the recoil. The silhouetted figure disappeared behind the swirling haze.

"Did I get him?"

"Hard . . . hard to tell," Carter said. "We have to get . . . out of here." His wound was weakening him.

"Hide here! I'll be right back."

"I'm coming with—"

"No time to argue! Save your strength to get out of here and make it to the safe house!" Kate rushed down the side of the nave, toward the bottom of the stairs, her sneakers drumming over the slate floors, her eyes searching, scanning, probing, struggling to detect her quarry through the inky cloud overhead.

Stroboscopic flashes abruptly erupted from the thick smoke in the vestibule, like unseen lightning. The flickering flames sealed the exit through the main doors.

She stopped, gazing back toward the altàr, barely visible in the smoke. They were trapped, unable to move forward or back.

Two bulky figures wearing black hoods emerged through the dark vestibule on the opposite side of the nave, their hands clutching Uzi submachine guns.

Dropping to one knee while lining up the larger figure in the Beretta's sights, Kate fired twice, the blasts deafening, the spent cartridges ejected through the opening on the top of the weapon's slide. The figure arched back just as the second one leveled the Uzi at her.

Diving as the blaring reports thundered inside the nave, she landed on her side, cursing the searing pain in the middle of her back from the blow inflicted by the first assassin.

Bullets swept by at waist level, striking wood, metal, and glass alike, splintering statues, shattering carnation-filled vases. Sparks exploded as rounds struck a brass pot, the sounds mixing with the roar of the swelling flames consuming the century-old wooden ceiling like a ravenous predator.

Keeping her finger off the trigger, Kate rolled away, landing in a semi-crouch fifteen feet away, closer to the altar, a hot wind swirling the smoke, brightened by tongues of fire licking the ceiling, reaching the columns. She estimated only minutes before the roof collapsed into the nave.

The gunfire stopped, followed by clicking footsteps, roaring flames, and the wailing of fire engines.

Peeking over the edge of a pew, Kate saw a figure racing toward the sacristy, obviously trying to get away before the fire sealed their last exit

She lurched forward still in a semi-crouch, partly shrouded by the darkness, feeling the heat on her forehead, her fingers curled around the handle of the semiautomatic, eyes glued to her target. She fired as the figure reached the steps by the altar, the rounds transferring their energy, propelling him forward.

Coughing, her burning eyes blinking as she made out the outline of Hollis Carter slumped on a pew, Kate removed her jacket and pressed the sleeve of her shirt against her mouth, breathing through it as she raced toward the young station chief. Her lungs rebelling, her throat seared by the hot smoke, she shook her CIA colleague.

"Let's go!"

Carter stirred back to life. She helped him to his feet.

Heaving, tears rolling freely out of his bloodshot eyes, Carter shouted, "The front doors . . . are ablaze!"

Kate pointed toward the sacristy, across the nave, next to the altar. "We have to go back! It's our only way out!"

They reached the altar in seconds. A huge burning beam broke loose from the ceiling above the vestibule, crashing over the pipe organ, its momentum powerful enough to crack the fire-weakened second floor, collapsing it. The gigantic organ and dozens of burning pews cascaded over the entrance in a scorching mass of dust and sparks and twisted metal. The array of brass pipes, like a thousand apocalyptic horns, blasted a brief, deafening sound that thundered across the nave. The structure rumbled from the phenomenal impact of several tons of wood and metal against the vestibule floor.

Dashing across the smoke-filled altar, she reached the sacristy, her skin burning from the intense heat, her lungs protesting the hot breaths inflating them.

She was about to push the door, but it was locked. Someone had bolted it and it could not be unlocked without a key.

"Stand back!" she commanded, aiming her 9mm pistol and blasting three rounds at the lock, cracking it while creating a shower of sparks. The heavy door swung open and a rush of fresh air streamed in, like a wind tunnel, filling the sacristy and continuing onto the main nave to feed the inferno.

Kate grabbed Carter's hand and jerked him forward. "Move! We don't have much time!"

They raced into the courtyard, landing on the gravel patch. She rapidly rolled away from the entry way, reaching the bushes to the left of the door, urging Carter to do the same. But the station chief staggered back toward the protection of the doorway, obviously concerned about a sniper.

"Get away from there!" she shouted while bracing herself for a sniper's bullet fired from a vantage point, but the impact never came. "The fire! Move!"

A gargantuan roar, like a primeval demon, surged through the church, getting louder, increasing in intensity, until it blasted through the only opening feeding the hungry flames with oxygen.

"Christ, Carter! Get the hell out of the—"

In a blur, a horizontal column of fire erupted through

the doorway, enveloping Carter, blasting him against the brick wall of the courtyard twenty feet away.

The young officer's screams echoed loudly over the roaring fire as he crashed onto a patch of frozen grass, flames shrouding him.

"Mother of God!" Kate mumbled as the fire receded back into the sacristy, only to reappear a second later. The blinding column swallowed Carter once again, before vanishing back inside the building.

She rushed toward him, shoveling snow over him, putting out the flames.

Kate felt sick, staring at a face that resembled fried bacon. Carter shivered, trembling from the intense pain, his bloated lips murmuring something Kate could not make out.

Controlling her emotions, momentarily forgetting about a sniper attack, she leaned down, pressing her right ear against his quivering lips.

"Kill . . . me . . . please . . ."

Kate Donaldson swallowed the lump in her throat, forcing savage control into her thoughts.

"Please . . . Kate . . . kill . . . me . . ."

Kate knew that Hollis Carter would not last another hour. Even the best medical care could not possibly salvage what had not been consumed by the flames.

Pulling out her Beretta, she pressed it against his forehead, swallowing hard. "May God forgive me for this."

Closing her eyes, she pulled the trigger. At once all movement ceased.

Shoving her emotions aside, realizing that such demons would catch up with her later, Kate stood, scanning her surroundings, spotting several fire engines arriving, their sires wailing. Figures in long, yellow coats leaped out of them, hauling hoses to the side of the church, roughly two hundred feet from where she stood. Multiple streams of high-pressure water projected toward the burning buildings, fighting the pulsating flames.

Kate Donaldson slowly walked away.

5

In the bedroom of a third-story flat overlooking Hyde Park, Kate Donaldson watched the images flashing on the small television set over the dresser while the contract physician stitched up her hand. The keeper of the safe house read a newspaper in the living room.

Her eyes stared at the rubble, at the destruction caused by a terrorist strike that had taken place right under their noses. In her mind flashed a vision of Carter, the man responsible for this mess, but also the man who had saved her life inside the church, and the man who had suffered such a terrible death.

The physician finished and left without saying a word.

She got up and walked to the window, flexing her hand, her mind considering her options, the implications of what had taken place, the reality of an operation technically under her command going astray. The mid-morning sun had burned off most of the fog, exposing a clear sky, darkened only by the distant column of smoke on the other side of the park. News of the bombing had already interrupted many regularly scheduled programs. The death count had reached seven hundred, most of them attendees and speakers at the Y2K convention.

What a mess.

She checked her watch, frowning not only at the sight of the bandage between her thumb and index finger, but also at the irony that it was exactly the time of her birth forty years ago.

Happy birthday to me.

The phone on the nightstand rang. The line was secure. She picked it up on the second ring.

"Yes?"

"Is the weather in London pleasant?"

"Not as pleasant as in Rome," she replied, completing the code.

"What happened?" the voice demanded. It was one of the controllers in Langley who would listen to her version of the incident, as well as of the few CIA officers who survived the bombing at the hotel, then review all of the files before forwarding a summary to Mike Costner. Costner was the Chief of Counterterrorism within the Directorate of Operations of the CIA, and Kate's boss. Costner would review the entire file and make a recommendation to *his* boss, the Deputy Director of Operations. From there, the report would be reviewed and further amended by the Director of Operations, who would consider the input from every manager along the reporting chain and make a final recommendation to the Director of Central Intelligence. The DCI would in turn settle on a final position for the Agency before briefing the president.

She spent the next ten minutes providing her assessment of the incident, carefully articulating her perceptions of every aspect of this mission, from its conception to the events leading up to the unexpected strike. Kate was well aware that everything she said was being recorded and would be scrutinized by a team of experts in Langley. In the end, this was a screw-up of phenomenal proportions, and Kate Donaldson's name was associated with this mess, regardless of the fact that Carter had purposefully excluded her from some of the decisions that in her opinion played a major role in the bombing.

The voice informed Kate that she would be getting a phone call from her boss before the end of the day. The line went dead.

Kate calmly hung up the phone and returned to the windows overlooking Hyde Park, but in her mind she saw a different park. Kate Donaldson saw Brackenridge Park, in the heart of San Antonio, her hometown. She had not been back for nearly ten years, and then it had been on a short mission to monitor the activities of a Russian expatriate who was illegally acquiring state-of-the-art drilling technology from a former Texaco employee.

San Antonio.

Kate sighed, remembering her explosive youth, going from foster home to foster home after her mother had died from a drug overdose. She never knew her father. At the age of twelve, she'd escaped her last foster home and joined a gang, where she had spent two violent years before reality caught up with her when her gang was ambushed by rival group, killing all of her friends and sending her to St. Rose Hospital with a concussion and multiple stab wounds, including one in her lower spine. That had been the turning point in her life, mostly thanks to a Catholic priest who visited her frequently as she learned to walk all over again. Six months later, at the priest's recommendation, the state placed her in a Catholic boarding high school, where she not only earned the highest marks, but also a scholarship to the University of Virginia. She had joined the CIA upon her graduation.

I've come all this way for this?

She continued to stare at the picturesque scene, listening

to the distant bells of Big Ben by the Thames. It seems like disasters always had a way of marking turning points in her life. Her mother's untimely death had forced her to mature much faster than other girls her age, also propelling her to a life of recklessness and crime. Then being nearly paralyzed had provided her with a new perspective on life, steering her back onto the right path.

Now this.

Perhaps it was time for another change.

She grabbed her jacket and headed for the door.

"Where are you going?" asked the keeper of the safe house, a CIA retiree who got to live in London for free. His face, deeply fissured by years of stress, regarded her under thinning white hair.

"Out." She reached for the door.

The keeper got in the way. Albeit old, he was still slim and moved briskly enough to command respect, even by a highly trained operative like Kate. "But the instructions from Langley are clear."

"And you have done your job by reminding me. I need to go for a walk. Please move."

"If Langley calls and you're not here . . ."

"Tell them I'll call them back."

The aged operative moved out of the way. "You can get in trouble for this."

Kate laughed. "I can't imagine being in more trouble than I already am."

6

Seven hours later, Kate Donaldson stood in the same bedroom, the phone pressed against the side of her face as a series of clicks on the line preceded Mike Costner's tired voice. The safe house keeper had left to get a few groceries.

"Kate?"

"Evening, Mike."

"It's still mid-afternoon here. Anyway, the director has reviewed your statement, as well as the recommendations from his senior staff. He's on his way to brief the president."

"And?"

"This is very difficult for me, Kate, especially because I've known you for so many years."

She forced a calm voice in the hope of reaching an understanding with her superior. "Decisions were made without my knowledge, including the approval of an increased budget by the director himself."

"I know, but you're still the officer in charge of that operation."

"On paper, Mike. *Only* on paper. I didn't authorize the recruitment of a British foreign national with a shadowy Bosnian past. To put it mildly, I was downright shocked when I learned about it this morning, as well as how much the director had approved to pay for his services."

"I'm sorry, Kate. But that is not how the director views it, especially in light of the recent finding from British intelligence MIA regarding Popov. He was found shot dead, along with his wife and daughters in the south of London three hours ago. Apparently the London police caught one of the killers, who turned out to be an independent contractor working under orders by Dragan Kundat himself to break the link in the investigation."

Kate felt as if she had just swallowed hot coals. Dragan Kundat was one of the most ruthless men in Yugoslavia, a former Serbian military general responsible for the slaughter of tens of thousands of civilians during ethnic cleansing sweeps through Bosnia-Herzegovina and Croatia. Dragan Kundat, a name fitting for a monster, reported directly to another monster: Slobodan Milosevic, Yugoslavia's president and in the eyes of many, the world's most wanted man, responsible for ordering and supervising the slaughter of over 200,000 men, women, and children in the Balkans, plus the atrocities in the province of Kosovo.

"British intelligence believes that the Yugoslavs were retaliating for NATO strikes, and Popov was the link."

"And Popov was recruited by Carter. I had nothing to do with it."

"As senior officer, you should have been more proactive in keeping tabs on this operation . . . look, Kate, face it, most of the officers under your command *died,* and because they did so during a mission, our government can't even claim the bodies. I've spent most of the day contacting families. And to top it all off, the Agency was tricked by Dragan's people. We recruited one of them and essentially gave him free reign of the operation to set up his strike. You have to agree that this is certainly not one of the CIA's finest moments.''

She sat in bed and closed her eyes, refusing to believe that the Agency was going to use her as the scapegoat on this one.

''I . . . I'm totally amazed that you're doing this to me. You know the extent of my role in this mission. You asked me to set it up for Carter and then walk away when he got his appointment in London to let him prove himself. You know that I was not informed of any changes made afterwards. The only thing that links me to this mess is the clerical error of not having my name removed as officer in charge.''

''I'm sorry, Kate. This one is out of my hands.''

Kate Donaldson kept her eyes closed, considering her next statement quite carefully. ''In that case, Mike, consider this conversation my official resignation from the CIA.''

Costner's voice suddenly climbed a few decibels. ''Hold on—wait a moment! You're taking this to an extreme.''

''Really?''

''We don't want to go that far.''

''Oh?''

''The director will be satisfied with a statement from you accepting responsibility.''

''Is that right?''

''It's pretty simple, Kate. You accept the blame and the Agency retains you as an employee.''

''No deal, Mike. I'm not taking the rap for something that I wasn't responsible for. You go and tell the director to shove his proposal where the sun doesn't shine.''

''Kate!''

''And something else: you keep letting young, inexpe-

rienced guns like Hollis Carter loose out there because of
agency politics, and I can personally guarantee you that
you will be having this exact same conversation with another senior officer in six months or less.''

"Kate, listen, you're taking this all wrong. We don't
want to lose you. You're a—"

"I was already considering leaving, Mike. Nineteen
years in this rat race is long enough."

Silence, followed by, "But—but you're still too young
to retire. Besides, espionage is your life. What will you
do?''

Kate expected that question. Costner was worried that
Kate, strapped for money, might consider selling her
knowledge of CIA practices and procedures to another intelligence service. "For one thing, you guys never let me
spend the money you've been paying me all these years.
Ever heard of mutual funds? Well, that's where it all went,
and it's doing quite nicely for me. Also, Mike, espionage
is what I *did* for a living," she added, emphasizing the
past tense. "I never saw it as my life, especially recently,
and certainly starting this minute."

"Kate, listen, you can't—"

"I just did, Mike. Have a good life. I'm certainly looking forward to the rest of mine. And by the way, as a
parting thought, you guys might want to figure out why is
it that the Serbs targeted a Y2K convention."

Silence, followed by, "What do you mean?"

"Why the elaborate scheme? If the Serbs wanted to retaliate for NATO bombings, why not just bomb a department store, or a theater, or a restaurant? Why try to blow
up a place under so much professional surveillance and
risk getting caught? There's more here than a simple retaliatory strike."

"See what I mean? You're meant for this line of work."

"I'm out, Mike. Pass the thought to your director.

Maybe he can do something with it. Then again, maybe not. Either way, *I don't care.*"

"Kate, you can quit the CIA, but you can *never* stop being what we trained you to be. You are an operative. You are a trained spy. You can't deny who you are."

"Bye, Mike." The former CIA officer hung up the phone and walked to the windows, staring at the dimly lit park beneath a crystalline sea of stars. For the first time today she smiled, suddenly realizing that she had just given herself the best birthday present of all: a life.

BOOK TWO

■

New Life

■

"Life is half-spent before one knows what life is."
—French Proverb

1

Austin, Texas. September, 1999.

The noon sun shone high in the heart of Texas, reflecting off the steel and glass high-rises crowding the downtown area. To the north of the skyscrapers, the large campus of the University of Texas expanded across dozens of city blocks, bound on the east by the legendary Longhorn Stadium and to the west by Guadalupe Avenue, also known as The Drag, filled with college kids and the shops they patronized. Just south of downtown Austin the Texas capitol, bearing a strong resemblance to the U.S. capitol, contrasted sharply with the modern architecture of the buildings near it. Congress Avenue extended south of the capitol, crossing the Colorado River, and continuing deep into south Austin.

Kate Donaldson drove across the Congress bridge, inspecting the gleaming white capitol while steering her way through the lunch traffic.

In the seven months since her voluntary retirement from her previous line of work, as she sometimes referred to it with her clients, Kate had rapidly adjusted to the laid-back style of this very unique Texas city, quite different from the fast-paced Dallas–Fort Worth area or the hopelessly overcrowded Houston. One look at both of those places had prompted her to keep looking for a high-tech place to settle down. She had also spent a week in Silicon Valley, opting out of that not only because of the extreme cost of living but also because of the crowds. Austin provided the perfect place to start up her high-tech security consulting business, and it also allowed her to live in the hill country, surrounded by crystalline lakes and rivers. Austin was a young city, energetic, clean, safe, and just the right size for someone who had spent almost two decades elbowing her way through the crowded streets of every major city in the world. Silicon Hills, as Austin was often referred to, was filled with high-tech corporations, many of them in need of her services.

Her break from the Agency had gone much more smoothly than anticipated. She had endured a week at Langley, going through multiple exit interviews with everyone from Mike Costner up to the director himself. After declining their proposals over and over, each CIA official had then turned stern on her, reminding her of the severe penalties that former CIA officers faced if caught deviating from the rules stipulated in their contracts. After turning in her ID and weapons, Kate had gone home and packed, realizing as she did so that the apartment in Bethesda which she had called home for the past ten years really meant nothing to her. It had always been just a place to drop her dirty laundry from one trip, sleep, and get ready for another trip. It had not been *home,* unlike the house she had purchased in Lost Creek, a suburb stretching into the hills west of Austin, which already felt like home even though she had lived there for only four months. The purchase, however, which she had done more on impulse than anything else, had significantly cut into her life savings, pressuring her to pull together her plans for the consulting firm.

Kate steered her Honda Accord into an empty parking space in front of Manuel's, a Mexican restaurant specializing in interior Mexican cuisine with a touch of Texas that was built into one of the many historical buildings flanking the wide Congress Avenue. She had been hooked on the place two months ago and since then had tried to set up all her lunch appointments there. Today she would be talking to Brandon Holst, founder and CEO of Holst Enterprises, a two-year-old software venture. Kate had bumped into Holst at a Lost Creek neighborhood association party two weeks ago. In the half hour that she had been able to chat with him before he had to leave, Kate had been impressed by the energy of the middle-aged Texan entrepreneur as well as by his unpretentious honesty. Holst appeared to be a what-you-see-is-what-you-get kind of man. He also seemed hard-working to the point of obsession, which had prevented him from developing a personal life—something that Kate Donaldson could certainly relate to.

She deposited a few quarters into the parking meter, forcing herself not to glance up and down the street looking for tails—as she would had done in her previous life—and entered the restaurant. It took a considerable effort to ignore those details which in the past had kept her alive. She had also forced herself to live without a gun, another difficult habit to overcome.

The smell of cilantro and freshly baked flour tortillas made her forget those nineteen years. She looked for Brandon but did not see him.

The hostess sat her at a table in the middle of the restaurant—in clear violation of her rules. No, correct that, of her *former* rules. Seven months ago she would have chosen a table in the rear, by the swinging doors leading into the kitchen, providing her with a clear view of everyone in the restaurant and with an alternative route out in an emergency.

As she ordered iced tea, a tall and bulky figure entered the restaurant, backlit by the noon sun. Dressed in black jeans, boots, a starched white shirt, and a large belt buckle, Brandon Holst resembled a gunfighter more than a software developer, missing only the cowboy hat and a holstered sidearm.

She waved.

Holst's eyes, as dark as his hair, blinked recognition. His square face, supported by a wrestler's neck, broadened as he grinned, pulling his bronze skin taut over the ridge of his cheekbones.

"Hi there," he said in a booming voice, matching his bear-like appearance. He extended a palm toward Kate.

"Hello, Brandon. Nice seeing you again." The former CIA operative shook it firmly, a bit amused at her fine hand disappearing inside Holt's massive grip.

"Same here, Kate," he replied, sitting down across from her at the small table. "How's Austin treating you?"

"Can't complain. There's a lot of opportunities here."

"You've got that right." He looked about him and flagged down a waiter, a young kid dressed in jeans, a dark shirt, and a white apron. "I'd like an iced tea too, please." The waiter nodded politely and walked away.

"That was a nice neighborhood gathering the other day," she commented.

"Nice group of people," he said.

"How long did you tell me you've lived in Austin?"

Looking in the distance for a moment, Holst said, "In Austin . . . let's see . . . six years at UT, plus fifteen at AMD before going solo . . . right under twenty-three years."

"But you grew up nearby, right?"

"Just west of here. A place called Marble Falls. About an hour drive."

"Marble Falls . . . that's right," she said, remembering their conversation, before she had passed him a business card in case he needed to improve the security of his business. In the two hours that she had spent at the neighborhood party of the large community, Kate had dispensed a dozen business cards to all kinds of individuals, from lawyers and doctors to CPAs and high-tech professionals, including Brandon Holst. So far five people had called to make appointments. Of those, Kate had contracted her services to three. Brandon was her sixth caller. "Tell me about Marble Falls," she added.

He leaned back, his face relaxing. "Great little place, but still living in the good old days, I'm afraid. No high-tech industries there."

"That's why you live in Austin?"

He nodded. "Computers are my life. But I guess I should consider myself blessed to be able to live and work so close to home. I come from a pretty big family. They tend the family ranch just outside of Marble Falls."

"Must be nice to have your family so close, and also be able to live near where you grew up," she said, also leaning back, sipping her tea, feeling a little jealous.

The waiter came back with his drink and spent a minute reciting the daily specials. Kate ordered her usual, chicken flautas. Holst had the same.

"So," she said, her tone turning businesslike. "Have you gotten a chance to read the proposal I e-mailed to you?"

"Some," he said, tilting his head. "I'm just not certain how much protection is enough. I don't want to overdo it. On the other hand, I don't trust one of my current clients. I want my work protected." He leaned forward. "And I mean beyond the vanilla security systems offered by the run-of-the-mill companies around town."

Kate studied him for a moment. "Who is this client?"

"All I can tell you is that it's someone very powerful, and who is not crazy about Sweeper making it into the commercial market."

"Sweeper?"

"The name of my custom software to fix Y2K problems. I've licensed it to this particular client, and now I'm contacting a few promotional agencies to license it openly."

Kate's ears perked up at the mention of Y2K. During her brief meeting Holst had mentioned that his company wrote web browser software, not Y2K code.

"I didn't know that's the kind of software that you wrote."

"I do mostly web browser stuff just to stay alive. The problem is that there's too many companies doing the same. The market's saturated. But Sweeper is very different, quite vital to help eliminate certain remnants of any potential Y2K bug."

"I thought there was no such thing as a computer program that could solve the Y2K problem."

Holst nodded. "That's right. There isn't one, and anyone who tries to tell you that there is such code is either totally ignorant of the problem or a con artist trying to take your money."

Intrigued, she set her elbows on the table. Twining her fingers, she rested her chin on her knuckles.

"I'd like to protect your software, but first I need to know a little more about what it actually does. The way I understand it, the Y2K bug has to do with the year field of a date being represented by two digits instead of four, so when 2000 comes, instead of going from 1999 to 2000, the date goes from 99 to 00, which could be misinterpreted by computers as 1900."

The waiter brought them a basket of chips and a bowl of salsa. Holst dug in. Kate didn't, not having gotten used to the Mexican hot sauce yet. Besides, she didn't need the extra calories.

"That's right," he said. "The problem exists not just on large networks and the hundreds of millions of personal computers, but also in embedded systems, which are particularly difficult to fix because they're usually isolated from a network, and many were written in old languages like Cobol."

Her technical background permitted Kate to follow the conversation, something she considered vital in her new line of work. She had to appear technologically competent in order for her clients to trust her with the security of their goods.

Embedded systems was the term used to describe commercial, industrial, and military applications that used computers in a self-contained environment. Embedded systems ranged from microwave ovens, fuel injector systems, washing machines, and anti-lock brakes to elevators, traffic light control systems, autopilot navigation systems, and even Tomahawk missiles. Any piece of equipment that utilized a small computer system to control its operation was considered an embedded system. They differed from regular systems in the simple fact that they were not networked, like the computers in a private industry or government agency, which could be easily accessed by a central system. Embedded systems were built, put into operation, and left there in an autonomous operating mode to carry out the set of commands programmed into their electronic brains. Embedded systems weren't typically upgraded, like PCs in an office environment. Therefore, many of them were still running the same old software downloaded when they first went into operation, which could be many years ago.

"What's the target of your software? Certainly not embedded systems."

"Embedded systems can only be checked manually, and

with a high degree of pain. My solution applies only to large networks that have already been checked either with manual tools, automatic tools, or a combination of both. Sweeper essentially combs through billions of lines of code very rapidly and flags any remaining Y2K non-compliant code.''

''How?''

He grinned, fine wrinkles forming around his eyes. ''That's what I'm trying to protect.''

''How many employees do you have?''

He inspected his large college ring. ''Thirty, plus two secretaries; and three security guards, one per shift.''

''How do you control what they bring in and out?''

''Daily container inspections. Pretty standard practice . . . look, Kate, before we go too far down that path, tell me why I should contract your services over so many other security companies in town, especially considering the fact that you've been in business in Austin only for a couple of months?''

She regarded him briefly. Holst had gone straight to the core of their discussion. ''My services go well beyond the plain-vanilla gadgets you can purchase at Radio Shack. Sure, I install security cameras, motion detectors, card-access locks, and even fingerprint- or voice-activated locks, but that is only *part* of the security solution. This is, by the way, what most companies will do for you. Problem is, they miss the other half of the security installation.''

Holst also set his elbows on the table. ''What's that?''

''The people working at your office, Brandon, or at least the key ones, need to be trained on basic surveillance patterns, on how to detect the telltale signs of wrongdoing, however subtle.''

''You're being too abstract for me. I need an example.''

''All right. If you watch people carefully, you'll notice that they all develop a pattern in their daily behavior. It's totally unavoidable because humans like patterns. You, for example, do certain things the same way every day. You're probably thinking of some right now, but there are many, many others that you do subconsciously, without realizing that you're doing them. One very easy way to detect wrongdoing is by establishing the daily pattern of every employee in your firm and then looking for deviations in that pattern. Is someone spending longer on the phone than in the past? Is someone taking just a bit longer for lunch than usual? Is someone spending a bit longer at the copier, the fax, or the coffee stand than usual? That doesn't automatically mean that they are doing something wrong, but those signs merit further surveillance to see what it is that made them deviate from their established routines.''

"Sounds like something out of a spy novel.''

"Unfortunately, it's very real, and you wouldn't believe how many companies wait until something goes terribly wrong before taking appropriate security measures, like the ones I provide. In addition to the training, we can also go beyond monitoring video cameras and phones by keeping close tabs on Internet access on the networked systems at your office. We can generate a list of the valid URLs that you would allow your employees to access. All other sites would be banned. Do you currently allow your employees to take work home? Like on laptops?''

He nodded.

"How do you know that they're not taking the source code of Sweeper with them?''

"Because not one employee can have access to the entire program. Only I posses the root password to access the innermost directory of the system, where the source code resides. I also keep one archive copy of the code in a safe at home.''

"That's actually very good, as a first step. But someone determined enough could force a core dump of your workstation and steal your password.''

A core dump was a built-in mechanism in every workstation where in the event of a crash, the system dumped its entire memory contents into a file, which could then be reviewed by skilled programmers to figure out what had caused the system to crash, similar to a high-tech autopsy. In that core dump, however, the system also included all of the keyboard commands entered since the last boot sequence, which often contained the user's password, or in Brandon Holst's case, the root password.

"I've never thought of that."

"We can install custom software to prevent illegal users from core-dumping your workstation and accessing high-privilege passwords. And even if someone did manage to get access to the main drive, where you keep the source code of your software, I can install a shield that will prevent anyone from reading it unless they have access to a special software password that will unscramble the data in the drive. We can also install special scanners at every entryway—not just to monitor the electronics equipment going in and out of the building, but going to the extreme of setting up an electromagnetic pulse generator that would erase all magnetic-type data carriers, like diskettes, tapes, and drives that have not been properly checked out. In summary, my services include the standard security hardware installations, plus personnel training, and specialty software and hardware tailored to your requirements and your budget."

Holst studied her with a half amused, half quizzical gaze. "I've sat through at least a dozen security pitches, and this one is the first that I actually like. How long have you been in the security business?"

"About nineteen years," she said.

"Doing this kind of work?"

"Pretty much."

"Where did you say you worked before?"

"I had a security business in Virginia."

As part of her exit interview, the CIA had provided Kate with this cover, as well as a phone number in case someone wanted to check her references.

"Nineteen years in this business . . . impressive. Are you a good shot?"

Kate narrowed her hazel eyes. "Excuse me?"

The waiter came with their order, serving Kate first, then Holst, who placed a napkin on his lap. "Smells good," he commented. "All this time living in Austin and never once have been here. I need to get out a little more often."

Kate didn't reply. She continued to stare at the large cowboy across the table. His firm mouth, normally curled, as if on the edge of laughter, made it difficult for Kate to tell if he was serious or not. *What does he mean, am I good shot? Does he know about my past? Is there a leak at the Agency?*

Holst dug in, cutting into one of the flautas—chicken, Monterey jack cheese, and sautéed mushrooms wrapped in a corn tortilla and then pan fried. "So, how good of a shot are you?" He grinned.

Kate had suddenly lost her appetite. "I'm not sure what's that got to do with—"

"If you're in the security business, you certainly should have some experience with weapons, right?"

She relaxed. "I've shot pistols before," she said, measuring her words. Since surrendering her weapons and ID cards to Mike Costner, Kate had not touched another gun, even though she could own one for self-defense in Texas. "But that has little to do with my contracts. I provide high-tech security services, not armed protection. I'm not in the bodyguard business."

"I see," he said, his dark eyebrows slanting in a frown. "For some reason I had you pegged as someone who could handle weapons. You know, being in the security business and all."

She smiled. "No, no. My specialty is in high-tech security, not firearms."

"Pity," he said with a heavy sigh, in which Kate detected humor, but his deceitful mouth didn't tell her if he was kidding or not.

"Why?"

"Because guns are my hobby. I was looking forward to us two going shooting."

"We can still do that . . . but only if it gets me the contract." She took a sip of tea.

"Tell you what," he said, his tanned face spreading into a smile. "Come by my offices tomorrow and give us your full pitch. Then we'll go shoot some pistols."

2

The range was isolated, secluded, hidden in the Texas hill country. They drove west on Bee Caves Road out of Austin until reaching Highway 71, turning right and continuing until intersecting Highway 620, where Holst swung right.

The software entrepreneur owned the largest Ford truck Kate had ever seen. It had front and rear seats and four doors, like a sedan, but it also had a long bed. They had driven back to Lost Creek in their own vehicles following her presentation. Kate had changed from a business suit to a pair of jeans, a T-shirt, and sneakers. She had met Holst at the entrance to the Lost Creek Country Club, where she left her vehicle and climbed aboard the truck, almost needing a ladder to make it up into the tall vehicle. Unlike her designer jeans, Holst wore a pair of Wranglers, a plain cotton shirt, boots, and the unavoidable thick belt and large buckle.

She gazed at the sparse vegetation dotting the hills beyond the tinted side window, relaxing as a Willie Nelson tune filled the large cabin. Cold air streamed out of vents on the dashboard. She had not felt this calm in years.

"The team was impressed," Holst said, right hand on the wheel, left hand adjusting his sun glasses as the road narrowed before approaching a weathered bridge.

"Glad to hear that. I really think I can help you protect your investment." She gazed down at a deep ravine beyond the rusted beams supporting the old structure, which creaked under the weight of the Ford. A stream flowed at the bottom, amidst boulders and debris.

"They were particularly impressed with your proposal for training. Assigning codes to states of awareness sounded like something out of a spy book, but in many ways it does have direct applications to my business. I should be operating in Yellow Mode while at work, always keeping an eye on people's activities."

"And if you combine the state-of-the-art hardware with the training, plus a few changes in procedure, you will have a nearly bulletproof system."

"Why only *nearly*?"

"Nothing is *fully* bulletproof. History has taught us over and over that if someone is desperate enough to achieve something, he or she will likely find a way to do it. Any system can be defeated, Brandon. It's just a matter of how difficult you want to make it to discourage potential breaches. But someone skilled, determined, and lucky enough will probably get in. Anyone who tells you otherwise is either ignorant or is lying to you."

"You're very different from anyone I've ever dealt with."

"How so?"

"For one thing, you never seem apprehensive or tense. Either you're not, which is amazing, given the high pressure of this industry, or you're remarkably good at hiding it."

Kate sighed. "The former, Brandon. For some reason this line of work is not getting to me."

"You don't worry about finding work? About paying your bills?"

"I focus my energy on doing the best I can. The rest always takes care of itself."

He glanced at Kate, fine wrinkles forming around his eyes as he grinned. "Like I said," he said, turning his attention back to the road. "Very different. I like that. It tells me you have nothing to hide."

Kate almost chuckled at that one, but she didn't allow her external appearance to change one bit. Nineteen years pretending to be someone she was not had left her with the uncanny ability to make people believe just about anything she wanted them to believe about herself. But that strange feeling of omnipotence also made her feel quite alone, because she could never share her secrets with anyone, unless she wanted to end up in a federal prison.

They reached an unpaved road to their left, by a sign that read AUSTIN SHOOTING RANGE. Holst steered the truck onto the unpaved road, riddled with potholes. No, make that *craters*, which he had to drive around to keep from getting stuck, even with four-wheel-drive.

A mile later they reached a dusty parking lot flanked by small hills and a shack. An unkempt man wearing a pair of soiled jeans, an equally dirty shirt, and a beard that made him look like a younger Ted Kaczynski greeted them. There was no one else in sight.

"Hey, Rich. Slow day?" asked Holst, getting out and opening the rear door, shouldering a backpack and picking up a duffel bag.

"Brandon? That's a surprise to see you out on a weekday. Ain't you supposed to be workin'?"

Kate noticed the holstered pistol dangling from his belt. He carried the gun like a cowboy, always keeping his hand next to it, even as he walked, giving the appearance that he would draw at any moment.

"Taking a break on a pretty day to show a pretty lady how to shoot," said Holst, winking at Kate.

She smiled.

"Works for me," the stranger replied.

"Kate, this is my friend, Richard Jones. Rich, this is Kate Donaldson. She's showing me how to protect my business."

"Protect your business?" Jones smiled, unveiling a row of yellow teeth beneath the messy beard. "All you need is something like this." He patted the side of his massive sidearm, which Kate recognized upon closer inspection as a Desert Eagle .44 Magnum, a highly reliable Israeli-made gun, its rounds capable of going through an engine block.

"Rich here's from the old school of 'bigger is better,' " commented Brandon.

"Damn right," he replied. "The man with the bigger gun always wins."

Kate wanted to point out that accuracy was just as important but chose against doing so. Instead, she settled for a heavy sigh and a stereotypical comment:

"Boys and their toys."

Her comment drew a laugh from Holst.

Jones just grinned. "You can laugh all you want, but Brandon here knows I'm right. This little baby's saved my life on more than one occasion."

Brandon shook his head and took Kate by the hand. "It's too early for one of your stories, Rich. Maybe later. Right now my friend and I have some shooting to do. See if she qualifies to handle my company's security."

Kate punched him lightly on the shoulder. Brandon winked at her again. This time she winked back and could tell that he liked that.

"Hey, did you ever get your CHL?" asked Jones.

Brandon nodded. "Three months ago."

"Where at?"

"Over at Red's indoor range."

Jones nodded. "It's about time. Now you're legal."

"CHL? What's that?" Kate asked.

Before Holst could answer, Jones said, "Concealed handgun license. The State of Texas lets you carry a concealed weapon as long as you take a course and pass a written exam and a shooting test. I've been trying to get Brandon to take his for a couple years. Looks like he finally got around to it."

"So all you have to do is pass a couple of tests and you get to carry a concealed weapon?"

"Plus a background check. We don't want any loonies out there carrying a loaded firearm." Jones grinned again, showing his decaying teeth.

Kate thought that was ironic coming out of this character.

Brandon nodded. "That's the law."

"You ought to get your friend to take the test, Brandon. Not very smart for a pretty lady to be walking around in this crazy world without protection."

"Really?" she asked, amused.

"Jones is right, Kate. You could get mugged."

"You don't say?"

"Seriously. That's why I carry this." Brandon patted the left side of his waist.

"Don't leave home without it," commented Jones, scratching his beard with a long fingernail.

Only then did Kate realize the small bulk by Brandon's waistline. "Have you been carrying all this time?"

"Always," he said, unbuttoning the button of his shirt right above his waistline, sliding his right hand beneath the cloth, and producing a small pistol. "Unless I'm going to a bar."

"Can't carry a weapon in an establishment that makes fifty-one percent or more of its income from alcohol."

"Or in a church or school," added Brandon. "Texas law."

Jones frowned while pointing at Brandon's weapon, which Kate recognized as a small-caliber Beretta. "Brandon, you're the only guy I know who has a license to carry a weapon but walks around instead with a rat shooter."

"This is a Beretta Tomcat," Holst said. "A 32-caliber pistol with the same bite of a .380 automatic."

"You'll have to fire five of yours to achieve the same effect as one of mine," the Unabomber look-alike said, patting the handle of his .44 Magnum.

"Not if I place them right," he said, replacing the weapon beneath his shirt, shoving it in his jeans, by his left kidney.

Kate was annoyed with herself for having missed Brandon's weapon. Her senses were definitely dulling from inactivity. *But that was the intent of your retirement, right? To get away from it all.* Still, she couldn't help feeling like she was losing something she had once treasured, something that had been such an integral part of her. Now, like steam escaping from a heated pool, Kate Donaldson sensed her trained instincts leaving her, abandoning her, and she found herself not liking that feeling.

"What are you shooting today?" Jones asked, reaching for a notepad on a rusted metallic desk just outside the shack.

"A few pistols. A Walther PPK, a Colt .45, and a Beretta 92FS."

Kate's ears perked up when hearing her old gun being mentioned. Her fingers tingled with the anticipation of holding a 92FS after so many months of inactivity, wondering if she could still shoot straight.

Ten minutes later they had finished stapling fresh targets to a large plywood board supported by a plain metal frame twenty feet down the firing range. They walked back to the table where Holst had left his backpack and duffel bag.

First he produced the Colt, then the Walther, and finally a stainless-steel version of the Beretta 92FS, Kate's favorite.

"How long has it been since you've shot a Beretta?"

Kate froze. "What makes you think that I've shot a Beret—"

"The way you're staring at it, like if it's some kind of long-lost friend. Here. Hold it."

She did, the irritation she felt for not being able to control her external features vanishing as she clutched the weapon. Her fingers remembered, moving automatically, engaging the safety, releasing the magazine, pulling back the slide, inspecting the action, verifying the empty chamber. Her left forefinger depressed the disassembling latch release button as her thumb rotated the disassembling latch clockwise. In one smooth stroke she pulled the barrel-slide assembly forward off the frame, inspecting the overall integrity of the barrel and recoil spring assembly, before reassembling the pistol—all in under thirty seconds.

"Looks fine."

"Are you *sure* you know what you're doing?" asked Holst, humor in his stare as he held a box of 9mm shells.

She made a face and took the ammunition from him, loading the magazine, which, unlike her old weapon, could hold only ten rounds. When Holst had first suggested to come shooting, Kate had planned to pretend to be an average shot, just good enough to get his business. But now, the former CIA officer felt she had something to prove to herself. Although some of her senses may have dulled, Kate hoped that she had still hung on to her marksmanship.

Holst handed her a small box of foam earplugs before snuggling a pair into his own ears.

She lined up the front sight with the upper-left chest area of the leftmost silhouette, firing five rounds in rapid succession, creating a tight cluster over the heart before quickly switching targets and firing the last five at the silhouette's head in a second tight group.

She set the weapon on the table, action open, reassurance filling her. Perhaps if she just reverted to Yellow Mode she might recover some of—

No! That's exactly what you're trying not *to do! You will never live a normal life unless you become normal, and normal people do not operate in Yellow Mode.*

She sighed, her feelings betraying her.

"What branch of the service were you in?" said a voice behind them.

She turned around in surprise. It was Jones, arms crossed, the bulky Magnum hanging from his belt, suspicious eyes regarding Kate Donaldson.

"I'm flattered," she replied. "But I've never been. My father was in the Marines. I had no brothers, so Dad taught me how to shoot."

Brandon Holst smiled. "Kate Donaldson, I don't care *how* you learned. With that kind of shooting you can protect my business *any* time."

"I told you I'm not in the bodyguard business. I don't even own a gun."

"You don't learn to shoot like that just by coming to the range," insisted Jones.

Brandon smiled. "Rich here used to be in Army intelligence. He's suspicious by nature."

"You're right," she said, thinking rapidly. "Except that Dad was really into guns, especially after he retired. He took me with him—actually, he *dragged* me with him, teaching me not just the basics, like shooting at stationary targets, but also at moving ones."

"There," said Brandon, extending his arms at the Unabomber look-alike. "A perfectly reasonable explanation. Rich, you're going to have to be less suspicions of everyone you meet."

Jones shifted his gaze between Kate and Brandon, before he drew his weapon and said. "All right, then. Let's do some real shooting. Think you can handle a *real* gun?"

3

Kate turned into her street in Lost Creek at five in the evening, following what she considered the best time she'd had in a while. She had shot over a hundred rounds with the Beretta before switching to the Walther PPK/S, using up most of Brandon's ammunition. Then she had switched to Jones's .44 Magnum, scoring better than even Jones, who continued to regard Kate with suspicion. By the end of their two-hour shooting spree, they had consumed over six hundred rounds. Afterwards, Brandon had driven her back to the country club, where she had left her Honda.

Tired, her hand throbbing from the prolonged recoil stress after a long period of inactivity, Kate reached her house moments later, fingering the large button on the remote control clipped to her sun visor. The garage door on the front of her house began to rise. Her house was the least expensive on the block. Kate had bought it not just because it was in her price range and it was located in a great neighborhood, but it was among homes one and a half to two times more costly—a factor that would make it easy to sell if she had to move quickly.

She closed the garage door after pulling in. The stairs in the rear led to the kitchen. She walked into the space between the front of her car and a large freezer, which had come with the house, as well as the refrigerator in the kitchen, appliances which Kate had used little since she hardly ever cooked. She unlocked the door and heard the beeping sound made by her alarm system, whose built-in delay gave her thirty seconds to disarm. Kate entered her four-digit code and the blinking red light on the control panel turned green, indicating that the system was ready to be armed again. She eyed the MEMORY light indicator, verifying that it was green, which meant her system had not gone off while she was away.

Kate dropped her keys and purse on the counter and poured herself a glass of cold water from a large bottle of Evian, one of the few items in her refrigerator, along with two bottles of Chardonnay and a carton of milk. She was dehydrated from being out all afternoon.

Closing her eyes as she drank, Kate realized she had not been this relaxed in years. Whatever apprehension she may have had before launching her security consulting firm had been washed away after landing her fifth contract, Holst Enterprises, for a hefty thirty thousand dollars, half of which would be pure profit after she paid for the equipment and the subcontractor to install it. The real value of her services, however, was in her experience. She knew just the right way to carry out a surveillance job and therefore knew precisely how to deploy cameras, how to interpret the recorded video, the most strategic places for motion detectors, the finest software firewalls in the business to keep hackers out, and the right training for both security guards and selected management.

A brief mental addition told her that in the two months she had been in business, Kate Donaldson had earned more money than in her first two years at the CIA. *No wonder so many spooks turn to the private sector.* The value of the experience she had taken for granted for so many years was priceless.

She headed for her bedroom on the second floor, walking across her living room, which she had decorated several weeks ago after completing her first job, which had netted her over nine thousand dollars. A octagonal cocktail table separated a burgundy leather sofa from a brick fireplace. A sofa table ran behind the sofa, adorned with carefully positioned knickknacks from recent trips to antique shops and a pair of silver frames displaying photos from her college days. On the wall next to the sofa hung her framed college diploma. Nowhere in her house did she have one item that reminded her of her past nineteen years, not only because of her agreement with the Agency but also because she didn't want to think about it.

Out of sight, out of mind.

She stepped into her bedroom and went straight to the bathroom, undressing and jumping in the shower, letting the hot water massage her back and her neck, further relaxing her. She breathed in the steam rising around her, enveloping her, soothing her, helping her forget about her past, about her assignments, about a life of deception, always pretending to be someone else, always assuming new identities, always concerned about making a mistake—however minor—and blowing her cover, endangering not just herself but those around her.

The water streaming out of the shower head washed away the old feelings of living under constant stress, the unbearable tension that stemmed from never being sure if she was safe, if a figure would emerge from the shadows and fire a hollow-point round through her spine. It was that uncertainty about the world around her that Kate detested the most, because it forced her to maintain a constant state of paranoia, affectionately known as Yellow Mode.

Yellow Mode. She toweled her hair dry, slipped into a pair of silk pajamas, and got into bed with a magazine on home decorating, also grabbing the remote and tuning on to a home decorating program, her mind forgetting about Yellow Mode as Martha Stewart came on. She'd never known what the famous home decorator looked like until decorating her new home had become a priority in her life.

A life.

Kate thought about the past weeks. It seemed that most everyone she did business with wanted to take her out. The owner of a CPA firm had taken her sailing on nearby Lake Travis last month. She had gone hiking with the owner of a small retail shop just last weekend. And now Brandon had taken her shooting. And all of them had invited her back.

Seven months after her fortieth birthday, Kate Donaldson decided that she was definitely well on her way to getting a life.

4

Brandon Jonathan Holst was a Texan, just like his father, and his father before him. He had been brought up to be honest, taught that a man's worth was measured not by the size of his bank account but by the value of his word, by his integrity, by his ability to keep a promise, by his willingness to help a friend in need. He respected straight shooters and despised those who didn't play with an open hand, who kept some of the cards to themselves, who operated according to a secret agenda.

And he had developed a fine nose to detect deceivers, users, manipulators, like the two men sitting on the other side of his desk this evening.

"I guess I just don't get it," said Holst, reclining his large frame on his swivel chair and crossing his left leg over his right, the tip of his boot touching the edge of the desk. "I have delivered a copy of Sweeper, just as you have requested. If the problem is bugs, please report them to the technical service hotline and Holst Enterprises will provide you with a patch to solve your specific problem until we release the next version of the program. It's a service included in the license agreement.''

The older of the two, Astor Kendell, a man in his fifties, with silver hair and a granitelike face, leaned forward, shaking his head. "Sweeper works just fine, Mr. Holst. In fact, it works *too well*, which is the reason why we're here."

Holst wasn't a deceitful man by nature, but he could *pretend* to be one in the presence of this crafty pair. "I'm afraid you've lost me."

"We are prepared to make you a very generous offer to purchase Sweeper outright," replied Kendell.

Holst pretended to think about it for a moment. After so many days dancing around the topic, Kendell had finally come out and said it, confirming Holst's suspicions. These two characters, and the government agency they represented, didn't want him to license Sweeper in the open market. To this day he still didn't know which agency they worked for, only that the payment he had received was in the form of a check from the Department of the Treasury, which narrowed it down to just about any federal agency.

"Why would you want to do that?" Holst asked, waving a hand in the air. "You have already been sold a license to service your entire agency. Isn't that what you wanted, to get your agency Y2K-compliant?"

"Let's just say we have our reasons," replied Lester Gallagher, Kendell's younger companion, a man Brandon's age, but with thinning hair and a pockmarked face.

"If you tell me those reasons, I may be able to customize Sweeper to serve your specific needs. There's no reason to purchase it outright."

Kendell pulled out a check from his coat pocket and slid it across the desk toward Brandon Holst, who remained sitting back, eyes on the silver-haired government man.

. "My agency is prepared to compensate you handsomely for your cooperation."

Holst stood, walking over to the glass panes flanking his door, staring across the cubicles to a man on a ladder installing one of the security cameras. He could also see Kate Donaldson's brown hair sticking just over the edge of the cubicle walls. She stood next to the ladder talking to the subcontractor.

He checked his watch. Almost dinner time.

Returning to his seat, Holst eyed the amount of the check and smiled cordially. The government men were not even close to the amount he could get through the licensing program. In addition, his company would get a lot of exposure in the field through licensing, just like Microsoft did during the early eighties, which would lead to future income and contracts. Slowly shaking his head, Holst pushed the envelope back to Kendell using an index finger. "Gentlemen, I'm afraid we'll have to continue this conversation some other time."

The government men exchanged a puzzled glance, before returning his attention to him.

"Is the amount not adequate? I'm prepared to negotiate," said Gallagher, setting his elbows on the table.

"Not now. I've got to get ready for a very important date."

5

A contractor's badge from Holst Enterprises clipped to the collar of her blouse, Kate Donaldson stood next to a stepladder as one of her subs installed a surveillance camera in a corner of the main cubicle area of Holst Enterprises, located in a one-story building in west Austin. The camera resembled a smoke detector.

She studied the hand-drawn diagram on the yellow pad she held in her hands. This would be the third and last camera to monitor this area, each fitted with a wide-angle lens for maximum coverage. The hidden camera sent a wireless signal to its own recorder in the basement. The recorders were housed inside a fireproof cabinet cleverly hidden behind a fake set of bookshelves packed with old computer manuals. By pressing on the correct manual, the fake bookshelves slid to the side, exposing the cabinet, which still required an access code to open. Two other concealed cameras covered the parking lot and one swept the foyer. In addition to the recording device, all cameras also broadcast their signals to a tiny handheld screen that the guard on duty could carry with him during his rounds. It looked and felt like a kid's video game. The wireless unit switched to a different camera every ten seconds, going through a full cycle once a minute.

"You can go home after you finish this one. I'll give the system a final check and call you in the morning if there are any problems," she told the man on the ladder.

"Yes, ma'am," he replied, a Hispanic in his late twenties, using a screwdriver to secure the fake smoke detector to the ceiling.

Kate headed for Holst's office at the other end of the cubicle maze, empty at this late hour. The founder and CEO of Holst Enterprises occupied a large office on the opposite side of the foyer, across the cubicle area. He had asked her out to dinner for the second time this week. The first time, two nights ago, they had gone to Carmelo's, an Italian restaurant on Fifth Street. Tonight, Holst had tempted her with Sullivan's, an expensive steak house. She had readily accepted, having enjoyed his company on each previous occasion.

She reached his office and saw through the glass panel next to his door that he had company. She knocked twice.

"Come in."

She stepped inside. Brandon sat behind his desk facing two men in business suits. They stood when she entered and turned toward her. Kate had never seen them before. Their stolid expressions told her they were not having a good meeting. One was quite old but in seemingly good shape, slim, muscular, with a full head of silver hair framing a hard face. The second looked to be in his forties, with thinning brown hair and a pock-marked face, and was equally well-built.

Alarms went off in her head, but she tried to ignore her

old instincts, her gut feeling that these two were more than businessmen. Maybe it was their stance, the way they kept their feet apart, providing the balance from which to launch a strike. Or perhaps it was their hands, free, ready. Or their Marines' necks and equally thick limbs. But mostly it was their eyes, cold, unemotional, watching her without interest, without conveying a single shred of how they felt.

Trained eyes. Balanced stances. Free hands. Professionals.

You're still too paranoid, she told herself as the strangers turned their attention back to Brandon Holst.

"Hi," said Holst, dressed in a pair of black jeans and a starched white shirt. "These gentlemen were just about to leave." He glared at both of them.

The well-dressed visitors stared at one another and headed out the door without acknowledging Kate. They held no attaché cases, or files, or laptops—nothing to compromise their hands. She watched them carefully as they made it to the other side of the cubicle area and into the foyer.

"Who were they?"

Holst frowned. "Clients." He reached for his sports coat over the credenza behind his desk and put it on.

She forced her concerns out of her tone of voice, settling for a simple, "They didn't look happy."

He nodded. "They never do. Always keeping me on my toes. How was your day?"

"Not nearly as busy as yours," she said, giving the door leading to the foyer a suspicious glance before looking at him, forcing herself to relax. "You had quite the entourage of people following you this morning." Kate had seen Holst early this morning, soon after she had arrived at the office with her subcontractor to continue their installations. The CEO had waved at her as he'd walked in the door, just before several employees surrounded him while discussing their technical problems. Like a football player rushing through the line of scrimmage, Brandon had made it to his office, where his assistant forced the mob into a line. He had spent the rest of his day solving one problem after the next, working through lunch.

He shrugged. "Just another beautiful day in the neighborhood. Looks like your man over there's finished."

The Hispanic climbed down the ladder, folded it, and disappeared into the foyer.

"We've installed all of the cameras."

Brandon Holst looked about him, a puzzled look pulling in his features. "I don't see any."

She smiled. "That's the idea. There's one in the corner over there, disguised as a smoke alarm."

"That's a camera?"

She nodded.

"Impressive."

"I was just about to give the system a final check. Want to see?"

He glanced at his watch. "Sure. The reservation isn't till eight."

The stairs at the far end of the building led either up to the roof, where Holst had built a sundeck and set up picnic tables for his employees, or down to the basement. Kate had learned from him that the leased building used to be an old brewery, explaining the large tanks lining the walls of the basement.

Holst had turned the cool and dry cellar into both an archive area for their software as well as a disk server facility, isolating the office area from the incessant humming of the larger computer hardware. Kate had installed the fireproof metal cabinet in the space between the archives and the servers. She stood in front of the bookshelves hiding the cabinet and pushed on an old Apple II owner's manual on the top shelf. The shelves magically moved to the right, exposing the safe-like cabinet, bolted to the floor. She entered a six-digit code on the keypad and the red LED above the pad turned green just as the latching mechanism released the lock.

"I feel like I'm in the basement of some government agency."

Kate smiled as she pulled on the door, exposing stacked Sony recorders, each slaved to a camera via a wireless receiver mounted on the rear of the safe. One shelf housed a nine-inch Sony display and a panel of buttons labeled A through F.

"When did you bring this in?" he asked, standing next to her in front of the cabinet.

"This afternoon. Pretty standard equipment. The first layer of your defensive system." She powered it on. The monitor came alive, as well as the recorders, which began to blink to indicate that they held no videotapes. She pushed button A and the screen displayed a high-resolution view of the foyer. The image moved slowly from one end of the rectangular room to the other, showing the guard station every fifteen-second sweep. She pressed another button, switching to a view of the parking lot. That camera also rotated, displaying a clear view of half of Holst Enterprises' lot, nearly empty at this hour in the evening, save for her Honda, his truck, and the contractor loading his ladder into the rear of a van. She switched to the second parking lot camera, her eyes narrowing at the two businessmen standing by the open doors of a dark sedan. The older one spoke on a cellular phone while making abrupt gestures at the building and also at the younger man, who scribbled notes on a small pad. The camera panned away from them, monitoring the rest of the parking lot, returning to the pair moments later. Kate pressed a button on the panel and the camera stopped its sweeping motion.

"You have strange customers, Brandon."

"They're just a bit eccentric. That's all."

The older man stared directly at the camera, obviously realizing that he was being watched. He motioned his associate into the sedan and drove off.

She felt the old familiar knot in her stomach that always came whenever she sensed trouble but could do nothing immediate to address it. That man had spotted a camera disguised as a malfunctioning floodlight a hundred feet away. That alone told her plenty about him.

She released the camera to continue its programmed motion. "How well do you know these people?"

"They pay their bills. That's as much as I need to know about them."

"These guys are . . ." she stopped herself, deciding to let it go. She knelt and ripped open a box of videotapes. Her mind, however, flashed the word she could not speak out loud, for it would expose her secret past.

Professionals.

"Kate? You were going to say something?"

She slowly shook her head. "It was nothing. Here," she said, handing him three blank tapes. "Unwrap them and shoved them into those." She pointed to three recorders over the monitor.

Kate removed the plastic wrapper from three additional tapes, loading them into the lower three recorders.

"How long do they last?"

"Forty-eight hours each."

"Really? How? They look like regular VHS tapes, just heavier."

"They're high-density tapes. They can hold many times more video than regular tapes, plus the recorders only snap one frame per second, stretching their recording length."

"Interesting," he said, inserting the last tape into a blinking machine. "What's next?"

She set the digital clock on the control panel, entering

the date and time. "All recorders reference this central time. Now all I have to do is this." She pressed a red button over the clock and the recorders began to hum, but their counters kept track of elapsed time, resetting themselves every forty-eight hours.

"What happens if someone cuts the power?"

She pointed to the large white metal box at the bottom of the cabinet. It had two green LEDs on top and a few switches. "That's the UPS," she said, referring to the uninterrupted power supply. "It can power all recorders and cameras for up to six hours. Long enough to record any crime."

"I'm impressed. What's next?"

"Tomorrow night we install the motion detectors and the custom firewall software on the key hard drives as well as all of your workstations to keep hackers from benefiting from forced core dumps. Then we start the training sessions for your selected personnel, the ones you want to operate in Yellow Mode. I also need to train your security guards on using the video equipment and the alarm system. Oh, we're also invading your office for ten minutes tomorrow to install a panic button under your desk. Pressing it will trigger a silent alarm directly to the police."

"Seems like you have thought of everything."

"Well, I still need to sell you on the EM scanners. They can be really helpful if someone tries to sneak out a diskette. When they get home all they'll have is garbage."

He shook his head. "I'm not sure about those yet. Let's see how this new hardware and training works out and maybe I'll be ready to take the next step."

"A sensible decision," she said.

"I'd like to think of myself as a sensible man." He pointed at his watch. "And sensible people are never late. Our reservation is in fifteen minutes. Shall we?"

Kate glanced at her black jeans and black blouse. "I guess this will have to do."

Holst grinned and winked. "You look great in anything, Kate Donaldson."

6

Sullivan's Steak House was located on Fourth Street and Colorado, in downtown Austin. They drove in separate cars and parked in adjacent spots on the dimly lit lot across the street. Kate had used the few traffic lights along the way to put on a touch of lipstick and eye shadow, both of which always had a transforming effect on the former CIA officer, bringing out her cat-like eyes and full lips.

The night air was cool and dry. Kate took a deep breath as she walked around her car to meet up with Holst, who was paying the parking lot attendant.

He glanced at her with quizzical eyes, his mouth curved up at the ends. "You look better every time I see you."

She laughed. "Amazing what a little makeup can do."

"I don't think the makeup has anything to do with it." That smile again, accompanied by warm and honest eyes glistening under the street lights.

"Thanks, but you're being too—"

A dark sedan drove slowly up Colorado, roughly a hundred feet from them, its rear window rolled halfway down. Although the interior of the vehicle was dark, Kate saw the glint of glass as the sedan, a late-model Mercedes, drove beneath a street light. She would have written it off as a person wearing glasses, but not when noticing the murky silhouette of a man lowering something from his face with both hands as the Mercedes accelerated and turned the corner.

Binoculars? Maybe a camera?

Her senses rushed from White Mode to Orange Mode—visual contact with a potential enemy. Her fingers ached to hold a weapon. Her legs urged her to seek cover. Her spine tingled in anticipation of a marksman's bullet. Someone was tailing them. The parking lot and surrounding building suddenly turned surreal as her senses became highly tuned to her environment, to the movement of people, of vehicles.

"Kate? Are you all right?" Brandon touched her left elbow. "You look as if you've just seen a ghost."

She inhaled deeply, forcing control in her external appearance and her voice as she said, "It's—it's nothing. Just got light-headed for a moment. I've been on my feet all day."

Kate couldn't let anyone in on her previous life. She could also not afford to do anything out of the ordinary to indicate that she knew she was being followed.

Brandon put his arm around her to provide the balance that Kate didn't need but didn't refuse either. She actually welcomed the proximity to this large man, if only because his sheer size might discourage her tail from launching an attack.

They walked side by side toward the restaurant, crossing Colorado Street, blending with the many couples going in and out of the popular restaurant and bar. Her mind, however, spun faster than a cyclone.

Who is following me? And most importantly, why? Why

is someone after me? Who ordered the surveillance? The Agency? Impossible. I've kept my nose clean. They have nothing on me.

Per her agreement with the CIA, Kate was to call a number once a month and leave a short coded message, including her current state of affairs, as well as any changes in home address or chosen career. She had done so religiously.

Did I make a mistake? Maybe the figure in the rear seat was just polishing his glasses.

Get real, Kate! You know a tail when you see one, and that was definitely a surveillance team.

Once inside, Kate insisted in getting seated in the rear, by the double door leading into the kitchen, puzzling not just Brandon, but also the hostess, who was planning on seating them at a cozy booth by the front—nice but without a back door in case . . .

In case of what? In case someone comes in shooting?

While she forced her paranoid mind into focus, Brandon Holst ordered a bottle of a Texas sauvignon blanc and a couple of appetizers. She went through the motions of keeping a light dinner conversation, asking him about his family's ranch, about his youth, about his career—questions targeted at making him do most of the talking while Kate did plenty of thinking, of calculating, of speculating.

By the end of her second glass her paranoia had dropped a couple of notches, allowing her to begin enjoying the evening, listening with growing interest as Holst explained to her how he had saved every penny he'd made for five years, and then went on to borrow twice as much to scrape together enough capital to launch Holst Enterprises two years ago, a company he still owned one hundred percent.

"But then we got our first big break," he said as the waiter brought their appetizers, stuffed mushrooms and half a dozen oysters Rockefeller. "A large high-tech company in town needed a better software tool to collect engineering-level data from multiple geographical locations . . . Austin, Sunnyvale, Manila, and Singapore, and perform complex analytical operations to monitor and adjust their manufacturing line.'' He took a fork and played with a stuffed mushroom. ''I was able to provide that software for them at a fraction of the cost of the competition and have it ready and fully debugged a month ahead of schedule.''

Well aware of the difficulty software companies have in adhering to their development schedules, Kate nodded, truly impressed. Heck, even the giant Microsoft failed to deliver Windows95 and Windows98 on time.

''How did you pull that off?''

He leaned forward, a mischievous look painted on his ruggedly handsome face.

''I cheated.''

She laughed. ''How?''

''I'd been working on such a tool for some time because I knew most large corporations had expanded their manufacturing across multiple geographical sites, pushing their existing data collection and analysis software to the breaking point. When the executives of this particular company, which shall remain nameless because of a confidentiality agreement, opened their door for bidding, I not only provided them with a very comprehensive bid, but also gave them a sample copy of what the program could do—while making them believe that my team had written it in the month it took for the company to go through the bidding process.''

She smiled. ''That wasn't cheating. That was being smart, making your own luck.''

She picked at the spinach over a baked oyster. It was delicious.

''Whatever it was, it was good enough to land us our first big contract. And to this day, they're still our customer, purchasing upgrades to their software every six months.''

The dinner progressed nicely, with Kate steering the conversation away from herself and allowing Brandon Holst the opportunity to talk about his life, which he did in a non-pretentious way that she found quite refreshing.

The potential of a surveillance team monitoring her moves increased her curiosity about the two operative-like men she had seen in his office earlier this evening. She maneuvered the conversation to the point where Holst might talk about it. But he didn't, obviously not wanting to discuss that particular client.

"Tell me more about your Y2K software," she said, sipping wine, regarding Brandon Holst over the rim of the glass. "Is it some kind of silver bullet to solve the Y2K problem?" In the past few days she had managed to get bits and pieces of information about this program that seemed so valuable that it had justified Holst Enterprises spending so much capital to protect it.

He smiled. "If by a silver bullet you mean some program that a Y2K non-compliant corporation can start running on Friday night, when everyone goes home for the weekend, and on Monday morning the problem is fixed, I have to tell you that such a tool is nothing but a pipe dream."

"Then what does your software do?"

"It reduces the problem by an average of fifty to sixty percent. So if a company has achieved a seventy percent compliance level, meaning it has thirty percent to go, my software has the potential, if properly used, to eliminate fifty percent of the remaining thirty percent. That company can go from seventy percent compliance to around eighty-five percent. That's significant, but it's no silver bullet."

"How does it do it?"

That smile again. "By making a computer understand that 99 in the year field means 1999, and that 04 means 2004."

"That's the end goal of any program targeted at addressing the Y2K bug. How does your program in particular actually achieve this?''

''Using a combination of common programming techniques in conjunction with a good understanding of how users will use the software. In the hands of properly trained personnel, the software turns into an incredibly powerful tool. I'm actually amazed that the large software companies haven't figured it out yet.'' Brandon cut a mushroom in half with his fork and ate it, chewing it slowly.

''Give me an example of one of your programming techniques.''

Swallowing with the help of a sip of wine, he said, ''Sliding windows.''

Kate raised her eyebrows. ''Sliding windows?''

''It's based on a pretty common Y2K programming technique called windowing. Essentially, you take all of the years from 00 to 99 and divide them into two groups, based on a carefully selected center, or pivot point. Pick a number from zero to 99.''

Kate shrugged. ''Twenty?''

''If we make our pivot point twenty, it means that any number from 00 to 20 will be assumed to be in the new millennium, or 2000 to 2020. Any number *higher* than twenty, will be assumed to be in the current millennium, or 1921 to 1999. You now have taught the computer a new way to interpret the data in the two-digit year field. That's the basis of *windowing*.''

''But all you're doing there is just postponing the problem right? Eventually we'll get to the year 2021, which the computer will interpret at 1921.''

''But it has bought you twenty years to fix the problem correctly, and by that I mean eliminating all two-digit year fields in place of a minimum of five or six digits.''

Kate regarded Holst across the white tablecloth, half-empty bottle of wine, glasses, and sparkling silverware.

''Why five or six? All we need is four, right?''

"Wrong. We need four up to the year 9999. Then we go through another reset to the year 10,000. Might as well think ahead this time, especially since memory space is so cheap."

"Never thought about that. It seems like a very distant problem."

Holst frowned. "That's what the first programmers said back in the sixties. 'Why waste space on more than two digits for the date now? The end of the century is still over thirty years away. Surely by then we will be using four digits for the date.' We're still not, and now we have to come up with patches like windowing to get by until a real fix is put into place."

"Windowing," Kate said, considering his explanation. "The key to making windowing a viable technique is selecting the correct pivot point, right?"

He nodded. "The right pivot point for, say, thirty-year home mortgages may be totally inadequate for a life-insurance company, whose contracts may span more than thirty years. A way to address that is by having sliding windows according to the particular application. There are, of course, the complications of trying to network systems that use different pivot points, requiring each system to display its pivot offset from a standard reference number, like fifty. Then, when users of different pivot-point systems exchange data, the software will automatically read this offset and adjust the incoming file to make its date compatible with the other files in that system."

"Sounds complicated."

"It does add a level of complication to a very complicated problem, but it also keeps the systems running while a more permanent solution is developed. Anyway, my technique of sliding windows takes the basic windowing principle to a higher level, mixing it with other techniques."

She set her elbows on the table, intrigued by the capability of his software. "What other techniques?"

"Now we're getting into confidential ideas," he said, lowering his voice. "The first one is time-shifting, a principle better explained with an example. The operation of subtracting 99 from 00 yields −99. However, if that operation was meant to yield the difference in years between 2000 and 1999, −99 is obviously the incorrect answer. But what if you represented the operation in this way?" He reached for the Mont Blanc pen in his pocket and grabbed the napkin beneath his wine glass.

$$00 - 99 = (00 + 6) - (99 + 6)$$

"Now, if we stick to only two-digit math and we resolve the math within the parenthesis first, as would a computer, we get the following:"

$$(00 + 06) - (99 + 06) = (06) - (05) = 01$$

Kate stared at the numbers, realizing the beauty of this simple trick. Adding 99 to 06 in two-digit math resulted in 05, because in two-digit math, the third digit was truncated. "I see," she said. "What you're doing is essentially bringing both numbers into the same century, and then doing the math to yield the correct number of years."

"You've got it. Of course, our situation is more complicated than that because dates are more than just numbers. For example, January 1st, 2000 is a Saturday, but January 1st, 2005 is not. So this simple time-shifting concept needs to evolve into something that comprehends the days of the week within a year, and also the fact that we have leap years every four years."

She nodded, realizing the complication.

"That was another challenge we had to overcome in the quest for the best method," he added. "However, as in all of our previous hurdles, the answer was embedded in the nature of the problem itself. After several brainstorming sessions, we managed to evolve the concept of time-shifting into its more refined version, which we called *encapsulation*. There is a cycle of seven for the days of the week, and a cycle of four for the leap years. When you multiply the two, you get a master cycle of twenty-eight years. The days of the week repeat exactly every twenty-eight years; thus January 1st, 2000 is a Saturday, as is January 1st, 2028.''

"I see," she said, marveling. "The encapsulation technique simply adds twenty-eight to two-digit years before performing any other calculations."

"Exactly."

"A simple and elegant solution," she said.

"A simple and elegant *patch*,"Brandon said, pouring wine into her glass, filling it halfway, then filling his to the same level. "Encapsulation, time-shifting, and windowing are techniques used to *patch* up existing Y2K noncompliant code and force it to be compliant for a few more decades, and at the price of making every piece of software out there far more complicated than it needs to be. The real solution is to do away with all two-digit years and replace them with five- or six-digit years, but that process may take at least five to ten years to complete. We're just buying us that extra time until we get around to fixing it right."

"So, all we're really doing is pushing out the deadline, right?"

He nodded. "That's what we humans always do, right? If we can't meet the deadline, let's find a way to push it out so we can get by until we get our act together. But even all of the techniques that I've mentioned have their shortcomings. Take encapsulation, for example. Adding twenty-eight to two-digit dates may cause other problems if those dates are buried in serial numbers that use the two-digit year field for other computations, like the serial numbers of products in a grocery store. Each product has a bar code number, say 8392-1856-99-60. The two-digit year field holds a 99, for 1999. The last two digits, which are called the check digits, are the product of adding every number in the sequence. Check digits are used to validate the rest of the serial number, like those in credit cards, Social Security numbers, and product stock numbers. Adding twenty-eight to the two-year field in this case will yield invalid check digits, which would result in the rejection of credit cards, or products.''

"Sounds complicated."

"That's because it is. Of course, the techniques that I've mentioned only work after you have figured out a way to *find* the two-digit fields representing dates. Often they're quite buried in the software application, like in the example I've just gave you, or much worse."

While Kate thought of an appropriate response their dinner arrived. She had ordered a lady's filet, just eight ounces and wrapped in bacon. Brandon had ordered a sixteen-ounce ribeye. He had ordered mashed potatoes as his side order; Kate had opted for steamed vegetables. At a glance her steak appeared burnt, but Brandon proceeded to explain that Sullivan's sears its steaks to keep the meat's natural juices from boiling out during the grill cycle. She cut her filet in half and realized how tender it was, cooked just to her specifications of medium rare.

They dug in. After a few bites of the most delicious steak she'd had in years, she said, "So, your software has a section that finds these non-compliant dates, right? And then another section that fixes them?"

He nodded with a mouthful, saying after swallowing, "Now you're grasping the larger picture. First you find the two-digit code, then you fix it, then you generate a report to inform the user how it was fixed and how he or she must now use their upgraded software. It's part software

fix and part human training to use the fixed code properly.''

"How do you find the non-compliant two-digit year
fields? It sounds like that would be the hardest part of the
job.''

"It is," he said, smiling. "But you don't expect me to
disclose all of my secrets in one sitting, do you?''

She smiled too. "I'm just trying to keep the conversation lively.''

"In that case," he said, pointing at her with his fork,
"why don't we talk about you?''

7

The moment they stepped back outside, Kate's apprehension returned. Her eyes scanned the sidewalk, the parking lot, the people immediately around her as well as those across the street, her trained eyes detecting nothing wrong, no hasty moves, no figures recessing into the shadows.

"I really enjoyed this," he said.

Kate sensed sincerity in his stare. So far, Brandon Holst had been the perfect gentlemen, always making her feel at ease, never pressuring her in any way, even to the extreme of suggesting taking separate cars on both dates to make her feel comfortable.

Dates? Kate felt way too old to be *dating*.

"I did too," she replied, not only sounding as if she had meant it, but actually meaning it, despite her short-lived paranoia episode. "Great food, good wine, and excellent company. Thanks, Brandon. I really appreciate this, and also your confidence by sharing some of your work secrets with me." She extended her hand, expecting him to shake it. Instead, the large cowboy kissed it.

Kate felt color coming to her cheeks and was glad they were in the murky parking lot.

"I'd like to see you again if you don't mind," he said with difficulty, obviously not used to doing this. "I really enjoy your company."

"I'll be in the office tomorrow," she replied, her professional side forcing words to her mouth. "There's still much to be done."

A part of her regretted those words the moment they came out, but the instinct that had kept her alive for nineteen years commanded her to stay away from personal relationships—something her enemy could use against her, hurting the people she cared for in the process.

He frowned. "That's not what I—"

"One step at a time, Brandon," she said, trying to find a middle ground between her conflicting inner forces, which had reverted her to her former profession the moment she had spotted that tail. But she liked Brandon enough to wish to leave the door open for a future date without making it sound like a commitment. "Let's see how the rest of the week goes. For the record, I also enjoy your company. I'm just—"

He put up a hand. "No explanation is necessary, and I apologize if I seemed too aggressive. I'll check with you toward the end of the week. Thanks for a lovely evening."

Kate studied his face for a moment. The ends of his mouth, naturally curved up, hid how he really felt. "Thank you," she finally said.

Holst waited until she had gotten in her car and pulled out before starting his own car.

In the darkness of her Honda, as she headed home, Kate Donaldson wished to have been more affectionate toward him. Not only was Brandon Holst a gentleman, a hard worker, smart, and an honest man, but she was slowly finding herself quite attracted to the tall Texan. But then, like an external force gripping her senses, her eyes shifted to the rearview mirror, checking for surveillance, spotting none. Her hand automatically rubbed her upper left chest, looking for the Beretta she didn't have. Kate exhaled, wondering if she would ever be able to completely shed her former life.

She reached her house a minute later, pulled into her garage, and went inside. All seemed normal at the Donaldson household. The alarm system told her she had had no uninvited visitors.

Heading upstairs, undressing, and getting in bed, she hugged a pillow and stared at the slow-turning ceiling fan. Perhaps it was just a coincidence, she told herself, but she realized that she had really enjoyed Brandon's company. For the first time in her life she had actually met a decent, hard-working, honest man.

Don't ruin it by being paranoid. The CIA is a thing of the past.

But was it? What if the Agency was now spying on her? *But why would they?* She had abided by the rules of her contract.

Reaching for the phone on her nightstand, Kate dialed a number she had long committed to memory, praying that it had not changed since her departure from the CIA. After three rings a tired voice came on the line.

"Yes?"

"Hello, Mike."

"Kate?"

"That's right."

"What—*why* are you calling me? You know the rules if you need to contact us. This is—"

"I wasn't the first to break the rules. Why are you having me followed?"

"What?"

"You heard me. I spotted the tail this evening, right outside the steak house."

Silence, followed by, ''Kate, I have *no idea* what you're talking about.''

''Really?''

''I swear to you. I have not ordered any surveillance on you. I've been quite satisfied with your periodic reports. You're sticking to your end of the deal and we're honoring ours.''

''I'm telling you, somebody was watching me today.''

''And it wasn't us.''

Kate peered at the wall of her bedroom.

''Look, is there any chance that you may have mistaken the tail?''

''After nineteen years?''

''Are you *absolutely* certain?''

Kate closed her eyes, forcing her mind to recollect every detail. She remembered the sedan, the rolled-down rear window, the glint of glass coming from inside the slow-moving vehicle, the figure in the backseat.

''Well?''

''Not a hundred percent.''

''Tell you what, then. I'll make a deal with you. If it happens again, contact me immediately and I'll have a couple of officers follow you for a few days to see if they can spot someone.''

She kept her eyes closed as she said, ''All right,'' before spending ten minutes declining Costner's multiple attempts to get her back to Langley. At first she had been annoyed, but then she felt strangely flattered that the CIA wanted her back.

Then she had frowned. *Not in this lifetime.*

She finally hung up, wondering if she was just being too paranoid. What if it was just a pair of eyeglasses and the man was removing them from his face to polish them? What if it was any other of dozens of possible explanations except for a surveillance team?

Relax. You're out of the game. Get on with your new life.

My new life.

Kate decided right then to make the next move tomorrow on Brandon Holst.

8

At her suggestion, Kate and Brandon agreed to go out the following Friday to see a play at the Zachary Scott Theater, by the shores of Town Lake, the name given to the Colorado river as it flowed through downtown Austin.

They stepped out of the Holst Enterprises building together, opting to take his truck and leave her Honda at the office, under the watchful eye of the newly installed security system on which Kate had trained all three security guards, each responsible for a different shift. The guards, all retired police officers, had not taken Kate seriously until she'd presented them with a couple of surveillance scenarios, which all three failed miserably. "On this job you can't think like a cop," she had told them. "You have to think like a burglar in order to defeat a burglar. You have to avoid repetition. Stay away from patterns. Go to the bathroom at different times every day. Never make your rounds at the same time, or for similar durations."

Brandon opened the door for her, waited until she had

climbed aboard, and gently closed it before walking around the front of the vehicle.

Five minutes later, the former CIA officer watched the city lights rush by as they cruised down Lamar Boulevard, toward the river.

"Do you know what I realized today, Kate?"

She sat sideways on the long front seat, facing him. "What's that?"

"That I've just about told you most of my life's story, but you haven't really told me much about you, even after I nearly begged you the other night at Sullivan's."

"That's because I've lived a pretty boring life."

He shot her a look, his rugged features softening with humor. "Somehow I *seriously* doubt that."

"What makes you say that?"

The burly cowboy shrugged. Kate thought he looked quite handsome in his Wrangler jeans and starched black shirt buttoned all the way up to the top button. For being such a mild-mannered man, he surely conveyed a sense of power. Or was it stability that she sensed every time she gazed at him, whether sitting at the helm of Holst Enterprises solving everyone's problems or at the shooting range, where he had surprised her with his marksmanship? Kate wasn't quite sure, but she felt certain that whenever she was with him a sense of comfort filled her, like if she were not alone anymore.

"Just because," he finally said. "The way you handle yourself, with an air of self-assurance that can only come from being totally confident in oneself. That's usually acquired only after facing and overcoming pretty serious challenges."

Kate didn't reply, wondering about a man who could see so much without knowing anything about her past.

"This afternoon, for example," he continued. "I saw you training the guards. I watched how you turned their skeptical attitudes around, how you manipulated their opinions to make them *want* to use the system, to make them *want* to adopt your security methods over their own—which, by the way, are based on a lifetime of police work.''

Kate shrugged. ''Those are different tactics than what's required to protect a building. On the street police officers are always on the move, making arrests, dispensing traffic tickets, solving domestic disputes, breaking up fights. The protection of a building involves a different kind of approach. They are now at the receiving end of someone else's attack. They have become stationary, no longer able to go to the troubled spot and solve the problem. They are now at the potential trouble spot and trying to prevent the problem from taking place. Their job is now to avoid having to call the police, to use the tools I have installed as a deterrent against all types of intruders, either physical or cyber.''

''See what I mean? You're incredibly certain of yourself. A person doesn't get to be this way by living a boring life.''

As they reached the intersection of Lamar and Barton Springs, just a couple of blocks away from the theater, Kate wondered if she should open up a little. She decided to give honesty a chance for a change, at least up until the point where she would violate a federal law.

''You're right about the challenges,'' she said with difficulty. After a lifetime of deception, honesty was a foreign concept to get used to. ''My life's been filled with them. I never knew my father, and my mother died when I was very young. After three years of hopping from foster home to foster home, I ran away and joined a gang, who became my only family. They taught me most of what I know about staying alive, about survival instincts.''

Brandon Holst didn't utter a word, even as he turned into the theater's parking lot and shut off the engine and the headlights. She told him about her teenage years, living in the streets of San Antonio, learning about guns, about knives, about loyalty, about blood oaths. She apologized for having lied to him about her father, about becoming proficient with weapons. She talked openly about her final days as a gang member, recalling with vivid detail the ambush, the sudden death of the only family she had ever known, the months recovering from her wounds, the visits from the priest, the life-saving decision to change her ways, the challenge of integrating herself back into society. The years at a Catholic boarding school followed, where she developed new friendships, new ideals, new dreams.

"After that came college, in Virginia, where I got my technical degree. The rest, as they say, is history," she said, purposely leaving out just the last nineteen years.

Brandon Holst was now also sitting sideways, facing her. Somewhere along the way he had reached over and held her hand. In the twilight of the truck's cabin, he leaned over and kissed her on the cheek.

"What was that for?" she asked, biting her lower lip.

"For being so brave. For having the courage to face the world alone, without anyone to support you, to cheer you on."

She smiled. "I did get some help along the way. I also was honored to have met some pretty wonderful people both in my old gang and also in school. I wish I could say the same about my professional life."

His eyebrows rose. "I guess I won't take that personally."

"That's not what I meant. I think you're a wonderful person, otherwise I wouldn't had agreed to go out with you."

"Going out? I thought these were just business entertainment." Humor filled his voice. "And we're doing a pretty poor job at that. The play's already started." He tapped his watch.

Acting entirely on impulse, Kate leaned over and kissed

him on the lips. Then she asked, "Does this happen during your typical business meetings?"

"Ah . . . no . . . not at all," he replied, obviously having been caught by surprise.

Kate enjoyed watching him momentarily lose his composure, not certain of what to do, like a teenager on his first date. As he readied to say something, she put a finger to his lips. "Just kiss me, would you?"

9

Almost two weeks later, on a Sunday afternoon, Kate and Brandon headed for his family's ranch in Marble Falls, where his family was hosting a barbecue to celebrate the birthday of one of Brandon's brothers.

The drive was quite pleasant, driving out of Austin on Bee Caves Road until reaching Highway 71, as if they were going shooting, but continuing past Highway 620, until 71 intersected Highway 281 a half hour later, where Brandon turned north.

Sparsely forested hills expanded as far as Kate could see. Mostly cedars, oaks, and a variety of cacti dominated the terrain, divided by miles and miles of barbed wire under a blazing afternoon sun. She wore shorts and a polo shirt. He had one of his customary pair of Wranglers, but wore them with a plain black T-shirt, which exposed the powerful arms she had felt wrapped around her the other night in his truck when they had kissed for nearly an hour, missing the play and then laughing about it. But they had done nothing more than kiss. Brandon's hands had remained glued to her waistline, never venturing north or south, and Kate had welcomed that. The cowboy had continued to handle himself like the perfect gentleman. That had led to another attempt at seeing the play the following evening. This time they had succeeded, even after having a brief repeat of the previous night. Their next date, four days later, had consisted of dinner and a movie. Afterwards they had gone to his house for a nightcap, Baileys on the rocks, which they sipped while sitting in his back porch overlooking the green belt running behind the hilly community. They had talked and gazed at the stars for almost two hours, their conversation floating from business to personal and back to business, mixed with moments of kissing and hugging, plus an occasional brushing of his hand over her chest. Kate had enjoyed the brief but intimate touch, which made her feel even more attracted to him. Their next date had been at her place, where she had prepared grilled salmon and vegetables, followed by a chilled California Chardonnay on her balcony, overlooking the Barton Creek green belt. Again they had kissed while sitting in a wrought-iron glider, his hands adventuring a little, but respectfully remaining over her clothes. Now, after dating steadily for just under three weeks, Brandon was bringing her to meet his family, something that Kate considered a pretty serious step in their relationship.

They drove through the middle of Marble Falls, which Brandon described as a typical small Texas town, with a Wal-Mart on the outskirts of town, the customary Dairy Queen restaurant, and an old-fashioned city hall building in the center of town.

His family's ranch was located down a gravel road projecting east of Highway 281. Brandon turned onto it, the truck bouncing as it left the asphalt road and cruised down the uneven terrain flanked by dense vegetation, tires kicking gravel, a cloud of white dust following them. After a bend in the road, they drove past a sign that read:

SEVEN DIAMONDS RANCH
JESSIE HOLST & FAMILY

"Seven Diamonds?" she asked.

"For seven brothers, including the one who left to pursue a career in software development."

A long, unpaved driveway extended beyond the sign, leading to a large two-story house.

A small crowd, all dressed in jeans, either long-sleeved shirts or T-shirts, and boots, walked up to greet them as Brandon pulled up behind a row of pickup trucks. Most of the people wore hats. Kate felt a bit out of place with her suburban outfit, but she didn't own a hat and it was still too hot to wear jeans. November in central Texas felt as hot and humid as July in Washington, D.C.

A few kids skipped stones on a nearby pond to the right of what Kate had already catalogued as a mansion. A young couple rode horses on the other side of the pond. Two teenagers threw sticks into the water and laughed at a yellow Labrador as it plunged into the greenish water to retrieve them.

Kate returned her attention to the group around her.

"Hi, darling," said the closest person, a woman in her sixties, the wrinkled skin on her face shadowed by a black cowboy hat that matched her black jeans. She wore a turquoise-colored shirt and an assortment of turquoise and silver necklaces and bracelets. Long silver earrings in the shape of spurs swung as she tilted her head and smiled. She held a bottle of Shiner Bock in her left hand.

"Hello," Kate said.

Before she could react, the woman hugged her. "It's so nice to finally meet you," she said in a voice cracked with age. Kate felt her trembling lips kissing her cheek, the smell of alcohol in her breath reaching her nostrils. Then the lady held her hand while turning to Brandon Holst.

"Now, Brandy, you never told me she was *this* pretty."

The software entrepreneur blushed. Kate looked about her, half embarrassed.

"Kate, this is my mom, Jessie."

"Nice to meet—" Kate began to say.

"Welcome to Seven Diamonds, sweetheart," Jessie Holst said, continuing to hold Kate's hand while walking in front of a group of people, sipping her beer. The elder lady went through the introductions, including all six of Brandon's brothers, plus an assortment of cousins, uncles, aunts, nephews, and nieces. Kate began to shake hands as the names came faster than she could register them. There was a Joey, a Sally, two Mikes, a Chuck, someone named Fernando, an Uncle Bob, and even a Cousin Kate.

The former CIA officer struggled to keep the names and faces straight, giving up after the tenth one.

"And that is Rich Jones," Jessie finally said, pointing one of her turquoise-colored fingernails at the Unabomer impersonator sitting on the front porch of the ranch house, beyond a rustic, waist-high cedar fence surrounding the large two-story stone structure. Then she leaned close to Kate and whispered. "He's not all there, if you know what I mean. But he keeps bandits and coyotes away from my cattle."

Kate was surprised to hear the word *bandit*. She thought that it had died with the Old West. As for coyotes, she wasn't sure she wanted to find out how common they were in the region. She gave Jessie a single nod, whispering, "I met him a few weeks ago at the shooting range."

Jessie turned to Brandon as the group broke up and wandered around the front of the property. Some crowded by a keg inside a yellow trash can filled with ice, next to a pair of guitars resting against a bale of hay. Others headed for a cedar fence bordering the south side of the main house, beyond which a large number of cows pastured on what looked like many of acres of land. A few gathered around a horse while someone inspected one of its hoofs. "You've already brought her shooting?"

Hands shoved in his rear pockets, and kicking dirt while lowering his gaze, Brandon nodded. "Just the other day."

"My, my, this is more serious than I thought. Did you know that a Seven Diamonds boy never brings a girl shooting unless he's serious about her?"

"You're going to scare her off, Mom," said Brandon Holst.

"Not a chance," Kate replied, holding his hand. "I'm not going anywhere."

Jessie patted her son on the back. "Looks like you've gotten yourself a good one, Brandy." She winked at her, smiled, and wandered off.

"And *that*," Brandon said once Jessie Holst got out of ear's shot, "is my mom, tough as nails."

"I like her," Kate said.

"She raised us after dad passed away when I was only ten. They don't make them any tougher."

"And sweeter," Kate added.

He grunted. "You wouldn't think she's *that* sweet if she'd gotten your butt out of bed every morning at five to do your ranch chores before the school bus came." He pointed at several ice chests beyond the small fence, right next to where Rich Jones sat. "Want a cold Shiner?"

"Sounds good."

They went through a small gate. Jones greeted them with a nod as he sharpened a stick with a buck knife. "If it ain't the lady who shoots like a champ but doesn't own a gun."

"Hi, Rich," Kate said, smiling with irony. "How's that Magnum of yours? My hand's still sore."

Jones nodded. "Somehow I'm sure that shooting hand of yours is just fine."

"You're not going to start *that* again, huh, Rich?" Brandon said, stepping up to her defense.

Jones shrugged. "Suit yourself, but my instincts have yet to fail me, even at my age."

"Yeah, yeah, yeah." Brandon shook his head as he lifted the top of one of the ice chests and inspected its contents. "Amazing," he said to Kate. "We're out of Shiners. It's going to have to be either Diet Coke or beer from the keg."

"I'll take the soda," she said.

"Sounds good." He snatched two and closed the lid before glancing at Jones. "We're going for a walk. Why don't you guard the drinks against conspirators?"

Jones sighed and returned to his knife and sharpened stick. They left him and his mistrustful attitude, strolling side by side sipping their sodas, reaching the group inspecting a horse's hoof. Jessie Holst was with them.

"What's going on?" Brandon asked.

"It's Daisy," said Jessie, referring to a large mare. "She's got hoof rot again."

Brandon handed Kate his Coke can and took a look at the front left hoof in the hands of Jessie Holst, who had turned it up, exposing the bottom of the hoof.

"We have been trying hoof grease for a few days and it has helped some, but it has not gotten rid of it."

Brandon produced a red Swiss Army knife, extending a tool that resembled a blunt knife. "I'll need a solution of one part bleach and three parts water."

One of the cowboys standing next of Jessie took off toward the ranch house. Brandon turned to Jessie, clutching the hoof against her lap. "Hold her steady," he said.

"I've got her."

He dug and scraped brownish matter from the center of the grayish hoof for a couple of minutes. The horse remained amazingly calm during what looked like a painful procedure. She wondered if Daisy was in pain. Halfway through the process Brandon gazed at Kate, almost as if he had been reading her mind and said:

"Don't worry. She can't feel a thing."

Kate was momentarily startled, in a way feeling annoyed that this man could see through her so easily. On the other hand, a sense of completeness filled her at the thought of another human being understanding how she felt without her having to say a word.

The cowboy returned with a glass filled with a milky liquid, which Kate guessed was Brandon's magic recipe for curing hoof rot.

Brandon poured it slowly on the track he had created after clearing the decayed section. The liquid began to bubble up.

"It's sealing and curing the wound," he said, waiting another five minutes before drying it completely and applying a maroon paste from a can by his feet. "The grease should do better now."

Jessie released Daisy, who trotted away. "You were always a natural, Brandy. We sure miss you around here."

"You can't afford me, Mom." He kissed his mother on the cheek before retrieving his Diet Coke from Kate, taking her by the hand, and leading her away from the group.

"Where are we going?"

"To a very special place. Just down that trail," he said, pointing with the can of soda.

"I've never met anyone like you," she said, not certain why she said it.

"Is that good or bad?"

"Oh, it's very good," she replied. "Very good."

On the way they chatted briefly with a few relatives, including two of Brandon's brothers, both equally burly. Kate learned that all of his brothers had gotten degrees in either agriculture or veterinarian medicine. They were also all married, and half of them with one or more kids. Brandon was definitely the odd duck, not only remaining single all these years, but also earning a degree not directly applicable to the daily running of the Ranch Seven Diamonds. Kate now understood why Jessie Holst had been so glad to see Brandon with someone.

The trail led to a pond in the far side of the property, towering oaks shadowing it.

"My brothers and I used to walk this trail alone many times when growing up, mostly after finishing our homework and our ranch work," he said. "I've always found it very peaceful. The pond's stocked with catfish. Makes for great fishing."

Kate inhaled the fresh afternoon air, listening to the distant chirping of birds and the clicking of insects, watching a mosquito hawk dance with the beams of sunshine filtering through the thick canopy of an opulent oak. Then she noticed it, on the wide trunk of the closest oak, by the water's edge.

"What's that?"

Brandon smiled, his eyes glistening with affection. "That's my family's history tree."

"History tree?"

"Come," he said, giving her hand a gentle squeeze. "Take a closer look."

The letters were well formed, lines made of bark carved from the tree. They started at the bottom, forming a circle around the base, where the grass pressed against the bark.

JEFF '57   BRANDON '59   HOWARD '60   STEPHEN '63

And so on. Then above each of the birth years were other significant events, moving up the trunk, forming a column for each of the seven boys.

"This is so neat," she commented, reading Brandon's column, her eyes scanning the markings, getting craggier and blurrier with age, with the passage of time.

HOLST INC.   '97

AMD   '81–'96

UT   '76–'81

MF HIGH   '72–'76

FIRST LASSO   '69

RODE HORSE   '65

19" 7 LBS

BRANDON   '59

"The story of my life," he said. "Not much of a social life, I'm afraid. Unlike my brothers."

Kate read some of the other columns, spotting marriages, followed one or more years later by the births of their children.

"Guess I never did find the right one," he added, pointing at the unmarked bark at the top of his column.

Kate looked into his eyes. "Sometimes it takes a little longer for the right one to come along."

Beneath that magnificent oak, the hill country's breeze swirling her hair, Brandon Holst put a hand on her face. "I think the wait has been worthwhile."

10

Kate Donaldson remembered many pivotal moments in her life, events that, good or bad, had shaped her views, her opinions, her life itself. She remembered each as it had occurred: the traumatic death of her mother from a drug overdose, the multiple foster homes, her escape to the streets, the murders of her blood brothers and sisters in her gang, the Catholic priest, her reforming years, the acceptance of the cards that life had dealt her, new friendships, new hopes, college, the CIA. Along the way she had met a few men that had crossed the boundary of friendship. Lovers, if only for a short while, affairs cut short either by death, as during her gang years, or by career aspirations later on. Each short-lived romance had left her disappointed, hardening her heart, lessening her hope for true love, if there really was such thing.

But tonight, as she surrendered herself in the arms of Brandon Holst, Kate Donaldson wondered if true love did exist after all. They had been sipping wine in Brandon's living room, just as they'd done in the past. They had talked about their lives some more, about their aspirations, their dreams. They had even joked about some of his relatives, about the paranoia of Rich Jones. But their conversation had turned to the carvings on the family oak tree, to that virgin section of bark at the top of his column of life. And at that moment, eyes locked, lights dimmed, the alcohol lowering their self-defenses, Kate and Brandon had embraced, had kissed, softly at first, then with passion, with meaning. This time his hands had wandered, had unbuttoned her blouse, had slid beneath her brassiere.

Kate closed her eyes to his touch, to his kiss, lying back on the sofa, feeling his body over hers, his hands undressing her, caressing her.

She shuddered as he entered her, her heart pounding like a piston, her body on the border of pleasure and pain, maybe because it had been such a long time, or maybe because Brandon's massive body was equally proportionate everywhere. But she slowly relaxed, breathing him in, her body stretching to absorb him, her legs wrapped around his thighs, her fingers running the length of his back as he swept over her, again and again, moving in unison, with harmony, transporting her to a place far away from her previous life. Kate let it all go, her paranoia, her loneliness, her former life, as Brandon shoved it all away with every thrust, unifying their feelings for one another, bringing unity to their relationship, erasing her past. Then she was on top, looking down at him, hands on his chest as she moved her lower body in a slow circular motion, feeling him deep inside of her. Eyes closed, her body spiraling up toward a climax, hands moving to his thighs, clutching them as she pulled him up toward her, Kate shuddered just as he came in a final thrust, hard, swelled, and erupting, hurting her as much as pleasing her.

She collapsed on his chest, breathing heavily, sweating,

her body tingling after being ravaged by this oversized man.

Neither said a word for several minutes. They just lay there, catching their breaths, Kate on top of Brandon, his arms around her back, her face tucked beneath his chin, her fingers toying with the hair on his chest.

"You know," Brandon began. "You go all of your life thinking that you're alive, enjoying the world, getting ahead, making a contribution through your hard work. But it is moments like this that put it all in perspective, suddenly realizing how very little I have *really* lived. Until this moment I simply didn't know what I'd been missing."

She raised her head and stared at him. "That's the nicest thing anyone has ever said to me. And the feeling is very mutual."

"I feel very certain about this, Kate," he said, commitment flashing in his eyes. "My life's been like a forgotten tome, its pages blank until its fortieth chapter. I hope that doesn't scare you off."

She slowly shook her head, feeling as if their physical union had sparked a new bond between them, one she had never experienced before, extending beyond the mere pleasures of the flesh. "There's been a few before you," she said, not really knowing why, perhaps it was the need to open herself to him, to share her whole self with him. "But the feelings I have for you were absent in them." She hugged him. "I'm also very certain."

She sat back up, hands on his chest, massaging him, her fingers exploring him.

He closed his eyes, enjoying her touch for minutes, before raising his hands to return the favor, rubbing her torso, her stomach, her breasts.

"What's that?" he asked softly, two fingers making a circle over a patch of scar tissue beneath her right breast, the place where she had been shot fifteen years go.

"Birthmark," she said, taking his hand, kissing each finger.

"Strange-looking mark," he said. "Looks a lot more like my gunshot wound." He pointed to his upper left shoulder, fingering his own circle of scar tissue. "One of my brothers nailed me by accident during a deer hunt."

She leaned down and kissed his scar before kissing him on the lips, hard, while rubbing her moist pubic hair against him in wide, lazy circles, making him forget about her bullet wound. He began to respond, grabbing her buttocks, entering her again. She gasped, again bordering on pleasure and pain, controlling her breathing, taking him whole, eyes closed.

Afterwards, they bathed together in his whirlpool tub. He hugged her from behind while lathering and sponging her with the care of a mother bathing an infant. Foamy water swirled around them as he caressed her, up and down her chest, between her legs, around her thighs. She kept her head back, resting it against his chest, unconditionally submitting herself to him. Then they switched, Kate taking a little longer to clean every square inch of his body, amazed at just how massive he was, even when relaxed. For a moment she wasn't sure if she should consider herself lucky or cursed, but figured that over time her body would adapt to accommodate him.

When she finished, they sat in the middle of the tub facing each other, smiling mischievously, like a pair of teenagers. Kissing, their wet, slippery bodies sliding against each other, they made love again. This time it hurt far less than before, allowing her to enjoy his endowment to the fullest. He remained on the bottom, letting Kate move at her own speed, at her own rhythm, extracting the kind of pleasure that made her forget about her past, about her future, focusing only on the moment, on a feeling of unity that she wished would never end.

Later, exhausted, they crawled into bed and fell asleep in each other's arms.

11

Kate woke up and reached for Brandon, but instead, her hand found a sheet of paper. Puzzled, she sat up in bed, sloe-eyed, half asleep. She checked her watch. It was almost five in the morning.

"Brandon?"

No response.

She picked up the sheet and switched on the lamp on the nightstand.

> *My lovely Kate,*
> *I had the most wonderful time of my life with you. I have just spent the last hour watching you sleep, and I realized that in this very short time that we have known each other, I've developed stronger feelings for you than anyone else I know.*
> *I'm sorry you will have to wake up alone, but it is a working day and I have a very critical meeting with my top client at seven (the two gentlemen you saw*

the other night) and have to get some work done be-
fore my day really gets started. Wish me luck. Come
by at lunch if you have time and I'll tell you all about
it. If you can't make it, then I'll see you tonight, as
well as every night for the rest of my life.
   Love,
   Brandon

Kate Donaldson stared at the last two lines.
Love, Brandon.
She checked her watch, Friday, November 15th, a date
that she would treasure forever.

A sense of completeness filled her as she read those
words over and over, trying to convince herself that this
was real, an honest relationship, one she thought she could
never have in her previous line of work.

Feeling light-headed, but not from lack of sleep, Kate
dressed herself, staring back at Brandon's king-sized bed,
the ends of her lips curling up.

12

Brandon Holst was a patient men, but this early morning he was quickly losing his patience. For the past week, he had tried to explain his position to Kendell and Gallagher a dozen times through e-mails, voicemails, multiple phone calls, and face to face for the past ten minutes, since the pair had intercepted him as he'd walked into the building. He was not supposed to meet with them until 7:00 A.M. and had arrived early to get some work done before that, particularly because his systems administrator had failed to come to work on Wednesday and Thursday, letting things pile up. Holst intended to call him at home today to find out what was going on. After two years of never missing a day of work, aside for scheduled vacations, Holst had found it quite odd that he had just stopped showing up for work without notice.

"I'm just not sure what else to say, gentlemen," Holst said, exhaling, hands on his lap. These two continued to insist on buying the software rights of Sweeper, something that Holst's gut feeling continued to tell him would not be a good business decision.

He was exhausted this morning, having spent an unforgettable night with Kate. His thoughts momentarily shifted to her.

"Tell us what we want to hear and we'll be out of here," said Gallagher, who had always come across as the brasher of the two.

"The answer is no, gentlemen. You have a license to use Sweeper at your agency. If you need additional licenses for other government agencies, I'll be happy to provide those to you at a discount."

Gallagher's face tightened with obvious anger, sitting back, arms crossed, glancing at Kendell. Holst didn't care. These two men could just vanish from his life as far as he was concerned. When they had first approached him months ago with the proposal to develop a program to help sweep through their software and flag any remaining noncompliant Y2K code, neither of them had put up any upfront cash as a development fee. Neither of them had been willing to give him a written contract to develop this code. They had simply thought it would be a good idea for him to work on Y2K software. Now, *months* later, after Holst had taken that recommendation and ran with it, investing a significant portion of his research and development budget to create what appeared to be a prized piece of code, the U.S. government had sent these two clowns back here in an attempt to purchase the program. Had they put up money and a contract up front, Holst would have had a contractual obligation to sell the software to them. But as it stood today, Holst felt he had been more than generous by selling them a Sweeper license at a significant discount. Beyond that, the software entrepreneur was not about to throw away the incredible opportunity of licensing this program, which would not only make Holst Enterprises a lot of money, but would also help his customer base get closer to Y2K compliance. The U.S. government had been unwilling to make a commitment before. Now Holst was not about to make—

The door to his office was kicked in, swinging on its hinges, the sudden gust of wind it created ruffling the papers on his desk.

A man in a dark jumpsuit wearing a terrorist-style black hood appeared in the doorway clutching a silenced submachine gun. His brown eyes studied the room from behind the holes in the hood. Holst recognized the weapon as a Heckler & Koch MP5, like the one Rich Jones had. Its muzzle was pointing straight at him.

"Stay where you are," the terrorist commanded in heavily-accented English.

Sitting behind his desk, Brandon Holst lifted his left leg, pressing the panic button Kate had installed weeks ago. Kendell and Gallagher remained sitting but turned their heads toward the threat.

"What do you want?" asked Holst, finding that he was not as alarmed as he should have been, perhaps because he had just alerted the Austin Police Department to the intrusion and patrol cars were likely on the way. Perhaps because he was so damned tired. Perhaps because he had grown up with guns at the Seven Diamonds Ranch, and had even been shot once accidentally by one of his brothers during a deer hunt. Maybe it was because he, too, was armed.

He suddenly became conscious of the .32-caliber Beretta Tomcat shoved in his jeans, pressed against his skin. He carried it with a round already chambered. All he had to do was flip the safety and pull the trigger. But his instinct told him to wait for the right moment. After all, the fact that the terrorist wore a hood told him that maybe he intended to keep him alive. Or maybe it was because he knew about the hidden cameras.

The terrorist moved aside as two others stepped into the

office, also clutching automatic weapons. One of them
wore the same color hood as the first one. The other wore
a brown hood. Aside for that, all three men dressed iden-
tically and appeared to be in similar physical space.

"Mr. Holst," said the terrorist with the brown hood,
also in an accent that sounded Slavic. "You have something we need. Now, all three of you step outside."

The government men looked at the terrorist, at one another, and then at Holst, who walked calmly around the
desk, holding his hands up by his chest, palms facing the
terrorists.

Outside, the brown-hooded leader stood in front of
them. The other two terrorists moved behind the hostage
trio, their black weapons no doubt pointed at their backs.

"Now," he said. "Why don't you take a walk down-
stairs, where the hard drive that contains Sweeper is located?"

Brandon froze, not certain how this man knew that the
disk housing his Y2K software was located in the old cellar. The comment threw him off balance. He no longer felt
certain of how much these terrorists knew about his operation. Did they already find some of his employees and
interrogate them? Was it possible that they had kidnapped
and forced the information out of his systems administrator? The fact that he had not shown up for work after two
years of never missing a scheduled workday, combined
with the terrorists' knowledge of Sweeper, surely suggested that. *Is he all right? Did they kill him? And how
much did they learn? Do they know the specifics of the
location of my Y2K software?* And why would a terrorist
group want this software in the first place? To sell it? Holst
couldn't believe that; pirated software was too easily trace-
able these days.

Before he could reply, he felt the end of a bulky silencer
pressed against his spine. "Move, Mr. Holst. We do not
have all day."

The terrorist behind him poked him again with the silencer. Brandon headed toward the stairs.

"And take a friend with you," the brown-hooded terrorist said, motioning Gallagher to go along. "In case you have second thoughts about cooperating."

Brandon reached the stairs with Gallagher by his side and the two black-hooded terrorists close behind, leaving Kendell alone with the leader. The software entrepreneur wondered how long before the cops showed up. He also wondered what would happen then. Would there be a standoff?

A moment later they stood in front of the disk drives, each resembling a standard-size personal computer, but without the monitor and keyboard, stacked ten high over a service table.

"Which one contains the Y2K code?"

Brandon hesitated.

"And no tricks, Mr. Holst, because you are coming with us to help us launch it. If you pick the wrong disk, we kill your girlfriend."

Brandon turned to the terrorist. *Kate? They have Kate?*

"That is right, Mr. Holst. We have your lovely Kate Donaldson with us this minute, so choose wisely. And to show you how serious we are . . ." The terrorist abruptly drove the bulky silencer into Gallagher's abdomen, doubling him over, before pressing the muzzle against the back of his head.

"No! Wait!" Holst shouted, pointing to a drive on the stack. "That's the one you want."

The terrorist lifted the weapon, and Brandon helped Gallagher to his feet.

"Good, Mr. Holst. I am glad to see that your systems administrator was correct in his claim. The disk server was down here. He just didn't know which one."

"The sys admin? Did you kidnap my—"

"He was most helpful . . . until he failed to tell us the precise location in the stack."

"You . . . you bastards!" Brandon Holst shouted, taking a step toward one of the terrorists, who shoved the end of the silencer into his stomach.

Now it was Brandon's turn to drop to his knees gasping for air.

"A foolish move, Mr. Holst. Very foolish indeed."

A minute later they were heading back up the stairs, Gallagher next to him. The terrorists, one of them carrying the disk server, walked behind them.

"Play it cool," whispered Gallagher. "They haven't shown us their faces. That means they intend to keep us alive."

"*Cool,*" Brandon mumbled, his abdomen burning from the blow. He unbuttoned the lower button of his shirt and slid a hand beneath the cotton fabric, pretending to massage the spot where the terrorist had hit him. "Cool is *exactly* how I intend to play it."

13

Kate steered the Honda into her garage at 6:00 in the morning. She walked up the steps leading to the kitchen and unlocked the door, her mind still clouded with recent memories. The alarm system beeped the moment she stepped into the kitchen. She turned on the overheads and was about to key in her code when she noticed the MEMORY light on her alarm system flashing red, telling her that the alarm system had gone off in her absence.

Brandon's face vanished as her operative mind kicked into high gear, rushing to Yellow Mode. The familiar surroundings of her home turned surreal as Kate automatically dropped to a crouch and reached for the gun she didn't have. She cursed under her breath, feeling naked without her Beretta. The alarm system was programmed to go off for three minutes when detecting an illegal entry, also notifying her alarm company. Then the system would reset itself, save for the blinking red light that told her someone had invaded her privacy.

Kate quickly disarmed the system to keep it from going off again. The moment she did so, a shadow detached itself from a living room wall, a pistol—two feet away—aimed at her left temple.

"Don't move," the stranger warned.

Trained instincts resurfaced with unparalleled clarity and swiftness. Kate stepped sideways, sweeping the air directly in front of her at chest level with the edge of her left hand, striking the man's wrist.

The gun went flying.

In the same fluid motion, she pivoted on her left leg and brought her right leg up and around, striking the hooded figure across the head.

The man groaned as he lost his balance, but quickly regained his footing, drawing a knife, its blackened edge protruding from the top of his fist.

Kate reached for one of the steak knives on the counter, holding it in her right hand with the blade also protruding from the top of her fist, just as she had been taught. She lifted her left arm, bent at the elbow, holding it in front of her chest, like a shield, the wrist facing her to protect major arteries.

Bending her legs for balance, her nervous system heightened by the adrenaline searing her veins, Kate moved sideways to the intruder, measuring him, sizing his capabilities, the way he moved, the way he tried to strike like a street fighter with rapid lunges and hasty retreats, which Kate evaded despite her eight-month repose.

The former CIA officer, however, did not mimic the graceful movements of her enemy. She stopped circling him, keeping most of her weight on the balls of her feet, heels just barely off the floor, allowing for rapid evasive motions while avoiding getting cut even on her shielding arm.

The intruder lunged again. Kate moved to the man's left, swiftly, like a world-class pugilist, avoiding the blow while jabbing with her own knife, the sharp blade cutting the intruder across his left forearm. Blood stained the blade of her knife. She ignored it, concentrating on her quarry.

The man didn't utter a sound, even as blood spurted onto the tiled floor. Instead, he lunged again, slashing a circular blow at waist level.

Instead of stepping away from the sweeping blade, Kate stepped in, blocking the assassin's wrist with her left hand while thrusting her crimson blade at the man's larynx. The intruder turned at the last moment, sustaining only a superficial cut to the left side of his neck.

The figures separated, regained their balance, and faced each other again. A third time the hooded man launched an attack, and again Kate blocked it, this time at the price of a cut on her shielding forearm, but gaining the opportunity to counter with another jab, inflicting a deep cut into the man's left arm, just beneath the shoulder.

He grunted, dropping the knife, rolling away from her, reaching for the pistol in the corner of the kitchen.

Kate lurched like a singed cat, ducking beneath his shooting arm as he tried to aim the gun, shoving her knife up, delivering a fatal blow like an uppercut, driving the eight-inch blade into the intruder's neck, snapping the larynx.

The man tensed before going limp, falling onto the tile floor a corpse.

Kate kicked the weapon away from him, her throat aching, her mind racing, considering the implications.

Who was he? What did he want?

He had obviously wanted to capture Kate alive, otherwise he could have easily shot her the moment she'd stepped into the kitchen.

Jesus, Kate. What are you going to do now?

Priorities.

Kate grabbed the pistol, a Sig Sauer 220, which her fingers searched automatically, pressing the magazine catch, verifying that it was fully loaded with eight .45-caliber rounds. She pulled on the slide, ejecting a ninth round already chambered. Reloading it and reinserting the magazine, Kate clutched the weapon in her right hand, muzzled pointed at the ceiling, finger on the trigger. She checked the entire first floor, verifying that nothing appeared to be missing, confirming her suspicions that this was not a burglar.

She reached the stairs, aiming the Sig 220 up, toward the upstairs landing while creeping to the second floor, checking her bedroom first and then the two guest rooms and connecting bathroom. Again, she found nothing missing, or moved, or vandalized, like it would have been during a search. Her house appeared in perfect order.

Except, of course, for the bastard you've just killed in the kitchen.

Damn.

The reality of her situation slowly sinking in, Kate returned to the kitchen. Blood was pooling around the dead man, its thick and inky consistency contrasting sharply with the white tile floor.

Careful not to step on the blood, Kate proceeded to check for identification, though she didn't expect to find any. First she removed the hood, not recognizing him, a man with thick dark hair and angular features of around forty, perhaps a little younger. His dead brown eyes stared at the ceiling. As feared, the stranger carried no ID on him, just the gun, the knife, and a lock-picking tool. Kate also found a telephone number, jotted across the inside of a matchbook. She recognized the local area code, probably an unlisted number where the assassin would call in to report.

She made a face. A professional would had committed that number to memory.

Pocketing the matchbook, Kate stepped back, crossing her arms, the .45-caliber pistol shoved into her jeans against her spine. Staring at the body sprawled on her kitchen floor, Kate considered her next move. She had to dispose of the body and clean up this mess right away. Calling the police was not an option. That would only complicate matters. This man was a professional assassin trying to extract information from her before killing her. The cops would never understand that, and also the fact that whoever ordered the strike was likely to try again. If the police tried to hold her in jail, it would make her an easy target.

She dragged the body to the bathroom, where she dumped it in the tub, before returning to the kitchen, grabbing a mop, and cleaning the pool of blood as well as the trail she had made when dragging the body.

Her thoughts drifted back to the alarm company. *Why didn't they get a call from the auto-dialer the moment the alarm went off?*

She checked to see if she had any messages, frowning at the large numeral zero in the answering machine's display.

She dialed the phone.

"Ranger American," said a male voice at the other end.

"Hi, this is Kate Donaldson. I've just got home and found the memory light blinking red, which means that someone broke into my house. Yet, no one from your company notified me."

"What is your personal code, ma'am?"

Kate gave it to him.

"Just a moment."

She waited, peeking at the floor she had just cleaned.

"Ma'am?"

"Yes?"

"The weekly log shows no activity at your site."

"I was here yesterday morning and all was well. Then I'm out all day and night and come home just now and find the memory light blinking."

"That's very strange, ma'am, because we show no record of an intrusion from your location, otherwise we would have contacted you immediately. We have a pager number and a cellular phone number. We also have instruction to send the police over if we can't reach you.''

Kate nodded while closing her eyes, well aware of the rules. The intruder had disabled the system somehow, preventing it from alerting the alarm company. But he had obviously been unable to reset the control panel, which had alerted Kate of his intrusion.

''Sometimes even the best of systems will malfunction,'' offered the voice in a comforting tone. ''Why don't you double-check all doors and windows and make sure the place is secured? If you want we can also send a technician in the morning to give your system a thorough check.''

''No, thanks. No need for that. I'll just reset it and see if it happens again. Goodbye.''

She hung up, her operative mind reviewing the facts as she returned to the bathroom, forcing control into her thought processes, recollecting the possible surveillance outside of Sullivan's. Then she remembered the stocky businessmen meeting with Brandon the other night. Alarms had gone off in her head then, and now, as she stared at the husky figure bleeding in her bathtub, Kate thought of the possible connection.

She suddenly felt as if she had swallowed hot coals. Brandon was meeting with those questionable businessmen just as a trained operative had tried to kill her.

Brandon! Oh, God! No!

Racing back into the garage, she got into her Honda and drove off.

14

The dawning sun brushed the sapphire sky with strokes of yellow and red-gold. Behind the wheel of her Honda, Kate Donaldson stiffened when spotting the flashing lights of four Austin Police Department police cruisers and one ambulance parked in front of Holst Enterprises. It was just before seven in the morning, and she saw no other cars, except for Brandon's truck and the vehicle of the swing shift's security guard, whose shift ended at seven. Four officers were unrolling yellow APD tape to seal off the area.

She got out, racing toward the entrance, dread filling her, a lump forming in her throat when two paramedics came out pushing a cart with a body covered by a blanket.

Before anyone could react, Kate rushed to them and pulled off the blanket, relief sweeping through her when spotting a stranger . . . wait, *not* a stranger. She recognized the pock-marked face. It was one of Brandon's clients from the other night. He had been shot twice in the chest. His fixed pupils stared at the sky.

"Hold it right there!" a police officer warned, a wiry man of short stature in his mid-thirties, with cropped dark hair. He got in between Kate and the startled paramedics, who covered the body and continued on to the waiting ambulance. He regarded Kate with narrowed blue eyes. "You can't do that, ma'am. You're contaminating the crime scene."

"But . . . but I work here. I know the owner very well," she said, finding it difficult to obey the officer.

"I've got my orders from the lieutenant, ma'am. No one's allowed on the premises at the moment."

"What—what happened?"

"Can't talk about that either, ma'am. See the lieutenant over there." He pointed at a Hispanic man in a brown suit smoking a cigarette while talking to the ambulance driver.

Kate approached him. "Lieutenant?"

The officer turned to her. "Yes? May I help you?"

"My name's Kate Donaldson. I work here. I was just coming into work . . . what—what happened?"

"May I see some ID, please?"

Kate produced her driver's license, as well as her Holst Enterprises' contractor badge.

The APD lieutenant inspected them both before glancing back at her. "I can't discuss the details of the investigation at this time. All I can tell you is that there was a shooting and some people were hurt. That's one of them over there." He pointed at the closing rear doors of the ambulance, which drove off without any sirens.

"What about Brandon Holst? Is he all right?"

The lieutenant narrowed his eyes at her. "How do you know he was in the building at the time of the shooting?"

"His truck," Kate said, pointing at Brandon's Ford. "It's parked right over there."

The APD officer nodded. "Of course. Mr. Holst was injured in the shooting. He's been taken to St. David's."

"How—how long ago was that?"

The lieutenant checked his watch. "About fifteen minutes—look, I'm sorry, but I can't discuss anything else with you until the investigation is over."

"I understand." Kate turned to leave, suddenly not caring about hanging around any longer. She had to get to the hospital immediately.

The lieutenant pulled out a small spiral notebook and flipped through several pages. "You said your name was Kate Donaldson?"

She stopped and nodded.

"How long have you worked here?"

"About two weeks—look, I really need to go see if Brandon is all right."

"In a moment, please. What do you do at Holst Enterprises?"

Kate thought about her answer carefully. "I'm a consultant."

"A consultant of what?"

"I provide Holst Enterprises with high-tech services on a contractual basis."

"What exactly do you provide in your high-tech services?"

"Customized software and hardware." She chose not to disclose anything else, including the knowledge about Brandon's early-morning meeting and the fact that she had recognized the body of one of the businessmen. She also chose not to alert the lieutenant about the hidden monitor cameras, hoping that they would miss them, just as they might dismiss the guard's handheld monitor as a video game. The small system only operated by first pressing a spring-loaded button on the side followed by a six-digit code. The moment the activation button was released the system shut itself off to conserve batteries. The police would not be able to activate the system without the code, which would prevent them from learning about the video system. Her instincts commanded her to hold back information, just as she had done for nineteen years, observing and gathering intelligence without releasing it to outsiders. Right now the Austin Police Department was an outsider. She would sneak into the building later and review the videos.

"We may need you later on for questioning, probably after the folks from the crime lab are through dusting the place. How can I reach you?"

Kate gave him her home number.

"Very well. Please try not to leave town in the next two days. I'll be in touch." The Hispanic APD officer, whose name Kate never even learned, headed for the building.

She found herself rushing back to her car.

15

All Kate remembered was that St. David's hugged the west side of IH 35 somewhere north of the Capitol. She headed north, checking the buildings as she cruised by them in the early-morning traffic. She spotted it as she crossed over Thirty-second Street.

She got off on Thirty-eighth and doubled back on the access road, turning right on Thirty-second and steered into the small parking lot adjacent to the emergency entrance.

She rushed past the double doors and into the emergency room. Fewer than a dozen people waited for medical attention. A teenager cried while holding on to his arm. A woman, presumably his mother, consoled him. A Hispanic couple watched a television set mounted on the wall. The man had a large lump on his forehead. Kate didn't look at the rest, her focus shifting to the nurse behind the counter scribbling on a notepad clipped to a board.

"Excuse me," Kate said. "I'm a friend of Brandon Holst. I was told that he was brought here."

With amazing calmness, the nurse, an African-American in her late fifties, tapped the keyboard of a computer and stared at the monitor for a moment before saying, ''He's in surgery.'' She returned to her scribble.

Kate controlled her temper. ''Do you know what kind of wounds he had?''

The nurse, visibly annoyed at Kate for taking up her time, looked up from her notepad. ''Are you a relative?''

''I'm his fiancée.''

''I can only release medical information to a relative.''

''I'm all he's got,'' she hissed, rapidly losing control. A half-dozen CIA interrogation methods crossed Kate's mind at she stared at the nurse. She forced herself to remain focused. ''Would you please tell me what's wrong with him?''

''I would if I could, but there's also a police block on that information.''

''Look, I know he's been shot. I just came from the scene of the crime. A lieutenant from the Austin Police Department sent me here. How else do you think I got here so soon? *Please?*''

The nurse hesitated for a moment, then glanced at the screen before leaning close to Kate and whispering. ''He had one gunshot wound in the chest. He got here just fifteen minutes ago. That's all I know.''

Kate inhaled deeply, closing her eyes. ''Any idea how long he'll be in surgery?''

The nurse shook her head. ''But you're welcome to wait. As soon as the doctor comes out I'll send him your way.''

''Thanks,'' Kate said.

She sat alone in a corner, her mind racing, considering the possibilities, the various angles. The man with the pock-marked face was dead. Brandon was wounded. What about the other businessman she had seen that evening, the older one with the granite-like face and silver hair? Was he also among the dead? And what about the security guard? Did he get killed? Or was he in another room also undergoing surgery? And who attacked them? One thing that Kate felt certain of was that it had been from the same group who had attacked her at home. But *why* were they attacked? Was this related to Brandon's revolutionary Y2K software? What should she do next? Her operative mind gave her the answer.

Priorities.

First she had to ensure the safety of Brandon. Somehow she felt hopeful that the cowboy's large bulk could take one shot, as long as they had not hit something vital. The fact that he had made it to surgery told Kate that maybe he did have a chance. It was now up to Kate to find a way to protect him. Her instincts also told her that whoever had done this would try again, which led her to the next item on her priority list: find the bastards who did this and make them pay dearly.

Find a way to protect Brandon. Then go after them.

Kate was about to reach for the cellular phone in her purse when she spotted a sign prohibiting its use inside the hospital. She got up and told the nurse she was just stepping outside to make a phone call.

Standing next to the emergency entrance, Kate dialed information and asked for the listing to the Austin Shooting Range.

Rich Jones picked it up on the fourth ring. "Austin Shooting Range."

"Hi, Rich. It's Kate, Brandon's friend."

A pause, followed by, "The shooting lady?"

"Yes."

"What can I do for you?"

"We've got a problem, Rich. Somebody shot Brandon this morning."

"What?"

"He was attacked at his office."

"Is he all right? Was it a robbery?"

"Don't know anything yet. The police are over there now. I'm at St. David's Hospital. He's in surgery."

"Damn! I'm going to kill whoever did this!"

"I'm glad you feel this way, because I'm going to need your help to do just that."

"What do have in mind?"

"It's no secret that we're both professionals, Rich, so I'll spare you the twenty questions. I was in the same business that you were in: intelligence."

A pause, followed by, "What do you need?"

"I need you near Brandon. I don't trust anyone else, especially after the way his company was attacked. And don't come empty-handed."

"Don't worry."

"Also, no offense, but I need you to look presentable. That messy beard and ragged clothes will draw unnecessary attention."

A sigh, followed by, "*Anything* else?"

"Yes. I'll be needing a backup weapon. Something small but with decent stopping power, like a Walther PPK."

"Backup weapon? I thought you didn't have *any* weapons."

"I got one this morning."

"How?"

"That's not important right now."

Another sigh.

"Come quickly," she said. "I have to get moving right away to go after those responsible."

"How?"

Kate stared at the phone number written on the box of matches. She thought of Brandon, of the life she could have with him, of the possibility of that life being shattered by the bullets of some bastard. Anger began to gain on her logical side, on her operative mind. Her training told her that anger was her ally, as long as she could *control* it, direct it, channel it to serve her own needs. Anger would inject passion and dedication into her mission. It would give her the commitment she needed to win. It would make her take higher risks than the enemy, therefore gaining an edge over the enemy.

"Kate? How are you going to find them?"

Determination filling her, she replied, "I'm not going to find them. *They* are going to find *me*."

Book Three

The Return
of the Warrior

■

"I came not to send peace, but a sword."
—Matthew 10:34

1

The man holding the baseball bat stood in the middle of the murky room. His eyes, icy, jet-black like the unruly hair reaching his shoulders, regarded the muscular men kneeling in front of him with lethal calmness.

The wooden bat felt balanced as he clutched it with both hands, like a professional ball player, swinging it in front of him as if warming up for his turn at the plate, listening as it swished across the air, its sound mixing with the short sobbing gasps of a man who had failed to follow his orders.

"I thought I had been quite specific about taking Mr. Holst unharmed," Dragan Kundat said, swinging the bat again, this time missing the goatee on his subordinate's face by an inch. "You have done the exact opposite, first shooting him and then leaving him behind."

"*Da!*" replied his subordinate in their native language, Serbo-Croatian. "*Ja sam izvini!*" *I am sorry!*

"*Kako zelite da umreti?*" *How would you like to die?*

"Ja sam izvini!" The subordinate repeated, perspiration beading on his bald head.

"Oprostite? Jeste li vi glup?" Excuse me? Are you stupid?

"Da! Veoma glup!" shouted out the terrorist, remorse and fear settling on his contorted features as he gazed up at one of the most feared men in Yugoslavia.

Dragan hesitated, gazing across the room at Mirko Todorovic, his second in command on this mission.

The stocky Todorovic stepped forward, a brown hood in his right hand, the silenced MP5 slung across his back. "It was Holst's fault. He fired at us, killing Rudolf. Then we heard the police sirens. Holst must have alerted them, somehow. We couldn't carry him and still get away."

"Don't you see that we need him? He wrote the *dvije hiljade godina* program!"

"And we can still get him. He is *not* dead," Todorovic said. "I've checked with the hospital. He will be out of surgery very soon."

"What about the *policija?* He will be under their protection."

"It will be difficult, but not impossible. And I need every man available, including him, and you."

Dragan considered his options. *"Ustati,"* he finally said, lowering the bat.

His subordinate complied, standing up, inhaling deeply.

As he did, Dragan drove the end of the bat into his groin, doubling him over. "Aghh . . ."

"Do not disappoint me again," Dragan said as his subordinate rolled on the stained concrete floor, both hands on his groin.

A moment later, the terrorist stepped into another room just as dark as the previous one, illuminated only by the pulsating glow of a portable computer connected to the external hard drive taken from Holst Enterprises.

Dragan put a hand on the right shoulder of Erik Haas,

an East German computer hacker lured to Serbia by Slobodan Milosevic's attempt to surround himself with enough
high-tech talent to steal high-tech secrets to bolster his
economy. Dragan remembered clearly how Milosevic had
first given him the assignment two years ago, providing him
with ample resources to go after the best, and the best in the
field were not always found at universities or large corporations. Some of the best software minds of the times were
often renegade programmers, hackers, just like Erik Haas;
brilliant minds either rejected or not yet recognized by the
corporate world. Those outcasts, filled with innovative
ideas, were easy prey for Dragan Kundat and his generous
recruitment budget. In the past two years, Dragan had visited just about every country in Europe, recruiting hackers,
purchasing software—sometimes legally, but more often *illegally*—bribing underpaid programmers and computer engineers to release Y2K technology and make a year's salary
in one evening. And in those instances when money had not
been sufficient, Dragan Kundat had simply acquired the talent the old-fashioned way: He had taken it.

"How is it going?" Dragan asked.

The German hacker looked over his shoulder before resuming his work. He was pale and lanky, reminding Dragan of emaciated Bosnians and Croats in Serbian
concentration camps during the early nineties.

"Look," Haas said in his adopted language, the Serbo-
Croatian that he had learned to master in the past two
years. He used a bony finger to push his horn-rimmed
glasses up his nose before adding, "The source code is
protected by a lock."

Dragan leaned closer to the screen.

HOLST ENTERPRISES, INC.
SWEEPER SOURCE CODE VERSION 2.0
ENTER ACCESS PASSWORD:

"Can you break in?" asked Dragan.

Haas shook his head. "Look at what happens."

He entered a random sequence of numbers and pressed ENTER. The screen changed to:

HOLST ENTERPRISES, INC.
SWEEPER SOURCE CODE VERSION 2.0
*** INCORRECT PASSWORD ***
*** ACCESS DENIED ***
ILLEGAL ENTRY ATTEMPT LOGGED IN SYSTEM
PROTECTED BY SOFTLOCK © 1999
DONALDSON SECURITY

The Yugoslav terrorist stared at the name, suddenly realizing that Kate Donaldson was responsible for the protection of the computer code. "Keep trying," he ordered.

"Can't," said the hacker. "I was able to decode a portion of the security code and it contains a counter, limiting the number of consecutive illegal entries to five before the security program reformats the hard drive, erasing all of the data. This was my second attempt. We need to save the last three for the real password, or at least educated guesses."

Dragan nodded, realizing that he simply had to kidnap both Holst and the Donaldson woman in order to be certain that they would yield the access key. Kidnapping just one might not work, because that one could simply refuse to cooperate if he or she considered the password more valuable than his or her life. But if *both* were captured, then Dragan could use one to convince the other to cooperate through torture, just as he had done so many times to force information out of captured villagers, or even soldiers, who cared more about what happened to a friend or loved one than to themselves. The fact that Holst and this woman had been intimate played beautifully into his strategy. But first he had to capture them.

"I shall get you help," Dragan said before storming out of the room and shouting orders to Todorovic. Then he prepared his contacts to get a message out to his superior.

Dragan's message, coded such that no one could understand it except for its intended receiver, was transmitted via an e-mail from Austin to Madrid, Spain, where it was forwarded to Moscow, before being rerouted one last time to Belgrade.

2

Belgrade, Yugoslavia.

Inside a windowless room in the basement of one of his luxurious safe houses sprinkled around the Yugoslav capital, President Slobodan Milosevic, dressed in a finely pressed Italian suit, reviewed the most recent report from his team in the United States before jotting a short response, which one of his personal assistants read before rushing off to convey the message.

Alone, Milosevic stood and paced the large suite, decorated in eye-pleasing pastels and accented with fine modern furniture and fake plants. His blue eyes, however, ignored the array of creature comforts and stared into the distance. He was considering his options, his struggle to make the world see the situation in Kosovo for what it was, contrary to the views publicized by NATO countries.

Milosevic walked alone, back and forth, chin up, hands behind his back, pondering, strategizing, using his life experiences as a platform from which to analyze his situation, his country's dilemma. He had been alone for a very long time. His father had abandoned the young Slobodan and his mother when the boy, whose name meant "freedom," was only five years of age. His father had then shot himself when Slobodan was twenty-one. His mother, a dour Communist activist, had hanged herself from a light fixture in her living room in 1974.

Alone.

Milosevic stopped by his desk, pouting, eyes narrowing, remembering his youth, his school years, his avoidance of extracurricular activities, his unyielding commitment to his studies, his loner attitude, his constant lecturing of classmates he felt weren't properly attired—beliefs and actions that prevented friendships not just during that portion of his life, but also later on.

But there were a few, he admitted to himself, a brief grin cracking his stolid face. One had been his wife, Mirjana, who, like Milosevic, also shared the tragedy of losing her parents at an early age. Another had been Ivan Stambolic, who became Milosevic's mentor while climbing the Communist ladder. It was Stambolic who positioned Milosevic in jobs of ever-increasing importance during the late seventies and early eighties, exposing him to many business, technical, and political aspects of Yugoslavia. It was Stambolic who had fought the Central Committee of the Serbian Communist Party, following his election to president of Serbia in 1985, to accept Slobodan Milosevic as its chief. And it was Stambolic who had sent his loyal deputy to Kosovo in 1987, when local Serbs were protesting their treatment by ethnic Albanians in that province.

Milosevic remembered that pivotal day just outside Pristina, Kosovo, when the local police began to disperse the protesting Serbs with batons and tear gas. Emotion for his fellow Serbians overcoming his natural serenity, the future president of Yugoslavia, patriotism searing his veins, had stood up against the ethnic-Albanian–controlled police force in the region. He followed that bold action with one of the most moving speeches of his life, enchanting the crowd, taking his first independent step to position himself in the ladder to the presidency.

Slobodan Milosevic had realized then the true meaning of the Yugoslav conflict, and he had carried that belief through the liberation wars in Bosnia and Herzegovina, and through his attempt to free the province of Kosovo from the clutches of the Muslim world. He had waved the Serbian nationalistic flag in the aftermath of Communism, when his people needed a new leader, a new figurehead to show them the path to the future, free from the threat of the neighboring Muslims.

Milosevic stared at one of many framed pictures on the wall next to his desk. He remembered this one well, from 1989, when he had rallied his Serbian followers in the Field of Blackbirds, just outside Pristina on the six hundredth anniversary of the terrible Serbian defeat at the hand of the Ottoman Turks in 1389. He had warned his followers that ethnic fissures were scarring Yugoslavia and could no longer be tolerated, lest they risk reverting back to the days when Muslims ruled their land.

Milosevic turned away in anger, eyes closed. He despised NATO, and *especially* the United States and their hypocritical stand on this issue.

How can they possibly dare force me to give up Kosovo, the cradle of my civilization, to these barbarians, to these . . . animals!

Milosevic saw his war in Kosovo just as American President Abraham Lincoln had seen the seceding South, feeling compelled to use his army's iron fist to force it to comply to his rule. The reasons to go to war with revolting provinces changed with the times, but the end goal was always the same: to preserve the Union.

Slobodan Milosevic, the man who was mocked as a future clerk by his schoolmates, the leader who refused to accept the views of foreign nations when it came to his homeland, the patriot who would rather die than allow the descendants of the Ottoman Empire take over his country, had exercised his only option—the same option that Lincoln had adopted in 1861—taking his nation down the only path he could possibly take: Wage open warfare against the rebels, against those threatening his nation's union, the very essence of his people.

War at all cost to cleanse my nation!
War at all cost to unite my people!

But in order to run a successful campaign against the Muslims, Milosevic needed a way to keep NATO from interfering. Unfortunately, he lacked the nuclear arsenal of Russia, his only ally in this holy war. Russia had waged such ethnic-cleansing campaigns against the Muslims in Afghanistan and Chechnya with little direct interference from NATO—beyond protests and covert operations. Milosevic also didn't have the luxury of relying on a large army, or powerful air force or navy to deter outsiders from intervening with his national affairs, like the North Koreans.

So the resourceful Milosevic had opted for a different weapon, one which he could assemble and deliver with surgical accuracy far easier than a suitcase bomb, but just as effective. He had elected to find a way to strike at the world's computer networks, which grew more and more vulnerable as they approached the end of the millennium. His years managing technical industries for Ivan Stambolic had exposed him to the high-tech world, and he knew how powerful yet fragile it really was. The same sophisticated programs that directed cruise missiles and laser-guided bombs against his land could be easily turned into binary garbage by the right computer virus, if properly delivered.

With the assistance of his allies in Russia, Milosevic had mounted a worldwide campaign to acquire Y2K technology for the sole purpose of building such a weapon.

"And we are so close," he mumbled, picking up the report from Dragan Kundat, reading it again. His operative had been only partially successful in retrieving what his scientists believed would be a crucial piece of software for his arsenal. This particular operation, which was offered to Dragan through his contacts in the independent contractor circles, promised to deliver the key to an efficient search of two-digit years. But as Dragan had also indicated, there had been complications, which included the death of one of the independent contractors who had first alerted them to the Y2K source, plus one of Dragan's own trained operatives.

But Dragan was far from giving up. The resourceful Dragan had fallen back on one of his contingency plans, which he was now in the process of executing.

Milosevic nodded, confident in his underling's abilities. He had given Dragan equally difficult assignments in the past, and the former Serbian colonel had delivered time after time, even against overwhelming odds. Dragan had masterminded and executed the operation in London, not only acquiring a gold mine of Y2K technology, but also preventing his enemies from accessing it by destroying the area, which was also quite effective at covering his tracks. Milosevic felt certain that Dragan would not let him down this time.

He will deliver again.

Milosevic picked up the short but stern reply he had jotted down for his aide to forward to Dragan.

Deliver or die trying.

3

Austin, Texas

Kate Donaldson parked her blue Honda near Congress and Fourth Streets, a few blocks away from the Four Seasons Hotel, overlooking the Colorado River. She had called ahead to make sure not only that there were rooms available, but that she would be able to find two connecting rooms.

Shouldering her burlap purse, Kate paid the parking lot attendant and headed not in the direction of the hotel, but up Congress, her eyes briefly landing on Manuel's Mexican Restaurant across the street. Momentarily aching with a mix of grief and anger, Kate turned right onto Seventh Street and continued until reaching San Jacinto Street. The Four Seasons was located at the south end of San Jacinto, as it reached the river. But before she could check in, she had to make absolutely certain that no one had followed her.

Old instincts resurfaced as she strolled one block down San Jacinto, toward the hotel, before casually turning left on Sixth Street, the legendary strip of bars and live-music nightclubs in Austin, in a way resembling New Orleans's Bourbon Street, but cleaner, without the strip joints. Businessmen headed for their afternoon appointments. Tourists walked the strip, snapping pictures, going into the shops, some getting an early start at one of many bars on either side of the street. Bartenders, waitresses, and bouncers headed for their jobs as the clubs got ready for the evening crowd.

Breaking into a sweat because of the heat and humidity, Kate Donaldson walked neither fast nor slow, her eyes looking at everyone without really staring. She inspected a group standing by the entrance to a bar, a couple walking in the middle of the street, and two cops drinking coffee at the corner of Sixth and Trinity. She noticed no sudden changes in stance or head movement. She spotted no instant recognition.

Kate strolled the area for ten minutes before she was satisfied that she had not been followed. She turned on San Jacinto and walked the three blocks that separated her from the Four Seasons. She briefly closed her eyes as she pushed a glass door open and felt a wave of cool air rushing past her, cooling the moisture on her cheeks. She silently welcomed it.

4

Fifteen minutes later, after checking in, Kate stood in front of Room 920. Inserting the flat plastic key into the electronic reader, she went inside, locking the door behind her.

A phenomenal view of the Colorado, stained in gold by the afternoon sun, momentarily caught her attention. Two double beds shared a nightstand opposite a desk and a color television. Pictures of adobe houses and oak trees hung over the beds, reflecting in the long mirror above the desk. A small round table flanked by two chairs by the panoramic windows blocked the view of the rooftops of nearby buildings. She set her burlap bag on the desk, catching herself in the mirror, and deciding that she'd better get some sleep soon. The brown circles encasing her bloodshot eyes were turning deep purple, making her look like a raccoon. Her eyelids grew heavy and her mind was becoming cloudy. But she still could not afford to rest.

A door next to the desk connected this room to the adjacent one. Kate unlocked and opened the door. She faced the second connecting door, which could only be opened from inside the adjacent room. She returned to the hallway, closed the door to Room 920, and went inside Room 922, a mirror image of the first room.

She opened the connecting door and walked back into 920. Unzipping the purse, Kate extracted a small roll of duct tape and a switch blade. Cutting a four-inch strip, she turned the knob of the connecting door of room 922 and applied the tape to the spring-loaded bolt to prevent the door from locking. Next, she grabbed a butterfly screw from the bag, wedged the butterfly between her thumb and index finger, pressed it against the side of the connecting door to Room 922, and began to turn it, driving it into the wood. Now she could close Room 922's connecting door from Room 920 without locking it.

She reached into her bag and removed a small black box attached to a thin metal cable that looped back into the box. She opened the connecting door and walked into room 920. The box was a transmitter, which once triggered would send a signal to a compact receiving unit still in the bag. Kate removed the DO NOT DISTURB sign from the inside knob of the door leading to the hallway, opened the door, hung it outside, and closed and locked the door. Next, she looped the transmitter's detection wire over the inside knob. If anyone touched the outside doorknob—contrary to what the sign outside requested—the transmitter would detect the minute vibration and warn Kate Donaldson of possible danger.

Before returning to Room 920, Kate increased the ringer volume on the telephone so that she would hear it if someone called the room. She then pulled on the hook to close the first connecting door. Cutting another piece of tape, she applied it to the door and the frame to keep the door from opening.

Using her cellular phone, she called the number on the matchbook.

The phone rang once, twice, thrice, and an answering machine came on. Kate listened to the monotone greeting of a stranger's male voice, before leaving a message which guaranteed her a visit from the perpetrators. She included her room number at the Four Seasons, 922, before hanging up. Then she called Rich Jones at St. David's, who told her that Brandon was out of surgery but remained unconscious following a two-hour-long operation to get a bullet out of the tissue adjacent to his left lung.

"So it sounds like he's going to be all right then?" she asked, hope straining her voice.

"Looks that way," replied Jones. "According to the doctors, he should be coming around any moment now. Fortunately for him the slug was only a 9mm, which wasn't large enough to damage the lung."

Kate nodded, swallowing a lump of relief. If the bullet had been from a .45 pistol, or God forbid a .44 Magnum, the story would have been much different.

Jones informed her that by unanimous agreement of the Holst family, Richard Jones would remain with Brandon at all times. In addition, the Austin Police Department had parked two officers outside the door to his room.

Clicking the receiving unit to her jeans, she switched it to vibrating mode. Yawning, hoping that no one would come near room 922 for at least a couple of hours, Kate Donaldson slumped on the bed. She had to force herself to sleep. Rest was a weapon, as powerful as the Sig Sauer she clutched in her right hand, or the Walther PPK pistol secured to an ankle holster, courtesy of Richard Jones when he had arrived at the hospital.

Her professional side now ordered her to rest, to recharge, to shove all emotions aside, to forget about Brandon, about their time together, about his touch, his smile, his—

Focus.

She shook her head. She could not think about him now.

She was no good to him unless she focused her operative mind, just as she had for nineteen years at the CIA, putting personal needs aside and concentrating on the job, on the mission.

The mission.

Kate Donaldson fell asleep to prepare herself for the most important mission of her life.

5

"Hurry up!" hissed Kate, nearly out of breath, raw fear devouring her as she clutched a stolen Smith & Wesson .38 Special while running with her decimated gang down a dark alley. The stench of urine and spoiled food reached her flaring nostrils, replacing the smell of gunpowder from her near-death encounter a block away.

Rusted garbage bins, alive with rodents and roaches, lined one side of the alley servicing a strip of rundown stores a mile east of The Alamo, in downtown San Antonio, Texas, all under a crystalline, moonless sky. A two-story brick wall, spray-painted with graffiti, faced the overfilled trash cans.

Dressed in a pair of stolen black Levis and a white T-shirt, the fifteen-year-old high-school dropout tightened the grip of a weapon she'd already fired twice tonight, once to persuade a convenience-store owner that she meant her threats, and once more when a rival gang opened fire on her gang as they left the corner store.

Bastards!

Kate felt raw fear in every step she took, her stolen sneakers splashing puddles of putrid water, her lungs filling with dead air, her young eyes taking in the images of a murky corridor that seemed to be closing in on her, just as the figures closed the gap behind her.

The crack of a gunshot reverberated down the back street, followed by a brief scream behind her and a sudden splashing sound.

Kate didn't look back. She knew the bullet had found its mark. *Ramon. They've hit Ramon!*

Instead, the teen glanced at the black revolver in her hand, adrenaline searing her veins, her heart hammering in her chest, her breath exploding through her mouth. Piles of garbage, brick walls, and graffiti merged into a blurry path from which there was no escape.

Another shot ripped the night in half, the deafening report drilling her eardrums, drowning the brief cry of Jeanny, a sixteen-year-old from Laredo, as she crashed against a garbage bin.

This time Kate glanced backward, saw her agonized death mask, saw the fist-size hole in the middle of her chest as she lay dying on the wet concrete.

She was all alone now. Alone with the figures in black converging on her.

Cutting left, Kate dove behind a garbage can, landing on her side. Something stung her left temple and for a split-second she lost consciousness. Imminent danger, however, brought her back around. Sitting up, she stared over the rusted edge of the garbage can.

Gunfire erupted from the incoming silhouettes, a round striking her right shoulder, making her lose control of her bladder.

And apparently her gun as well.

It was nowhere to be found.

"Bastards!" she barked, feeling light-headed, dizzy, but

refusing to surrender. Her left hand reached behind her back, producing a switchblade, clutching it as she lunged like a singed cat.

A hand grabbed her wrist, twisting it, forcing her to release the weapon. As she did, a fist struck her solar plexus with crippling force.

Bent over, gasping for air, her abdomen ablaze, her wounded shoulder burning, Kate collapsed against the rusted can, a wide-eyed stare landing on her would-be executioners.

The figures peered at her with their angered eyes, their muscles pressed against their T-shirts.

One of them, a Hispanic teenager about the same age as Kate, took Kate's own switchblade, holding it in front of her.

''Hey, little girl, have you ever been fucked by a knife?''

As multiple hands held her down while others pulled on her jeans, Kate heard the sound of sirens ringing in her ears.

Then she felt the cold steel pressed in between her legs.

6

Kate Donaldson sat up in bed, wide-eyed, gasping. Sweating, trembling, she clutched the Sig 220, aiming it up, at nothing in particular.

She blinked, taking a deep breath, calming herself. She was having the nightmare again. But the ringing continued.

She closed her eyes, listening carefully. The phone was ringing in the adjacent room.

Getting up, she staggered to the door leading to the connecting room. It was three in the afternoon. She had slept for almost four hours.

Holding the Sig in her right hand, she opened the first door, pressing an ear against the second door, confirming that the phone was indeed ringing, her professional training ordering her to let it ring and then check the voicemail.

She went inside Room 922 exactly two minutes after the phone stopped ringing, noticing the flashing red light on the phone.

Someone had left a message.

She pressed the voicemail button and was rewarded by a short recorded greeting, followed by a series of beeps, and then a monotone voice.

"Eight P.M. tonight on Sixth Street, by Esther's Follies. Bring the password. Come alone."

Kate knew the place, a popular variety show at the corner of Neches and Sixth. She hung up, returning to the adjacent room, careful to tape the first connecting door to the frame to hold it in place and then bolting the second door.

She gazed at the white cotton curtains framing a sinking sun. A wave of apprehension scourging her, the former CIA officer frowned. The fish had not only failed to bite, but it had also thrown its own line at Kate Donaldson in the hope of reversing her trap.

Professionals.

But so are you, and you know the access password, the key they seek to get access to Sweeper.

Kate checked her watch. She still had five hours before the meeting. St. David's was only fifteen minutes away. Rather than calling to check on Brandon, Kate decided to pay him a short visit. Her professional side advised her not to go. Seeing Brandon would allow her emotions to surface, distracting her from her current objective. But her emotional side longed for his touch, for his smile. Besides, there was nothing she could do between now and the meeting at eight. Shoving the Sig into her jeans by her spine and covering it with her T-shirt, she left her room.

7

Brandon Holst had never felt this bad in his entire life, not even after one of his brothers had shot him with a rifle.

He opened his eyes and watched ceiling tiles rush by, realizing a moment later that he was being wheeled down a corridor on a cart, probably in a hospital.

His mouth felt dry and pasty, and his chest burned, almost as if someone had poured acid on it and let it eat through his skin into his core. Feeling thirsty but unable to speak, he gazed about him. A man dressed in white held a chart while walking to his right. A uniformed officer strolled along his left side, and another in front of the cart. He could hear someone behind him, probably the person pushing the cart.

He remembered the shooting.

What were you doing, you idiot? He thought, regretting the impulsive move to pull out his gun and shoot the terrorists, who very quickly overpowered him. At the time he had been angry. No, fix that. He had been totally, royally

pissed off and had lost his head. That was it. He had not
been able to control his emotions and had just wanted to
blast them all to hell. Instead, he had been able to shoot
. . . twice? Yes, two times, recalling the reports, amplified
by the enclosed area. He still remembered his ears throbbing from the piercing noise, right before an invisible force
had lifted him off the floor and shoved him against the
wall.

Bastards.

The terrorists had then left him behind, perhaps because
of the nearing police sirens. Maybe getting shot had been
his ticket to avoiding being kidnapped, assuming that had
been their intention. Maybe he had made the correct decision after all, even though the throbbing in his chest currently conflicted with that thought.

Now here he was, probably just out of surgery, the dry-
ness in his mouth and the incredible thirst telling him that
he had been administered some kind of anesthesia.

What about Kate?

The thought pierced his mind with the same intensity as
the sunshine stabbing his eyes while being wheeled
through a corridor full of windows.

Where is she? Is she all right? The terrorists had said
that they had her. Did his foolish move put her life in
danger? Were they now punishing her for what he had
done?

Stupid. Stupid. Stupid.

That was the only word that came to mind when thinking about his foolish act. *Why did I shoot? Why?* He had
already given them what they wanted. After that they
would have probably cut him and Kate loose. Or would
they?

Never negotiate with terrorists.

He had read that somewhere, perhaps heard it in some
TV show, or—

"Mr. Holst?"

Brandon heard his name but couldn't tell which direction the sound had come from. He shifted his head to his left, then to his right, and back to his left, his eyes finding the man holding the notepad. He was speaking to him. They had stopped moving.

"Mr. Holst, blink twice if you can hear me."

Brandon blinked twice.

"Very good, sir. You did very well on your surgery and are just going through the side effects of the anesthesia. You'll feel much better in a few more hours, and should be able to sit up by tonight. We're going to take some X rays now, all right?"

Two more blinks.

"Good. We're going to check out your ribcage. The bullet was deflected by your ribcage, missing your right lung by a fraction of an inch. We had to clean up some of the bone debris, but fortunately it didn't harm any vital organs. You're a very lucky man, Mr. Holst."

Lucky man? Brandon Holst didn't feel very lucky at the moment. Someone had kidnapped Kate, stolen his Y2K software, and shot him.

How can I possibly feel lucky?

At least you're alive.

As groggy and pain-racked as he felt, Brandon Holst did admit that he had survived, that he had been given a chance to—

Brandon heard a spitting sound, then another, and many more after that, very similar to the ones he had heard as his body was lifted off the floor at this office and thrown against the wall. He looked about him but could not find the uniformed officers escorting him. Instead, he saw three men in dressed in white, like orderlies, only they did not look like part of any hospital's staff. Their rugged faces, washed in apprehension, looked about them as they rushed him down a corridor.

One of them, a man with long and tangled black hair,

glanced at him with the coldest eyes Brandon Holst had ever seen. "Do not worry, Mr. Holst," he said in the same heavily accented English as the terrorists who had kidnapped him. "We will take very good care of you . . . and of your software."

8

Kate Donaldson steered her Honda in the parking garage and walked across the street to the main entrance of St. David's Hospital. Jones had indicated that Brandon was in Room 333. She walked up to the information desk.

"May I help you?" asked a young blonde in a white uniform.

"How do I get to Room 333?"

Pointing a finger to her left, she replied, "Elevators are at the end of hall to your right. Go left when you exit the elevators. The room should be at the end of the hallway, near the emergency stairs."

Kate headed down the narrow hall, anticipation increasing her heartbeat. She reached the elevators and pressed the UP button just as he heard a noise behind her. She turned around and watched a few doctors and nurses load up their trays as they walked single file down the cafeteria self-service line.

She blinked in disbelief when spotting Rich Jones, his

unkempt beard neatly trimmed, sitting at front of the cafeteria. Puzzled, she quickly approached him.

"Rich, what in the world are you doing down here?
Where is Brandon?"

He finished chewing a bite of cheeseburger and washed
it down with a sip of soda before saying, "I couldn't get
anyone to deliver food up there."

She felt sick. "What about Brandon? Who is guarding
him?"

"There's two cops outside his door. I know them personally. They come to my range all the time. They're both
ex-Marines. Relax. He is being cared for."

"Are you *kidding* me? I thought you weren't going to
let Brandon out of your sight!"

"Calm down, would you? The cops are armed and—"

"Let's go! Now! Brandon's a target. I *always* want
someone who knows him with him at all times!" They
fast-walked toward the elevators, which were still hung up
several floors above them.

Hastily, Kate scanned the area and spotted the red sign
at the far end of the hall. She rushed toward it.

"Follow me!"

Zigzagging around startled orderlies and nurses, Kate
made it to the emergency stairs and bolted up the concrete
steps, reaching the third floor thirty seconds later with Rich
Jones in tow.

She pushed the door open and raced down the wide
corridor. "I don't see any cops, Rich!"

"I . . . I don't understand! They were here just a moment
ago!"

She rushed inside the room, dread filling her at the sight
of an empty hospital bed. She checked the bathroom,
which was also empty, and raced back outside, leaving
Jones mumbling something incoherent.

"Nurse!" she shouted, spotting two uniformed women
leaning against a circular counter in the middle of the hall-

way. Both turned to her, exchanged a puzzled glance, and started toward Kate.

"Where is Brandon Holst? He was supposed to be in Room 333!"

"Calm down, darling," the older of the two nurses said just as Jones caught up with her. She was tall, with curly white hair that reminded Kate of Barbara Bush. "Mr. Holst was taken down for X rays a few minutes ago."

"What about the APD officers?"

"They went down with him."

Kate inhaled deeply, trying to suppress deep-rooted feelings of paranoia. "Where is the X-ray room?"

She told her and Kate found herself once again fast-walking to the fire stairs, climbing down to the first floor, and moving toward the rear of the building, where the X-ray lab was located.

"Wait up," Jones said, walking behind her. "See, I told you that there was nothing—"

"I'm not sure what kind of military intelligence service you were in, Rich!" she snapped, cutting him off. "But where I come from you never, *ever,* leave your post, even if that means going hungry for—"

Kate froze when they reached a glass door labeled X-RAY LABORATORY. Beyond it she spotted the bodies of two uniformed police officers sprawled on the floor, blood pooling from the bullet wounds in their backs. Next to them she also found a dead nurse, her white uniform crimson with blood flowing from two chest wounds. A fourth body, belonging to an orderly, was sprawled over the counter, half of his skull missing.

There was no sign of Brandon Holst or of the hospital cart that the orderly would have no doubt used to transport Brandon down here.

"Call security!" she screamed at Jones as she glanced in both directions, drawing the Sig, clutching it over her right shoulder, muzzle pointed at the ceiling tiles. Her eyes landed on the red EXIT sign over a set of double doors at the far end of the corridor.

She raced toward it, her sneakers thudding on the vinyl floor. She kicked open the metal doors, the afternoon sun stabbing her eyes. She blinked several times, adjusting her eyes to the bright light. A narrow walkway connected the doors to the side parking lot of the hospital. The upper deck of IH 35 projected beyond the hospital grounds.

Kate felt needles in her gut the moment she spotted an empty hospital cart at the end of the walkway, by the edge of the small parking lot.

Jones raced outside seconds later, breathing heavily. "I've called security! They . . . they should be here any moment."

"He's gone! Damn it! *They've taken him!*"

"Oh, God," said Jones. "I'm so sorry, Kate. Those ex-Marines were very good. I thought—"

"There's no time for that now! Stay here and deal with the cops! Don't mention me at all. I was never here! Understood?"

"What about—"

"Damn it, Rich! Do you understand? No mention of me! Got it?"

"Yes, but—"

"Return to the range. I'll be in touch." She began to run toward the other side of the building, where she had left her Honda parked.

"Where are you going?"

"To get him back!"

9

Dusk in Austin. Gold and yellow shafts of light forked across the Texas sky as daylight slowly gave way to darkness. The sinking crimson ball disappeared beyond the western rimrock, staining the glass and steel buildings downtown, also bathing the campus of the University of Texas and the capitol with its dying light. Streetlights flickered before coming on, their glow steadily growing from dim gray to bright yellow, gleaming above college students, tourists, and locals heading for a night on the town. Headlights converged in the dark as a mix of rental cars, taxis, police cruisers, and private vehicles fought for the right to cross the busy intersections against the wave of humanity flowing out of hotels and parking garages.

Sixth Street at night.

Kate Donaldson sat alone at a table at a café across Sixth Street from Esther's Follies, anger swelling inside of her at the thought of Brandon being kidnapped by whoever had done this, and just hours after undergoing surgery.

Although he had weathered the operation quite well, she knew that he was still in dire need of medical help, of antibiotics, of painkillers. She remembered when she had been shot in East Germany, fifteen years ago, a 9mm round fired by a KGB agent during an operation long forgotten. The round had gone through cleanly, also missing her lungs, leaving the scar tissue beneath her right breast that Brandon had spotted the night before. She had been out of commission for weeks, recovering from the operation.

Kate watched the line of people formed to get into the nine o'clock show already extending around the corner. Sipping coffee, she forced her mind to relax, to forget about Brandon for the moment, to use the anger as a weapon, as a way to take on more risk, to do the unexpected, to turn the hunter into prey.

Anger is a weapon.

Her predatory eyes surveyed the crowd. She looked for patterns, for people who seemed to be, like herself, also studying the mob walking both sides of the street, going in and out of clubs, snapping pictures, negotiating with street vendors, watching three African-American teenagers do a tap-dance number on the sidewalk while their audience threw coins and dollar bills into a large cowboy hat.

Kate no longer had her burlap bag, having left it at the hotel. She needed her hands free this evening, limiting herself to carrying the two guns, her license, a credit card, her keys, and four hundred dollars in cash from an ATM withdrawal.

She kept her eyes on the hat, guarded by two additional kids, one probably around eleven, the other topping thirteen or fourteen. Kate also spotted a policeman standing at a street corner a block away, and two more leaning against the railing adjacent to Esther's Follies, roughly a hundred feet from her.

Although the lonely officer at the corner did concern

himself with keeping an eye on the crowd all around
him—as he should—the two standing by the railing kept
their attention fixed only on the few pedestrians venturing
around the popular comedy club.

Odd.

She spent the next five minutes closely inspecting the
two officers, without drawing any attention to herself, just
as she had been tutored, noticing their lack of concern
about everyone around them—except for those hovering
around Esther's Follies.

After leisurely taking another sip of cafe latte, the seasoned operative checked her watch.

Eight twenty.

She looked back at the cops, who were now constantly
checking their watches while gazing at the people near the
variety club.

She dropped her eyebrows and grinned. One was blond,
muscular. The second just as intimidating but completely
bald.

Taking a final sip, she got up and casually strolled into
a nearby shop, purchasing a few postcards, a small ashtray
in the shape of Texas, and two key chains shaped like
jalapeno peppers before walking back out to the noisy
street five minutes later. The plastic souvenir bag hanging
from her left hand, Kate approached the tap-dancing show
across the street from Esther's Follies, merging herself
with the crowd, slowly inching her way up to the donation
hat on the floor.

The oldest of the two kids guarding the hat, stained
jeans and T-shirt hanging loosely from his skinny frame,
glanced up at Kate as she pulled out a bill from under her
jacket and inconspicuously flashed it at him.

The huge round eyes on his face quickly zeroing in on
the fifty-dollar bill, the teenage boy whispered something
to his younger friend and then followed Kate away from
the crowd.

Stopping next to a streetlight, Kate looked down at the teen. "What's your name, kid?"

"You can call me Joe."

She smiled inwardly, guessing him to be around thirteen. He reminded Kate of herself at that age, street-smart, already having to take care of himself. "You want to make an easy fifty in two minutes, Joe? Nothing too dangerous."

"Bullshit," he replied. "There ain't nothing I can do for fifty bucks in two minutes that ain't dangerous."

Kate tilted her head at the kid, the bill in her hands as she told him what she wanted him to do.

"Why would you want to do a thing like that?"

"I have my reasons."

"You're nuts, lady. If I get caught, they'll send my ass to a detention center."

"Do it for seventy bucks?"

Joe made a face and blurted, "What if I get caught?"

Kate gave him credit. He was smart. "You won't. I'll give you plenty of time to get away before I start screaming."

"But what if I get unlucky and get caught anyway? There's cops around, you know?"

"I won't press charges. They'll have to let you go."

Hands in his rear pockets as he kicked a pebble on the concrete sidewalk, Joe shrugged while saying, "I'm not sure about—"

Kate put the money away. "I'll just gonna have to find someone else who—"

"A hundred."

"What?"

"One hundred," Joe repeated. "I'll do it for a hundred bucks."

Kate pretended to choke, a hand on her forehead. "One *hundred* bucks?"

Raising his chin at the former CIA officer, Joe insisted, "And not a penny less."

Looking in both directions, Kate let her hands drop to her sides and said, *"All right.* Go and get ready. I'm going to start walking away from the crowd. You start coming from—"

"No way. The money first, lady. *Then* I'll do it."

Smiling internally but pretending to debate the issue, Kate said, "How do I know you just won't run away with the dough?"

"How do I know you'll pay me later?"

Kate rubbed her chin. "All right. I'll meet you halfway. You can have fifty now, and I'll put the other fifty in the bag. Deal?"

"Deal. But that fifty better be there when I look for it a block away."

"It will."

Nodding, the kid grabbed the fifty-dollar bill, watched Kate shove another fifty into the souvenir bag, and went back to his younger friend guarding the hat. He whispered something to him and then walked across Sixth Street, waiting for Kate to take her position twenty or so feet ahead of him.

Her back toward the questionable police officers, the souvenir bag hanging loosely from her hand, the ex-operative began to make her way down the street, smiling inwardly when she heard Joe's hastening steps.

The tug was firm, quick, without hesitation. Kate felt certain that this kid had done this before.

Waiting ten seconds while several people looked in her direction, Kate screamed, "Thief! Someone stop that kid! Help! Help!"

More heads now turned in her direction as Kate scanned the streets, pleased to catch a glimpse of the fake officers slowly moving *away* from the action, obviously not wishing to get involved, confirming Kate's suspicions.

She waved both hands in fake disgust as the kid disappeared around a corner. "You can have it, kid!" She shouted. "Just a few cheap souvenirs!"

And a hundred bucks for a minute's worth of work. Kate felt she had done her charitable act for the week. *Good luck, kid.*

She went in discreet pursuit of the two pretenders, ignoring the questions and stares from those around her. Twenty seconds later no one remembered the incident and Sixth Street returned to normal, except for Kate and her prey, who walked down Neches, toward the river, and turned right on Second Street, heading toward East Austin, going beneath IH 35 and straight into the least desirable part of town, especially after dark.

Several blocks later, Second Street narrowed and grew murkier. Mosquitoes buzzing in her ears, Kate remained a block behind, moving carefully, quietly, with practiced ease, her quarry never once leaving her sight. A light breeze tunneled down the old street, cooling Kate's face, blowing the flying invertebrates away, swinging an overhead sign that hung at the end of two thin chains in front of an antiques shop.

The hard muscles of her thighs pumped against the jeans as she took a few steps. Checking her rear, not favoring the thought of getting surprised, Kate Donaldson kept one hand inside her jacket, curled fingers feeling the Sig's checkered plastic stock.

A block later the fake policemen turned right, toward First Street, which bordered the river. Kate immediately cut left on a murky alley halfway down the block and raced down to First, garbage cans rushing by, the stench making her grimace, her sneakers splashing across puddles left over from an earlier rain. She sensed movement among the piled garbage and realized, without stopping, that an army of rats dominated the refuse. In disgust, but without losing focus, she reached the corner and turned left, fastwalking up the deserted and poorly-lit street.

An abandoned warehouse across First Street, most of its windows covered with rotting plywood, blocked the view of the Colorado River. An overgrown field separated the warehouse from a weathered, two-story brick building, its windows also boarded up. This section of Austin east of IH 35 went downhill quite rapidly.

Stopping at the corner, Kate once more checked both sides of the dark street, verifying that she stood alone, her ears detecting nearing footsteps—two sets of them. Up First Street she could see the distant glow of the vehicles cruising on IH 35. Their muffled noise mixed with the conversation from her nearing quarry.

"So, what do we do now?" a booming voice asked from around the corner, the sound echoing against the rotting warehouse across the street.

"Head back and wait for instructions," replied a second voice.

Her back pressed against the corner, her weapon gripped firmly above her right shoulder, muzzle pointed at the dark sky, Kate held her breath as the figures approached, as their shadows neared the corner, crossing her field of view. Her options were limited. She could risk jumping out and ordering them to drop their weapons, but if they were really good, Kate would not be able to react fast enough if both of them drew their sidearms at the same time. Contrary to popular belief, it is quite difficult for one armed person to cover two armed individuals. Besides, the last thing she wanted to do was discharge a firearm, drawing unwanted attention. She wanted to question them on the spot, not have to move them somewhere else. Whatever method she had to use to disable them, it had to be a silent one.

Standing sideways to them, springing forward, the former CIA officer lunged, the middle and index fingers of her left hand extended like a snake's tongue, striking the blond's eyes. In the same motion, she shoved her left sneaker in between the blond's legs, driving it upward with resolve. The man's face cringed into a mask of agonizing pain as he dropped to his knees, a hand on his face and the other on his groin, a slight moan escaping his lips.

Before the bald figure could react, Kate had already recoiled her right leg and extended it toward the man's face, heel up, toes pointing down.

She connected, crashing the sole of her sneaker against the cheekbone. The bald man brought both hands to his face, pain-racked, blood dripping through hairy fingers.

Kate recoiled once more and side-kicked him again, this time in the exposed solar plexus, smashing the web of nerves between the waist and the lower ribs, doubling him over, making him collapse on the oil-stained sidewalk, gasping for air, convulsing, his pants soiled with urine.

Pivoting on her right leg, the street turning in a swirling blur, Kate, in a semi-crouch, brought her left leg up at waist level, striking the side of the blond, who collapsed on impact. Instead of landing on a patch of grass next to his partner, the blonde rolled over, cracking his skull on the edge of the sidewalk, going into convulsions. His eyes rolled to the back of his head as the spasms ended and all movement ceased.

Kate knelt next to him and felt for a pulse but detected none. Frowning, she checked the bald man, exhaling in relief when she detected one.

Reaching for the handcuffs strapped to the bald man's side, Kate quickly cuffed him behind his back and, timing herself with the sporadic traffic flow down First Street, dragged him across the street, into the overgrowth next to the abandoned warehouse, out of sight from the street.

Exhausted, her arm and leg muscles burning, Kate Donaldson pulled off the man's sneakers, used the strings to secure his feet, and stuffed one of his socks into his mouth to keep him from screaming.

She glanced across the street, wondering if she should

also move the blond who, dressed as a cop and dead, would certainly draw attention.

Kate dragged him into the bushes, out of sight not just from the street but also from his partner. She returned to her quarry, lying unconscious next to the rusted, corrugated-metal wall of the warehouse. Although his left cheek was already swelling from the kick, the jaw seemed intact, meaning he should be able to verbalize the answers Kate planned to extract from him.

"Wake up, sleeping beauty," Kate said, slapping him.

Bulging biceps and pectorals worthy of a championship body builder pumped against the shirt of his uniform as he struggled to break loose, the veins in his massive neck pulsating as he tried to spit out the dark cotton sock. His angular face turned to his captor. Slanted, almost Asian eyes, brown in color, glared at Kate Donaldson.

"Listen carefully. I'm going to remove the sock. If you scream, I'll shove it back in your mouth and you'll start losing body parts. Understood?"

She got a nod.

"Where is Brandon Holst?"

His face turned impassive, expressionless, his eyes staring into the distance.

Kate reached for the man's belt and extracted his own semiautomatic, a Sig 220, just like the one she had taken from the assassin at her house. She did a quick search and also found an ten-inch stainless-steel blade, razor-sharp on one edge and jagged on the other with a rubber handle sporting finger grips to prevent the user from losing control. This certainly was *not* the kind of knife a regular police officer would carry. This one was a favorite of the U.S. Special Forces, the Rangers, and the SEALs—as well as several terrorist organizations. It was designed to inflict far more damage coming out than going in.

"Nice," she said, holding it up against the wan street

light. "You should be able to do some damage with this. What do you think?"

No response.

"Did I mention I'm quite handy with knives?"

The comment grabbed the bald man's attention. Lying sideways on the knee-high grass, he gazed up curiously.

"Blondie was pretty stubborn, I have to admit," Kate said, speaking not to the man but to the knife. "In the end, however, his knife and the rats in that alley got the best of him." She lowered her eyes to meet his.

The man began to breath heavily.

"As you probably know by now, I'm *no* girl scout. The man you sent to my house learned that the hard way when I shoved a knife up his throat, just like I'm planning to do to you if you don't start talking. See, I *don't* play by the rules."

Waiting for that to sink in, Kate added, "Now, I'll ask you once again. Where have you taken Brandon Holst?"

No response.

Without warning, Kate jammed the sole of her right sneaker against the man's scalp, shoving him into the weeds. Pulling his left ear, she drove the steel edge a quarter of an inch into its base—just enough to show her conviction but without inflicting permanent damage.

Resembling a fish out of water, the bald man began to wobble and jerk on the tall grass, blood spurting off the side of his head from the small cut, his contorted eyes wildly gazing around him.

Grabbing him by the lapel with her left hand, the right holding the bloody knife to his face, Kate hissed, "Why did you attack him? And me? *Why?* Answer me, or I'll cut it off and make you eat it!"

"The software . . . my contact needed help with the software."

Sitting him up, blood running down his neck, soaking his shirt, Kate cut off a section of his pants and wrapped it around his head, field-dressed the wound. The assassin now looked like a buccaneer.

"Where is he?"

"With the drive and the main team . . . in Houston."

"Is he all right?"

"I don't know. He's with a separate cell."

"Who do you work for?"

Wincing in pain, his chest swelling in erratic spasms, the man mumbled, "They're always . . . monitoring us. They'll kill me . . . and my family . . . I can't."

"If you choose to cooperate with us, we'll guarantee your protection."

"Who . . . are you with?"

Kate regarded the man, who resembled a young and muscular Telly Savalas. "CIA."

Inhaling deeply and blinking, obviously forcing himself to focus, he said. "There are many cells, and buffers within each cell . . . I receive instructions to carry out certain tasks, but I never see my controller."

"Were you involved in this morning's attack at Holst Enterprises?"

He shook his head. "Different cell. I was assigned to follow you."

"Why?"

"To gain access to the software key protecting the Y2K code. The other cell was able to retrieve the drive from Holst Enterprises housing the code, but it can't be read without the access password of the shield that you've installed. I was told by my controller that only you know how to decode it."

Kate nodded, glad that at least one of her precautions had paid off. But she also knew that no shield was one hundred percent bulletproof, and this password was also known by Brandon, who was either unconscious or claiming he didn't know it. On the other hand, if she had convinced Brandon to let her install the EM scanners, the information on the drive would have been erased the moment the high-tech thieves left the building with their loot.

"Where in Houston? And why there?"

"A seaport. The team is getting ready to return home."

"Where exactly is he being held in Houston?"

"I don't know the exact location. Only that he is aboard a vessel."

"What's the vessel's name?"

"They haven't told me that either. See, I only—"

A silent round pierced the man's undamaged ear, exiting through the bandaged side of his head, before impaling itself into the ground in an explosion of dirt and grass. The energy of the slug created enough pressure inside the skull to pop both eyes out of their sockets, followed by brown liquid, which also spurted from his nose, mouth, and ears as the man collapsed on his side.

Her right hand automatically reaching for the Sig 220, Kate went into a frantic roll down the side of the warehouse as the ground erupted to her right and her left, two rounds punching dime-sized holes into the corrugated-metal wall as someone from a vantage point adjusted his fire. She didn't stop rolling, her back, elbows, and knees stinging from the multiple impacts against the uneven terrain, her eyes searching for an opening in the warehouse . . .

There!

A board of plywood had partially separated from the rusted sheet metal, creating a two-foot-wide opening.

Kate ceased rolling and surged into a deep crouch, plunging head-first through the opening, scraping both shoulders as she dove through the break.

Adrenaline searing her veins, her throat boiling dry, a fusillade of rounds hammering the thin wall, splintering the plywood, Kate Donaldson smashed her torso against the concrete floor, tearing her jacket, skinning her left elbow and knee.

Standing, ignoring the pain, her heartbeat pounding her temples, she pivoted a full revolution, scanning the warehouse with the clutched pistol, squinting to see in the pitch-black interior, giving up after a few seconds.

She was trapped, unable to move forward, to seek cover, to find temporary shelter. And she couldn't go back out without risking—

Footsteps. Kate heard footsteps, felt her heartbeat thundering inside her chest, behind her ears, saw the shadows of two men hustling up to the side of the warehouse as she stood next to the broken window, back pressed against a supporting beam, weapon over her left shoulder. The same darkness that prevented her from venturing inside the old structure now shielded her from anyone looking in, as long as she remained quiet.

The hooded figures marched directly toward her, silenced Uzi submachine guns held in classic combat fashion, right hand beneath the handle, index on the trigger, left hand under the bulky silencer. The pair moved together with expert ease, diagonally from each other, making it difficult for anyone to take them both with a single burst.

Dropping to one knee, clutching the weapon with both hands, the former CIA officer slipped behind the steel stanchion and lined up one of the incoming figures between the gun's sights. She fired once, twice. The reports thundered inside the metallic structure, hammering her ears, the muzzle flashes momentarily lighting the interior of the cavernous room.

The figure arched back, but before she could switch targets the second figure had returned the fire, guided by Kate's muzzle flashes from inside the warehouse.

A round struck the stanchion at eye level, a shower of sparks and steel shards lashing her face. The feral scream of metal on metal screeched in her ears.

"Aghh!"

She fell back, half-blinded, clawing at her eyes. Her
head crashed against an unseen, hard object, her vision
blurring from the impact, from the tears assaulting her
eyes. Engulfed by an ocean of darkness, pawing on all
fours, fingers groping for her lost weapon, Kate heard the
scraping of cloth against wood and metal, followed by
footsteps, the sounds mixing with her own breathing. The
second assassin was inside the—

A stabbing pain on her side made Kate cringe in un-
believable pain as the blow lifted her light frame off the
floor, sending her crashing against another unseen object.
She landed on her stomach, the darkness spiraling from
the kick to her abdomen, the pain inducing uncontrollable
spasms, bile reaching her throat, her bladder muscles
weakening.

The assassin grabbed her by the hair and the waist of
her jeans, snatching her off the floor with incredible ease,
hurling her toward the opening with animal strength. She
put her hands in front, shielding her face as she smashed
into plywood head-first, taking the rotting plank of wood
along with her as she shot out of the window like a missile,
crash-landing against the open field, the tall grass cushioning the impact.

Gasping for air, scourged, her ribs ablaze, tears blinding
her, Kate Donaldson saw a blurry image approach her, saw
a leg swinging back, braced herself for—

The powerful kick connected right below the sternum,
her bladder muscles loosening on impact, her lids twitching, her mind momentarily blanking out. A witches' brew
of blood and bile rose up her throat, exploding through her
trembling lips.

Everything was happening too fast now. Two blurry figures converged on her. Instincts overrode her thought processes. Still heaving, Kate's right hand reached for her
backup piece, the Walther PPK, her thumb flipping the

safety as she brought the weapon around, aiming it at the center of the closest blur, firing once, twice.

A cry followed the blur dropping from her field of view. The second figure dropped to a crouch, a hand clutching a dark weapon already aimed at Kate.

The muffled spits of silenced rounds grazed the night air. Kate braced herself for the impact but it never came. Instead, the figure in front of her arched back, collapsing over the weeds a second later, twitching, bleeding from his ears and nose.

Then silence.

Blinking rapidly, Kate inhaled once, twice, controlling the spasms, her mind racing as she surveyed the area around her with the slim gun. Who had come to her rescue? Why?

No time to analyze!

Move!

With great effort she stood, cringing from the stabbing pain in her ribs as she took a deep breath, the acrid stench of her own vomit nauseating her. She checked the two bodies. One still held the gun he had aimed at Kate just seconds before, a .45 caliber Sig 220. The second had an identical gun in a chest holster.

Just like the assassin at my house.

The pattern told her they belonged to a well-funded group. The question was *who?*

Verifying that both Sigs were loaded, Kate shoved one into the small of her back and ejected the magazine from the second, pocketing the ammo and throwing the empty weapon in the tall grass.

She staggered up First Street, toward IH 35. She needed a place to rest, if only momentarily, before resuming the hunt. But she also had to avoid drawing attention to herself.

Her house was out of the question. The place was compromised. She could go back to her hotel room. After all, the enemy only knew that her room was 922. She had registered Room 920 under a different name. If they came back looking for her, it would at least give her another opportunity to capture someone alive, hopefully for long enough to extract more information. She now knew that she was dealing with a foreign agency, maybe even a terrorist group controlling different cells. And they were taking Brandon somewhere from Houston aboard a sea vessel.

But when?

And which vessel?

Is he being taken care of? Is someone providing him with the medication that he needs to survive after surgery? To prevent an infection? Or is he slowly slipping from lack of care? What if the wound reopens from moving him around? What if he starts to bleed?

Stop it!

Kate closed her eyes, feeling like shouting out loud in anger, in frustration. Only her training kept her from falling apart. She had to assume that Brandon was being looked after by whoever kidnapped him, if only so that he could in turn assist them in understanding his complex Y2K code. She had to believe that, for only then could her operative's mind focus on her new plan.

Kate needed information, and fast. She still felt she held something those terrorists needed, something that she felt certain they would not leave without. The shield on Brandon's Y2K software would point at her as the owner of the access password. And if she continued to assume that Brandon was either unconscious or unwilling to assist them, Kate hoped that her knowledge of this password would give her enough to lure them back into another trap.

Priorities.

First she needed transportation. Her Honda was compromised, so she opted for an old Ford Taurus parked a block from the intersection of First and the highway, in

front of a weathered house. She briefly inspected the car.
It appeared to be in running condition.

Without hesitation, she grabbed a rock from the field
across the street and broke the window behind the driver's
seat, unlocking the door, sliding behind the wheel, just as
she had been taught, just as she had done dozens of times
to get access to transportation in an emergency. Her hands
reached beneath the dash, fingers finding the correct wires,
bypassing the ignition.

The Taurus started on the second crank just as a light
came on in the house, followed by shouts. She put it in
gear and rushed off, glancing at her rearview mirror,
watching two figures stomp out of the house and shake
their arms at the departing car.

10

Kate drove the stolen Taurus in front of Holst Enterprises, where she spotted no sign of the police in the area, except for the long strips of yellow tape wrapped around the building to seal the crime scene.

She dumped the Taurus three blocks away and returned on foot, avoiding the well-lit sections of the street, preferring the shadows created by the oaks and cedars blocking the street lights at each corner.

Kate moved with practiced ease, ignoring the pain in her abdomen, reaching the back of the building uneventfully. A delivery dock faced the alley she had used to offload the security hardware weeks ago. A wide metal door connected the dock to the shipping and receiving area. A keypad next to the door controlled the motor to lift it.

She keyed in the eight-digit code that she had been given at the beginning of her contract, praying that it was still valid. The red light above the keypad turned green, the motor whirled to life, and the heavy door began to lift into a hidden track in the ceiling.

Kate waited until the bottom of the door cleared the floor by a few feet before going under and pressing a red button on the other side to command it back down. At the same time, she rushed to the alarm pad by the empty guard station, across the small shipping and receiving area, and deactivated the system, preventing it from sending a warning signal to the alarm company.

Now it's time to watch the show.

She went straight to the basement. To her relief, the fake bookshelves, stuffed with computer manuals hiding the video cabinet, had fooled the Austin Police Department. Kate reached for the ancient Apple II owner's manual in the top shelf and pushed it half way. The shelves moved out of the way and Kate entered the code on the vault's keypad, gaining access to the video equipment.

She powered up the Sony monitor and slaved it to the first of six recorders, labeled A—the one that covered the foyer. The master counter used as reference by all six recorders showed 38:02:00, meaning that just over thirty-eight hours had elapsed since the last forty-eight-hour period. Kate did the math in her head and figured that the crime was committed sometime after five in the morning, and it was now just past ten at night.

She rewound the counter to 21:00 and pressed PLAY.

The blank monitor flickered a few times before displaying an image of the foyer, along with the security guard sitting behind the counter, all at the rate of one frame per second. She fast-forwarded it, watching the rapid sweeping motion of the video camera at ten times the regular speed. At 5:45, the camera picked up Brandon Holst, followed by the two men in business suits, going in the foyer. Kate recognized them immediately as the same two men she had seen with Brandon the other night. The older man with the silver hair was dressed in a light suit. The younger one with the pock-marked face, whose corpse she had seen being wheeled out this morning, was dressed in a dark suit.

The guard stood and handed the visitors the entry log pad and a pen. Each man filled it out and received a badge, which they clipped to the lapels of their suits before following Brandon Holst inside.

Kate switched to one of the interior cameras and picked up the trio exiting the lobby and heading toward Brandon's office. They closed the door behind them.

She frowned and switched back to the foyer, where the guard continued to sit behind the counter. Again, Kate fast-forward for another few minutes, when the guard abruptly stood, only to be forced back down as his chest erupted from the bullets fired by an unseen enemy.

She leaned closer to the display, her breath caught in her throat when spotting three hooded men bearing silenced MP5 submachine guns. They rushed past the dead guard and into the cubicle area. Kate switched cameras, catching them running down the center of the cubes, toward the closed door of Brandon's office.

The men took their positions around the door before one of them kicked it in. A moment later Brandon and the two businessmen exited the office. Two of the hooded figures forced Brandon and one of the businessmen, the younger one, toward the basement, presumably to get the drive housing the Y2K code. The third figure remained with the second businessmen, the one with the silver hair, who lowered his arms the moment Brandon and the others disappeared from view. Just then, the hooded figure lowered his weapon and removed his hood, which was brown in color, unlike the others, which were black.

"Animals," Kate hissed, realizing that Brandon's clients had set this up to get their hands on his code.

She froze the video, staring at the frame, wishing she had the equipment to enhance the image and get a better picture of the terrorist. All she could tell was that he had closely cropped hair and an intense look in his eyes, which matched his hasty movements as he spoke with the businessman. It looked as if they were arguing.

She continued watching, fast-forwarding as necessary, changing cameras, trying to get the best angles as she pieced together a most disturbing story. By the time Brandon reappeared, flanked by the two terrorists, one of whom carried a hard drive, the third terrorist had already slipped his brown hood back on, which told Kate that he really wasn't planning on killing Brandon, otherwise why keep his face hidden from the software entrepreneur? But then something happened. Kate sensed it just a moment before the video image displayed the terrorists turning their backs on Brandon. The software entrepreneur reached inside his shirt and produced a pistol, which Kate recognized as the little Beretta Tomcat.

No, Brandon. No.

Unlike the .45 caliber round of her Sig, which delivered enough punch to require only one per target, The Tomcat's .32 caliber round required at least three bullets to inflict the equivalent shock to the victim's nervous system. Based on the flashes picked up by the camera, Brandon managed to fire his weapon twice at one of the black-hooded terrorists before another one, also wearing a black hood, fired back, sending Brandon flying against a cubicle wall just as the terrorist that Brandon had hit fell on the floor. At the same time the businessman with the pock-marked face tried to stop the firing and got hit multiple times in the chest. The silver-haired businessman kicked the submachine gun out of the black-hooded terrorist's hands while pulling out his own gun and shouting something at the group. He checked his friend's pulse and shook his head. Then they all turned toward the windows, as if hearing something. The surviving trio rushed out of the building.

Kate switched cameras and caught them racing across

the parking lot, disappearing in the shadows of the trees lining the street.

She returned to the inner camera, watching with despair as Brandon staggered to his feet, just to collapse again, clutching his chest.

Her throat constricting, she ran a finger over his image on the screen, unable to control a single tear rolling down her left cheek, reaching the corner of her mouth. She tasted it, forcing herself to remain in control. A moment later the police arrived, explaining the terrorists' hasty retreat. Kate decided that Brandon must have used his panic button soon after the terrorists had burst into his office.

Leaving everything just as she had found it, Kate returned the cabinet to its original state and left the building, her mind going through the data she had just gathered, anger filling her at the thought of Brandon having been the victim of an open terrorist strike to gain access to his technology.

Once again, her operative mind forced priorities in her thoughts, in her actions, as she rushed away from the building, away from the scene of a terrible crime. The questions, however, pounded her mind, her logic. She concentrated on those questions that might result in finding Brandon. *Who are they? Where are they? What do they plan to do with the software? Sell it to the highest bidder? Profit from the research of Holst Enterprises?* A tool like that, according to Brandon, could be worth a fortune. Was that their primary objective? Was it merely money? Or was their motive something more deceitful than that?

Kate frowned. Almost two decades in the business had taught her to think the absolute worst of people, particularly terrorists, who were often driven by ideologies more than by money. But what other uses could Brandon's Y2K software have beyond addressing part of the millennium bug in systems? How could someone use that software for anything other than what it was intended?

She thought of two possible sources to answer that question. One was Brandon Holst, currently kidnapped. The second was the terrorist group itself. Both answers were in the same place: Houston. But not for long. The contract assassin had mentioned a vessel, the strong possibility of it sailing very soon.

As she raced past the stolen Taurus, which was too hot to use because the owners would have certainly contacted the police by now, Kate began to formulate a new plan. For that plan to work, however, she had to get to her hotel room without being spotted by the men she felt certain would have been left behind monitoring the area in case she showed up.

Back to the Four Seasons.

Kate took a long route to get there, hailing two taxis, the last of which drove her around town for twenty minutes. She sat sideways in the rear seat, constantly checking the traffic behind her, making certain that no one followed her, either potential enemies or whoever it was that had saved her life back at the warehouse. Her professional mind ordered her not to trust anyone, even those who'd saved her life but chose to remain out of sight; they too could be her enemies, only enemies who needed her alive for a little longer in the hope that Kate would help them gain information.

The taxi dropped her off three blocks from the hotel. As an added precaution, Kate walked aimlessly for ten minutes, until she spotted a new vehicle, old enough not to have an alarm system, yet presentable enough to avoid drawing unwanted attention while she steered it into the parking garage at the Four Seasons Hotel.

Cruising down Sixth Street, Kate drove past Esther's Follies on the way to the hotel. The comedy club was letting the audience out after the show ended at eleven. She continued toward her destination, her operative mind rehearsing a show of her own.

11

Kate Donaldson drove her stolen Mercury Sable directly into the underground parking garage beneath the Four Seasons Hotel at midnight. She selected a spot near the service elevator, where she easily found a service entrance.

Sneaking inside the laundry room, empty at this time of the night, she entered an adjacent janitorial room, where she quickly changed into a maid's uniform and grabbed a couple of pillows. Directing the elevator to the tenth floor—one floor above her own—she pretended to bring them to a guest.

The pillows served two additional purposes. They allowed Kate to hide the Sig 220, which she kept in her right hand, sandwiched between the cushions—and, in the event that she had to use the .45 caliber pistol, the foam in the pillows would serve as a makeshift silencer.

Kate stepped out of the elevator and headed for the adjacent stairs. Climbing down to the ninth floor, slowly, with caution, she tiptoed toward her own floor to avoid telegraphing her presence.

She reached the stairwell landing and inched open the metal door, peering down a long and empty corridor. An ice machine rumbled across the hallway, amidst a few vending machines. Rooms 920 and 922 were halfway down on the right-hand side. Walking casually, as a maid would while in the process of delivering two pillows to a guest, the former CIA officer left the protection of the stairs and ventured into the open, her right hand shoved in between the cushions, gripping the Sig 220, index finger resting against the trigger.

A figure emerged from a nearby room, large, built like a football player, his bulk pressing against his jogging suit. He held a plastic ice bucket. While shifting the Sig between the pillows to point it at the potential threat, Kate relaxed her facial muscles, making herself appear non-threatening as they approached one another.

"Evening," he said with a slight nod.

"Good evening, sir," she replied, keeping the muzzle pointed in his direction the entire time. She glanced over her shoulder and verified that he had continued down to the ice machine at the end of the corridor.

The moment he disappeared from view, Kate shoved her card key into the slot over the doorknob of Room 920, going inside, immediately dropping the pillows and scanning the room with the Sig, letting the spring-loaded door close behind her. Everything appeared to be just as she had left it a few hours ago.

Carefully, she unlocked the first connecting door, verifying that the second door was still being held in place by the duct tape. Pressing an ear to it revealed nothing. The room was silent. Just to make sure, she dialed it, setting the phone down while returning to the door and listening for any movement aside for the ringing. After four rings her call went to voicemail.

She hung up and went inside Room 922, the Sig 220 leading the way, her professional side assuming it could be compromised. Only after searching it thoroughly did she allow herself to reach the large windows overlooking the river, unlatched the double locks, and slid one of the panels open. A cool breeze swirled the lace curtains as she gazed outside, ignoring the tranquil scene, the full moon reflecting its light on the slow waters of the Colorado River. Kate focused her eyes on the narrow landing lining the bottom of the windows and continuing along the side of the building. She could use it as an escape route in an emergency to hop over to another room.

Leaving the window wide open, Kate returned to Room 920 to start the next phase of her plan.

12

Kate washed her soiled jeans and T-shirt in the bathroom sink, leaving them hanging beneath the heat lamp while she showered. The hot water stung the cuts on her forearms and sides. Kate endured it, breathing deeply, forcing her mind to relax, ignoring her bruised ribs. That had been the closest call she had had in her entire life of field operations, and she had survived it only because someone else had intervened.

But who? And most importantly, why?

Steam fogged the glass walls of the shower. Kate shook her head while lathering her arms, the soap and hot water disinfecting the cuts. Her professional side told her that the answer to those questions would come eventually. For now, she had to focus on staying alive while continuing to gather information like pieces to a puzzle, each by itself incomplete, but capable of unraveling this mystery if combined with other isolated pieces of data. Each new strand of information would get her one step closer to finding

Brandon, to rescuing him from the terrorists, to getting him the medical attention she feared he was not—

Stop thinking that way! He is fine. The terrorists need him alive! They need him to understand the Y2K code. They will do everything possible to keep him alive, to nurse him back to health.

And so Kate Donaldson continued to explore her logic, to think geometrically, considering all of the angles, all of the possible sides of this multifaceted mystery. The clues she had gathered so far provided her with only limited information. Sweeper was valuable enough for someone to be willing to kill to get it. That someone, who had managed to take the software, belonged to a foreign network and was planning to sail out of Houston, dragging a wounded Brandon Holst along. A third party was also involved, watching and intervening from a distance, probably also interested in the software and hoping that Kate's work will lead them to it. Was there any chance that this third party was in any way associated with an agency from the U.S. intelligence community?

Kate shrugged, familiar with this early stage of a mission, when questions far exceeded answers. She needed to gather more data, more clues to this enigma until she could tip the balance to the other side and unveil the truth.

And the truth shall set you free.

The trick was staying alive during the search for the truth.

After drying herself, she stood in front of the mirror to inspect the damage. Aside for the cuts, she had two large purple blotches on her torso, where the brutes had kicked her, but luckily they had only bruised her ribcage. It would hurt when she moved, but she would manage. She also had a number of bruises on her thighs, ranging in size from a penny to a quarter. Fortunately, her face had survived largely unscathed, except for a couple of minor cuts just above her eyes. She exhaled in relief, not out of vanity, but because facial bruises always drew unwanted attention.

Her jeans and T-shirt were still damp. Kate put on the maid's uniform and checked her weapons. The Sig had a full magazine of seven .45 caliber rounds, plus one already loaded in the chamber. She also had a spare magazine with another seven rounds. The Walther PPK that Jones had given her came with seven rounds plus one in the chamber. Kate had shot two, leaving her with six.

Two guns and twenty-one rounds.

It'll have to do.

Walking through the connecting doors into Room 922, Kate once again dialed the local number on the back of the matchbox, waited for the same monotone greeting to end, and said, "I have the access password and you have Brandon Holst. I want to make a trade. No tricks this time. Enough people have died already. Return Brandon to St. David's and I will in turn provide you with the password, which I'll leave at my hotel room at the Four Seasons. Room 922."

She hung up and checked her watch.

One o'clock in the morning.

She was tired. Her body demanded the rest that the professional in her refused to take, and the rumbling in her stomach reminded her that she had not eaten for almost twenty-four hours.

Stop complaining. Brandon is in far worse shape than you.

Kate frowned, once again regaining focus. If she couldn't give her body rest, then at least she could give it nourishment, which was another weapon often overlooked by younger operatives.

Snagging the hotel's menu next to the phone, she dialed room service, which according to the brochure in her hands provided twenty-four-hour service. She placed a small order and was promised delivery within thirty minutes.

Sitting up in bed, her stomach continuing to make noises, Kate stared at the Sig Sauer. The black pistol didn't have any scratches or nicks. It also lacked a serial number, making it untraceable. The number had not been ground off, as criminals often do. This had certainly been a factory job. It also looked brand new, like the gun she had taken from the assailant at her house, telling her that the group after Brandon's software had been recently armed and had good connections with the German manufacturer. Unless, of course, the guns had simply been stolen from the assembly line before the numbers were stamped on the frames.

Kate spent the next half hour pondering her situation, playing out various scenarios, selecting those which seemed to match her observations to date. A light knocking on the door made her jerk.

"Room service," called out a male voice.

She inspected the uniformed waiter through the peeping hole. Although the room the terrorists knew about was next door, Kate could not take any chances, even when the waiter appeared harmless.

"I'm indisposed at the moment. Please, leave it by my door and slip the total under the door. I'll be paying cash."

The waiter complied, and Kate slipped three tens back to him. The waiter thanked her and walked off. Waiting two full minutes before opening the door, she inspected both sides of the empty corridor before picking up the tray and setting it on her bed.

Keeping the Sig next to her, Kate ate a big salad, followed by a bowl of broccoli and cheese soup, and finished up with a fruit salad for dessert.

Her hunger satisfied, she resumed the analysis of her situation. As she did so, footsteps in the hallway made her reach for her pistol, jump out of bed, and tiptoe to the door. She peered through the peeping hole. Muscles,

T-shirts, military cuts, and Sig 220 pistols filled her fish-eye view of the corridor. She tightened the grip on her own Sig as she held it over her right shoulder.

She spotted the bulky cylinders protruding from the muzzles of their guns.

Assassins. Two of them.

Slowly, she cocked the gun with her thumb, waiting.

The men gathered in front of the door to Room 922. One of them swung his pistol at the door and fired. The sound of multiple hammer blows stung the silence, echoing loudly. Wood splintered, cracked. The door gave as one of the men crashed against it, followed by hastening footsteps.

Adrenaline searing her veins, Kate counted to ten before quietly leaving her room, checking the hallway to make sure no one was posted at either end of the long corridor. She peered into Room 922.

As expected, both assassins stood by the open window, looking out, their backs to Kate.

"Don't turn around!" she shouted, the Sig lined up on the closest man. "Drop the guns!"

One of them began to turn around. Kate shot him in his torso as he attempted to bring his weapon around, the report deafening, the smell of gunpowder hanging in the air. The man let go a brief cry before collapsing onto the floor.

The second assassin obeyed, releasing his grip on the silenced Sig, which fell onto the carpeted floor with a muffled thump.

"On your knees, hands behind your head, fingers interlocked."

The figured obeyed.

Kate approached him, her ears ringing from the blast of a .45 caliber pistol in such enclosed quarters. She retrieved both weapons while keeping her gun pressed against the back of his head.

"Where is Brandon Holst?"

"Who?" replied the stranger, his hair as dark as his eyes as he turned his head to gaze at Kate over his left shoulder.

She smacked the muzzle of the gun against his scalp hard enough to make her point.

"Aghh! Stop!"

"I told you not to turn around."

The man's grunting mixed with voices in the hallway. She didn't have much time. Soon hotel security would arrive, followed by the police.

"On your feet. Move it!"

She shoved one of the silenced guns in her jeans, by her spine. The second went in front, the long muzzle pressed against her lower abdomen. Covering both guns with her T-shirt, Kate grabbed the small room-service menu from the desk and folded it over her shooting hand clutching the Sig.

"Keep your hands by your sides. Walk normally. Let's go. Now!"

"Where are you taking me?" the stranger asked as he headed for the door. He was in his mid-forties, tanned, solidly built, with a boxer's nose and eyes too close together for his square face.

"You and I are going for a little ride."

13

Kate Donaldson sat sideways in the front passenger seat, the Sig pointed at the stranger as they exited Highway 71 thirty minutes later, near Bastrop, a town thirty miles south of Austin. She ordered him to turn into a secondary road that cut through the hill country. The moon hung high in the dark sky, bathing the towering pines flanking the deserted road with dim gray light.

They reached a Y in the road. To the right it turned into a gravel road. To the left it narrowed but remained paved.

Kate ordered him to go right, the stolen Mercury Sable bouncing as it cruised at thirty miles per hour over the uneven terrain, the high beams cutting through the night. Loose gravel pounded the vehicle's underside, occasionally bouncing off the doors and windows as the assassin steered them through the winding road. After a few minutes she spotted a weathered sign about a town five miles ahead.

"Where are we going?" he finally asked, the hardened features of his square face tightening.

Kate ignored him.

"Look. I'm just doing this for the money. I have no idea—"

"Shut up and drive."

Kate saw a break in the woods a minute later. "Stop. Put it in reverse. Go back about a hundred feet."

Extending beyond the shoulder Kate saw a section of reasonably flat, dry ground, flanked by knee-high vegetation.

She ordered him to steer the sedan into the opening, bouncing on her seat as they crossed the low shoulder. The vehicle's headlights forked through the woods. A pine resin fragrance streamed through the sedan's vents as they continued roughly another fifty feet before coming to a stop next to a creek.

"Get out and leave the lights on and the engine running."

Outside, she ordered him back on his knees, hands behind his head, fingers interlaced.

"Time for a heart to heart," she said, pacing behind him, the leaves cushioning her steps. Mosquitoes buzzed around them. "Who do you work for?"

"Look. I tried to tell you that I'm just an independent contractor. I'm not affiliated with any agency."

"Who is your controller?"

"Never met him."

"All right," she said, pulling out one of the silenced guns. "Take off your shoes and socks."

"What?"

"*Now!*"

He did.

"Lie on the ground facedown, hands behind your back, legs spread apart."

After he had complied, Kate used one of the man's socks to bind his wrists before kneeling in front of him. "Who is your controller?"

"I told you I—"

She shoved the second sock into his mouth, walked behind him, and pressed the muzzle against the small toe of his right foot.

"Last chance,"

"I really don't know what—"

She fired, the spitting sound mixing with the metallic grinding of the firing mechanism as the exiting bullet shoved back the Sig's slide, extracting and ejecting the spent cartridge before the slide returned, chambering a new round.

The man moaned, crashing on the leaf-littered ground after Kate had shaved the tip of his smallest toe.

Stepping on his back, she forced him to stop moving. "Now, listen very carefully. That was your one and only warning shot. From here on out, every time you give me a wrong answer you lose a full toe. When you run out of toes we'll move to your hands. After that we'll get more creative. Maybe you'll get to find out what your balls taste like. Now, for the third time, *who* is your controller?" She removed the sock from his mouth.

The stranger coughed, breathing in short sobbing gasps.

"All right," she said after several seconds. "If that's the way you want to do it . . ." she began to stuff the sock back in his mouth.

"No . . . wait . . . I'll tell you . . . . *stop!*"

She stopped. "I'm listening."

"A broker . . . my contact in Houston. He called me this afternoon . . . put me on standby. Then he phoned again right after you left the message in the answering machine."

"And?"

"Please. You need to understand that . . . they will kill me if I—"

"You should be more worried about what *I'm* going to do to you if you don't cooperate. Do you want me to shove the sock back in your mouth?"

The dark-haired man closed his eyes and shook his head, controlling his breathing. Kate tied the sock firmly around the end of his foot, stopping the blood loss.

"Thank—"

"What else?"

"I was ordered to . . . capture you alive."

"Who was the other man with you?"

He shrugged. "Never seen him in my life before."

"I warned you."

"Please! You have to believe me. That's the way the broker works. He never pairs us with people we know, and we never know the entire scope of the operation, just our own piece."

Kate considered that for a moment and chose to accept his explanation. Many intelligence communities, the CIA included, approached field operations in a similar manner, never letting operatives know the whole picture in case they got captured. Kate had always hated operating under such conditions but could not argue with the logic behind it. But just like on a battlefield, where the sergeant knew more than the grunt, and the lieutenant more than the sergeant, and so on, the trick to gathering intelligence was to capture higher ranking officers from the other side, debrief them, and then launch a counterstrike. The caveat was, however, that the enemy would realize that an officer had been compromised, along with the operations he was privy to, and switch their tactics to follow an alternate plan. The trick to a successful intelligence-gathering operation was to capture the officers without the enemy knowing they had been compromised. Accomplishing that was an art mastered only by the most experienced of operatives.

"All right," she said. "Where is Brandon Holst?"

"I don't know who that person is . . . I swear it."

Kate hesitated, once again wondering about how much information an independent contractor would be given, deciding that if he had been hired just to kidnap her, he might not have been told anything about the creator of the software. She decided to change her line of questioning away from Brandon for the moment.

"What are they planning to do with the software?"

"What software? I was contracted to bring you in. That's it."

She was rapidly losing her patience with this man. "What do you actually know?"

"After securing you I was to call a number to get information about the drop and collection of my payment."

Kate thought about it for a moment. She had captured a grunt and was getting nowhere. It was time to lure in the sergeant. She pulled out her cellular phone. "What's the number."

"But—"

"I'll tell you *exactly* what say."

The contractor gave it to her. She dialed and then gave the phone to him, telling him exactly what to say. A minute later she hung up.

"You did well," she said, glancing down at him, sitting on the ground, resting his back against the car's front bumper.

"Not bad for a dead man," he said with a heavy sigh.

"If you do your part, I'll see to it that you get protection from my agency."

"Who is your agency?"

"That's not important at the moment, only that it's powerful enough to guarantee your protection."

He nodded.

"What's your name?"

"Call me Jacobs."

"How's the foot, Jacobs?"

"That's the least of my problems right now."

"Good," she replied. "Because it's time for another ride."

14

Deception—an art that Kate Donaldson had learned to master long ago—was another weapon often overlooked by younger operatives, who relied far too much on their physical strength and firepower to carry them through an assignment. Today, Kate used deception to buy herself an edge over the enemy.

She approached an abandoned warehouse in East Austin, just a few blocks from the place where she had nearly been killed hours before. Kate walked in front, beneath the grayish gleam of streetlights. Jacobs remained next to her clutching an empty Sig Sauer, which muzzle he pressed against Kate's side, just as they had rehearsed. Kate also held a Sig .45 pistol, but fully loaded and beneath the dark windbreaker she had purchased on the way over, keeping it pointed at Jacobs.

They had stopped at a twenty-four-hour drugstore to get a dressing for his toe and makeup for her. Kate had used the cosmetics not to enhance her looks but to give herself a few bruises and a busted lip.

Deception is a weapon.

The cracked sidewalk on which they walked, overgrown with weeds, bordered a waist-high chain-link fence. A weathered FOR SALE sign, fastened to the fence with rusted wires, told Kate that the windowless warehouse beyond the empty parking lot had not been used for some time. They reached a gate, secured to the fence by an old chain. Upon closer inspection, Kate noticed that the chain had been cut, indicating that the meeting was still on.

Using her free hand, she removed the chain and pushed the gate, which creaked open. Beyond it a cobblestone walkway, also overgrown with weeds, led to the only door on this side of the two-story structure, washed by the streetlights.

A figure appeared in the doorway, roughly fifty feet away, carrying a long object. A second person stepped behind him, holding what Kate thought looked like a pistol.

"Stay where you are," the man in front warned in a heavy Slavic accent, before aiming the object at Kate, who recognized the flashlight a second after the blinding light stung her pupils. She closed her eyes, trying to minimize the impact the flash would have on her night vision. The Slav shifted the beam toward Jacobs before switching it off. He waved them over.

"You have become a real nuisance, Miss Donaldson," he said in a heavy Slavic accent.

Kate momentarily chilled when hearing the foreign accent, remembering the incident in London, the unexplained connection between the bombing of a Y2K convention in retaliation for NATO air strikes against Serbian troops.

Shoving aside the distracting thought, she faked a cough and leaned slightly forward when she was within a dozen feet of the stout man, his closely-cropped red hair framing a rugged face, slits for eyes, and—

The terrorist!

This man was the terrorist who had worn the brown hood at Holst Enterprises the day of the shooting!

Kate controlled her emotions, sticking to her original plan. She spotted a small gun in the redhead's other hand. "Where . . . where is Brandon Holst?" she asked, stopping a safe distance from him and his partner, pretending to be in pain, coughing slightly, conveying weakness.

The man's hard features relaxed. "You know something that my superiors need. Give it to me now and I'll kill you quickly. If you resist, I have been instructed to use any method possible to extract the information."

"Where is Brandon?" she repeated, hoping that her vulnerable state would compel the red-haired man to release a tidbit of information.

"That is not important. My employer needs the password. What is it? Tell me or those bruises will be nothing compared to what I will do to you."

"The password . . . for Brandon. That was the deal." She coughed harder.

"Bring her inside," the second man said, as big as the first and with a similar Slavic accent. He was completely bald but had a well-trimmed goatee. The accents continued to bother her.

"What about my payment?" asked Jacobs, holding Kate back.

"You will get it when—"

In a single fluid move, Kate pushed Jacobs aside and leveled the Sig at the pair of Slavs, something she hated doing because they were both armed. "Drop them!"

The bald man began to raise his weapon at Kate, pulling in his goatee as he scowled.

Her instincts took command of her actions. Kate shot him once in the face without further warning, the muffled spit of the silenced Sig mixing with the snapping noise of the firing mechanism. She trained her gun on the second

Slav even before the limp body of his associate collapsed on the walkway like a sack of potatoes.

The red-haired man looked confused, shifting his gaze from Jacobs, who stood to the side with the empty Sig still in his right hand, to Kate, who kept the pistol trained on his head, and finally to his disfigured partner bleeding on the ground.

"Last warning," she said, leveling the semiautomatic at his face. "Do you also want a face-lift?" These people had pushed her operative side back into the real world, and Kate Donaldson had surrendered herself to it, acting on polished survival instincts without hesitation, without remorse, without concern about taking a life if that got her closer to her objective.

The Slav complied, releasing the gun.

"Now kick it over to me."

He did, the dark weapon skittering over the cobblestone, stopping a few inches from her left foot.

Keeping her eyes on her quarry, Kate picked it up. It was a .380 caliber pistol, like Brandon's Walther PPK, but built by Sig Sauer, the preferred weapons manufacturer of this shadowy network.

"Take his flashlight," Kate ordered Jacobs.

The Slav hissed at Jacobs, "Your life won't be worth spit after this stunt you have pulled on us."

Kate's unlikely ally picked up the flashlight and shone the light in his face. "Tell me something I don't already know."

"Inside," she said. "How many more?"

The Slav didn't reply.

"Turn around," she ordered.

The moment he did, Kate hit him behind the right ear, shocking the web of nerves below the skin hard enough to knock him unconscious, but without killing him. His large bulk dropped unceremoniously on the stone floor.

"You sure have a way with men," Jacobs mumbled.

"Leave him here," she said, pocketing the small Sig. "Peek inside the warehouse."

"Can I at least have a gun?"

"You have a gun."

Jacobs made a face. "C'mon, lady."

"Maybe later. Right now you have to earn my trust."

Jacobs sighed, staring at his empty weapon. "Great. I guess I'll just get my ass shot if there's someone else inside."

"You should have thought about the risks of this profession before getting into it. Now move."

She kept the contract assassin in the sights of her pistol as Jacobs dragged the dead Slav to the doorway, pushing him inside while dropping to a crouch and peering beyond the entryway. The corpse landed on the floor a few feet past the entryway.

Hastening footsteps echoed from inside the structure, followed by the sound of a door being shut.

"Someone's in there!" Jacobs shouted.

Before Kate could react, she heard an engine coming to life, followed by screeching tires.

Swinging her weapon in the direction of the street, she spotted a sedan racing toward the corner, fishtailing as the driver negotiated the turn, disappearing from sight.

"Looks like one got away. We don't have much time," she said. "Come with me inside."

Jacobs didn't move, staring at the street corner.

"What's wrong?" she asked.

"It's all over for me now," Jacobs mumbled, staring at the warehouse. "The one that got away will report what he saw, what he heard. Might as well kill me now."

Kate understood Jacobs's predicament. He had definitely crossed the line and could not go back. That knowledge, however, told her that she could now trust this man. Jacobs had no place to go but with her.

"Here," she said, handing him the small Sig .380 automatic she had taken from the unconscious Slav. "Looks like you're stuck with me for good."

Jacobs inhaled deeply, exhaled, and took the gun. He spent a moment checking it and then followed her inside the building.

Kate scanned the murky room, roughly thirty feet square, illuminated by a single light bulb hanging at the end of a cord in the far corner, next to a wooden table and an armchair which, upon closer inspection, sported leather straps. Kate trained the flashlight on the table and saw a couple of syringes and several vials.

She grinned.

"What's so funny, lady?" he asked.

"Have you ever seen a chemical interrogation before, Jacobs?"

The contract assassin shook his head.

"Then you're in for a real treat."

She had captured a sergeant. It was now time to find the lieutenant, and if she got lucky, maybe even the captain. For a moment she wondered who was the captain of this kidnapping operation.

15

Dragan Kundat stood on the bow of the merchant vessel under a crystalline sky, a sea breeze swirling his long hair. The ship left the Houston Ship Channel and entered Galveston Bay. The Gulf of Mexico extended into the darkness beyond the bay.

His eyes gazing at the array of lights marking the shore as well as the vessels cruising the bay at this late hour, the Yugoslav terrorist crossed his arms, his mind racing through his plan, the one that would take him to Havana, Cuba, where he would board a plane to Madrid, Spain. From there a prearranged flight would take him and his cargo to Istanbul, Turkey, with a final hop in a chartered craft to Belgrade. With luck, he would be back home in less than forty-eight hours.

Dragan frowned.

Luck.

The former colonel of the Serbian army peered into the darkness, broken by a well-lit ship coming up to their right, its lights diffusing in the night, bringing the relatively smooth waters alive. He despised those who relied on luck to carry out any portion of their battle plans. Luck was what he hoped the enemy would count on, allowing him and his Serbian troops to win, to uproot, to eradicate, to cleanse.

Cleansing.

Dragan remembered the war in Bosnia, recalled the ethnic cleansing, the systematic elimination of Muslims and Catholics from areas under Bosnian Serb control.

The bright ship turned out to be a luxurious yacht, apparently anchored in the middle of the bay, its main deck as well as a few passengers clearly visible as the merchant vessel cruised a mere four hundred feet from its bow. Three blondes in nightgowns shouted and waved as they passed a bottle around.

Dragan ignored them, closing his eyes, the female screams bringing back memories of the justified exterminations for the benefit of Serbia. He remembered the villages in Croatia and Bosnia, remembered the firing squads, the mass burials, the boiling dust shrouding bulldozers as they buried the evidence, the necessary transgressions committed by one ethnic group against another.

Selective massacres of specific groups within a population had been a tool to scare the balance of that population away from the targeted area, therefore "cleansing" it, ridding it of unwanted ethnic or religious groups. In most cases, Dragan Kundat, under orders from Slobodan Milosevic himself, had extended the terminations to all males of military age, which minimum age the Yugoslav colonel had set at twelve years. And to breed out the unwanted races, Dragan has also ordered the widespread rape of every Muslim and Catholic woman older than twelve years of age, impregnating them, planting Serbian seeds on non-Serbian soil.

Dragan opened his eyes, peering at the American whores on the yacht.

Rape. *Silovati.*

The terrorist took a deep breath, remembering the contorted faces of so many women, gang-raped, from that point on carrying in their wombs not just their own humiliation but the humiliation of their race, of their people. *Silovati* was the ultimate weapon for ethnic cleansing, guaranteeing that the violated women would never return to the place where they had been ravaged, would never consider living in an area where Serbs lived, retreating to isolated, unwanted regions to raise their bastard children. Those women, marked for life, would also be less willing to become intimate with another men, assuming any non-Serbian man would want to be with them and their half-Serbian children.

And Dragan Kundat had enjoyed every moment, every scream, every writhing, trembling non-Serb female body that he had entered, violently, with crushing force, especially the younger ones, barely beginning to develop into women, sometimes ripping them apart, leaving them to die from internal bleeding. He had made them scream, shout, tense, convulse, cry in agony across the mountains of Bosnia and Herzegovina, in the lush valleys of Croatia, across every Serbian-held enclave in those revolting states. He had raped mothers in front of their daughters and daughters in front of their mothers, before shooting their husbands, fathers, sons, and brothers. He had bred them out in meadows, in forests, in the snow, in the center of countless villages, in front of their people, of their elders, of their children, even inside their own places of worship, showing them that they were never safe, would *never* be safe unless they left and never returned.

Dragan Kundat savored the memory, the visions, for they brought honor to his people, to his race, to his slaughtered family.

Tears reached the rugged terrorist's face as he remembered the ethnic Albanians who had killed his parents twenty years ago, in Pristina, Kosovo, when he was a teenager. Dragan remembered with a great deal of pain the night he'd killed for the first time.

Dragan, too young and stupid to know any better, had fallen in love with a beautiful ethnic Albanian girl. Against his parents' constant warnings, he'd continued to see the girl in secrecy for several weeks, in the process getting her pregnant. He had planned to run away with her, perhaps seek refuge in Italy, away from their intolerant society. Unfortunately for Dragan, her father found out everything and had gone to his house to kill him, but Dragan had not been home. Instead, the angered father had attacked Dragan's own father, stabbing him. When Dragan's mother had gone to his rescue, the girl's father had stabbed her as well. Dragan had learned that day the Serbs and Albanian Muslims could never coexist, could never overcome hundreds of years of hostilities deep rooted in their history, with each generation adding another layer of aversion. The same day that Dragan buried his parents, he had also learned that his girlfriend had been stoned to death by her family and relatives. In retaliation, the teenage Dragan had used his father's gun to kill her parents before going off to join the Serbian army.

"Dragan?"

Dragan Kundat turned around. One of his subordinates wore an alarmed expression across his Slavic face. He knew this one well, having rescued him as a young Serbian teenager in Bosnia after his family had been murdered by the Muslims.

"How is our passenger?" he asked, regarding the brown-haired Serb, his young eyes gazing at his mentor before looking into the distance.

"Drugged up to keep him quiet, as you have requested."

"Keep him that way until we reach international waters. Any news on Haas and the access password?"

"No. But there has been a . . . *komplikovatien.*"

Dragan worked for a man who did not like *komplikovatien,* complications. And as generous as Slobodan Milosevic had been to the former Serbian colonel, Dragan knew how unforgiving his superior could be.

Dragan took a deep breath. He had to get Milosevic out of his mind and focus on the problem at hand. His instincts told him it had something to do with the latest attempt to abduct the woman, who, based on the last report from a subcontractor, had been abducted and on her way to be debriefed by one of Dragan's top agents.

"Todorovic?" Dragan finally asked.

His underling nodded. "He has been taken hostage by the woman."

Dragan closed his eyes. In spite of his training, of his experience, of his many years turning the tables around on his enemies, it never ceased to amaze him how easy it was for certain people to turn the tables on him. Kate Donaldson appeared to be one of those people, stubbornly refusing to yield to his superior rule.

"How can it be?" Dragan finally said, struggling to control his anger. "The word from the subcontractor was that . . ." he let his words trail off in the sea breeze, knowing quite well that circumstances had gone out of his direct control. His experience told him he now needed to step back and find a way to perform a reasonable amount of damage control. But first he needed to control the demon turning loose inside of him, whirling around his core, scourging him at the thought of Todorovic in the hands of this woman, this witch, this American *prostitutka!*

"How long has he been abducted?" was all he managed to say, knowing quite well the serious repercussions if this woman broke Todorovic, forcing him to confess. Such concern was the main reason why he had not allowed Todorovic to enter the picture until *after* he had gotten assurances that the situation had been secured. It was now obvious to Dragan that Kate Donaldson had either turned the subcontractor, or somehow managed to free herself from capture and turn the tables. In either case the result was the same. Todorovic had been turned from an asset into a liability because of how much he knew on this operation. He had to be silenced immediately.

The young Serb hesitated, checking his watch before replying, "He was taken at least an hour ago. But he was wearing his transmitter. We have managed to track them. A team is following them."

Dragan Kundat, the Serbian colonel, the terrorist, the rapist of Bosnian women, turned his face to the sky, as dark as his soul, as cold as his calculating eyes as he shifted them to his subordinate, who broke eye contact. His soft gaze was no match to Dragan's armor-piercing stare.

"Get ready to execute the alternative plan the moment we clear the bay and enter the Gulf of Mexico."

He nodded.

"And order the team to strike immediately. Take no prisoners. Understood?"

Dragan Kundat continued to study the sea, a frown curving down the ends of his lips. He had always been good at *making* his own luck, at controlling his own destiny. He had the software and Brandon Holst. Assuming that Holst knew the access password, Dragan really didn't need Kate Donaldson to convince the executive to yield the software key. He just needed to *create* the illusion that Kate Donaldson would undergo severe torture unless he cooperated. The terrorist felt confident that this deceptive tactic, which had worked well so many times before, would not fail him. Right now it was more important to break the investigative chain than to capture Kate Donaldson or salvage Todorovic.

Dragan pulled a small piece of paper from his pocket, reading the short but quite stern message from his president.

Deliver or die trying.

Sweeper was the key to the success of his superior's cyber-weapon. Failure to deliver it meant disappointing Milosevic. Few men had disappointed the Yugoslav president and lived to tell their story. Everyone feared Milosevic, even Dragan Kundat, who on more than one occasion wondered when he would be promoted to a higher and safer position in the government, where the risk of failure was far lower than in field operations. But he had not brought himself to ask his superior. In Milosevic's government you did not ask for anything. You only received and *thanked.*

Dragan had never been good at just waiting for opportunities to be handed to him. Making his own luck meant taking advantage of opportunities. On more than one occasion he had wondered if the only real way to move up in Yugoslavia would be by *making* room at the top, by assassinating Milosevic, by eliminating his reign of error, his grip on the general population. Dragan felt that Milosevic was the safety pin. Once removed, his entire house of cards would come crumbling down, opening the door for a new strongman, like Dragan Kundat, highly respected by the Serbian army, which served under his command in Bosnia and Herzegovina. In addition, one of Dragan's best friends and a former comrade-in-arms, Ivan Goseliv, was the chief of Milosevic's state police. Between the two of them they could gain control of the armed forces, restoring order to the streets following Milosevic's assassination.

Could such strike be possible?

Dragan stared at the night sky, deciding that the very first step toward achieving any career move was by executing his current task to Milosevic's satisfaction. Once he had returned to Yugoslavia, he would consider the possibility of setting such plan in motion. But he had to be careful. Many men before him had tried to displace Milosevic, only to find themselves at the receiving end of his anger, a fate that was worse than hell itself.

16

Kate Donaldson and Jacobs stood in front of the Slav, safely secured to a chair in a motel room in south Austin. She had selected the room carefully, on the first floor, facing the rear parking lot, making it easy for them to carry their unconscious guest inside. The room had two double beds sharing a nightstand. The bathroom was located in the rear, with exposed double sinks and a private room for the toilet and the shower.

Kate had used her knife to shred two hotel towels into straps, binding the red-haired man to a chair facing the beds.

Jacobs had gone into the bathroom a few minutes ago and came out moments later while Kate sat on a bed facing the Slav, sprinkling water onto his face from a glass of water.

The Slav's eyes opened. He blinked, trying to focus them, before wincing in obvious pain.

"My head," he whispered.

Kate stabbed the purplish swelling behind his right ear with an index finger.

He jerked on the chair, his square face contorting in pain.

"Does it hurt?"

Eyes flashing contempt, the man did not reply.

"Where is Brandon Holst?"

"Nowhere you can ever find him."

She pressed the wound again with her finger, making him wince again.

"Whore! You will pay for this!"

"Really? How?"

"My people are very powerful. They will track you down and kill you like a pig, just like we shot your boyfriend."

She fought the overwhelming desire to kill him right then, as well as the impulse to tell him that she had seen the whole thing on video.

"And who are these people that you're referring to?"

"Go to hell."

Kate shook her head, stood, and slowly walked to the nightstand. "I guess it's time for this." She held up the soft-sided case she had found next to the chemicals inside the warehouse. "Remember?"

The Slav turned to Jacobs. "Do something, imbecile! You work for us! Stop this nonsense!"

The contract assassin shrugged. "I never took any payment from you, so technically I'm not under your control. And right now I'm contracting for her, who happens to hold better cards than you do."

"Be careful," the Slav said, turning to Kate, a hint of concern now staining his heavy accent. "If you do not know how to do this, it can—"

"Quiet."

She held up two vials. One contained sodium pentothal, a heavy barbiturate. The second was Dexedrine, a powerful amphetamine. She looked at Jacobs, standing to the side, arms crossed, watching with interest.

"Lower his pants."

"Huh?"

"His pants. Lower them."

Jacobs unbuckled the man's belt and pulled down his trousers all the way to his ankles. He wore white boxer shorts underneath.

"You're making a big mistake," he said. "Both of you! You will be—"

Kate smacked him across the face. "Instead of complaining, why don't you help yourself? Don't you get it? It's *over* for you unless you cooperate, like Jacobs did." She filled one of the syringes with sodium pentothal before approaching him. "Last chance."

"They control my life," the Slav said, fear breaking through his indifferent stare. "They will kill me and my family if I cross them. I have seen them do it before."

"Who? Tell me and perhaps we might be able to help you and your family."

"I . . . I can't tell you what—"

"You *will* tell me," Kate said. "And depending on what we learn, I might give you an extra dose of this barbiturate and kill a few brain cells." She held the syringe filled with sodium pentothal up in the air.

"This is your last chance," said Jacobs. "Save yourself, man. You are trying to protect people who obviously don't care about you."

Kate noticed that Jacob's words had a strong impact on the Slav. He started mumbling.

"Speak up!" Kate barked.

The Slav, his body secured to the chair, raised his head and looked at Kate with a pleading stare. "You won't understand," he said.

"Try me."

"These people have control over all of our lives. They

can turn around and destroy anyone as fast as I can snap my fingers. They probably know that I've been compromised already. If I talk, they will know because you will go after them, and they will in turn kill my family.''

"We've covered that already," replied Kate, reflecting on her own situation. "What else?"

"They have total control of my life, my wife, my kids. Right now I bet his people are with them, in Belgrade. If something out of the ordinary happens—"

"In *Belgrade*? Is that where this network is from?" Kate could barely ask the question as the parallels between London and this situation increased.

"Please ... try to understand. If you do something against the network based on information you've learned from me, they will slaughter my boys, rape my wife and oldest daughter, turn them to prostitution. I've seen it done before.''

"What is your name?"

After a moment of hesitation, he said, "Mirko Todorovic.''

"Are you a Yugoslav?"

He closed his eyes. "Serbian."

"Why is Milosevic interested in Y2K software?"

"I . . . I don't know. Please, I beg you. Understand that I am bound by blood agreements. I love my fam—"

Kate used her free hand to grab his lapels. "It's too late for such thoughts! You should have thought about it before you joined that organization. Right now those bastards have shot and kidnapped my boyfriend, and have also stolen his technology. I will find him *and* get even if it's the last thing I do.''

Without another word she injected half of the sodium pentothal solution subcutaneously, near Todorovic's femoral artery and waited a few seconds. The heavy barbiturate had the desired effect. His body relaxed. Kate kept the syringe filled with Dexedrine on the bed. She would inject small amounts of the strong amphetamine every time he started to fade away under the influence of the barbiturate, keeping him in that state long enough to extract all the information she could. This approach worked simply because the mind's natural tendency was to tell the truth.

Dreamers never lie.

Kate Donaldson counted on that basic human trait. Lying came into play during the waking hours, when external reasons compelled the brain to block the truth and instead release an altered version, depending on the situation. The sodium penothal simply forced the subject into a state of *near sleep,* lowering the mind's natural defenses, thus allowing the natural flow of information to take place.

She turned to Jacobs and whispered, "Don't say a word. I'll do all the talking from now on."

The contract assassin nodded, his face displaying a mix of curiosity and skepticism.

"Can you hear me?" she asked in a soft voice, just as she had been trained at The Farm. She had to formulate her questions such that Todorovic could answer them in a few words.

Todorovic didn't respond. Kate leaned down and repeated the question. She was worried about having given him a larger dose than necessary. Under other circumstances, she would have started with a smaller dose and worked her way up, but right now she was racing against time. She desperately needed solid information that would lead her to Brandon Holst.

"Hear . . . you," he mumbled, his eyes going in and out of focus, his head tilted to the right.

"You are with friends, understand?"

"Friends . . ."

"Good," said Kate in a very compassionate voice, "you

are my friend, and friends should call themselves by their first names. What is your first name?'' she asked to double check the information she had acquired earlier.

''Mirko . . .''

Kate nodded approvingly.

''Hello, Mirko, my name is Kate.''

''Kate . . .''

''Now tell me, Mirko, how old are you?''

''Forty-one,'' he replied, drool coming out of the corner of his mouth, running down his chin.

''Who do you work for?''

''. . . work . . .''

''Who is your superior?''

''Dragan Kundat.''

Kate found it difficult to hide her shock. Dragan Kundat, the same Serbian monster who had coordinated the bombing in London that ended her CIA career, was again involved in another Y2K scheme.

What in hell is going on?

Why was the government of Slobodan Milosevic interested in Y2K technology? Until now all Milosevic had cared about was raping Yugoslavia to satisfy his lust for power and money. In the years since he had become president, he had turned Yugoslavia into a kleptocracy which enabled him and his ministers to plunder the nation's resources and fatten their bank accounts at the expense of killing the economy. Why would he consider Y2K software important? Certainly not to get his country compliant. Yugoslavia had far too many other problems to worry about computer glitches. Its people were starving, homeless, enduring an inflation rate that reached three digits, making wages earned in the morning totally worthless by the afternoon.

Milosevic's priorities had always been clear: first and foremost, remaining in power while also amassing a large fortune; second, everything else that protected the first goal, including a strong army and police to enforce his orders on a defenseless population.

Kate gathered her thoughts. She could only keep Todorovic under the power of the barbiturate for several minutes before taking a break, lest she risked causing permanent damage to his brain.

"Where is Brandon Holst being held?"

"Houston . . . in Houston."

"Where in Houston?"

"Houston . . . Houston."

"Mirko, I need you to help your friend Kate. She needs to know *where* in Houston is Brandon Holst being held?"

"Ship . . . cargo . . ."

Her mouth turned dry from anticipation. "What is the name of the ship?"

"Jaka . . . Jakart . . . Jakartmphhh . . ." Mirko began to fade into a deep sleep.

Kate was losing him. She gave him a small dose of Dexedrine to pump him back up some, but not a lot, otherwise he would become too conscious and his defenses would awaken, fighting back the natural impulse to tell the truth.

"What is the name of the ship?" she asked when he stirred again.

The sound of broken glass drowned his answer.

"Shit!" shouted Jacobs as he dropped to the ground.

Kate dove for cover as a pear-shaped object bounced against the wall, hit the nightstand, and skittered between the two beds.

Grenade!

She landed hard on the worn carpet, her legs kicking to push herself into the bathroom, to get away from the nearing explosion.

But the blast never came. Instead, the room filled rapidly with smoke.

Kate remained close to the ground, holding her breath,

feeling the cold tile against her elbows as she crawled in front of the double sinks, next to the open door, and into the bathroom. She scrambled inside the room, smoke stinging her eyes, burning her nostrils.

She closed the door behind her, momentarily isolating herself from the madness outside. She grabbed a towel and turned on the shower, wetting it, wiping her face before wrapping it around her head, like a veil, leaving only a slit to see through.

Where is Jacobs?

The thought entered her mind only now, after she had gotten herself to safety, deciding that the contract assassin would have to take care of himself.

Kate turned off the lights and sat against the corner of the shower, grabbing both the Sig 220 in her jeans and the Walther in the ankle holster, one in each hand, both aimed at the door.

Gunfire erupted outside, followed by agonizing cries and more gunfire, some silenced, others deafening, like thunder.

Someone kicked in the bathroom door. It swung on its hinges hard, fanning smoke into the bathroom before crashing against the wall. Her guns aimed at the doorway, Kate Donaldson saw no target.

Confused, her throat now on fire from the smoke, even with the wet towel as a filter, she blinked to keep the tears from blurring her vision.

A figure suddenly loomed in her field of view, like an apparition within the smoke, large, muscular, wearing a mask, hands clutching a silenced submachine gun.

Without hesitation, Kate Donaldson fired twice with the Sig, keeping the Walther in reserve, her mind keeping track of how many rounds she had left. The reports inside the small bathroom stabbed her eardrums as the assassin arched back, propelled by the .45 caliber rounds, hitting the opposite wall.

Her ears ringing, Kate jumped off the shower, landing in a deep crouch on the tile floor beyond the doorway, in front of the double sinks, pressing her right wrist over her left at perpendicular angles from each other in front of her, which maintained the Sig pointed straight ahead and the Walther to her right, increasing her chances of neutralizing multiple targets in parallel.

A near miss buzzed in her left ear like an angered hornet before striking the mirror over the double sinks.

Kate jumped into the bedroom, firing both guns multiple times, buying herself time to land, to roll, to search for a target, spotting two: one by the broken windows, veiled by the smoke; the second in between the beds, standing over the bullet-riddled bodies of Jacobs and Todorovic.

Time seemed to slow down as she watched both figures swing their weapons toward her. In the same instant she fired both guns at perpendicular angles, hitting the closest man but missing the one behind the broken windows, striking glass instead, which shattered on impact, shards falling over the windowsill.

The Walther's final round shoved the slide all the way back, displaying an empty weapon. She dropped it, both hands now on the Sig as she stared at the assassin's muzzle, realizing it was too late to bring her weapon around. She braced for the impact but instead heard the muffled report of a gun coming from the parking lot.

The assassin lunged forward, as if possessed by an invisible force, landing on the closest bed, blood spurting from his back.

Her throat on fire from the smoke, Kate clambered toward the sinks, hiding beneath them, her nearly empty Sig aimed at the front of the room, the ringing in her ears intensifying, like sirens, making it very difficult to hear anything except for very loud noises.

She waited, coughing, her burning eyes focused on the

weapon's front sight. Someone had shot that last assassin, saving her life.

But who? Was it the same person who saved my life back at the warehouse?

Why did he save my life? And why doesn't he show himself?

She forced herself to focus, to peer through the haze, to keep the front of the room in her sight. Then she heard a faint voice calling out her name. The distant voice begged her to stop shooting, to lower her weapon.

Kate coughed hard, surprised that she could not hear herself, suddenly realizing that the mumbling was actually someone screaming from outside the room.

"Who are you?" she shouted. "Identify yourse—"

A figure opened the door, slowly.

Kate blinked twice, her finger on the trigger, following the dark shape through the suffocating smoke, recognizing the silver hair, the rugged features.

"You bastard! You're one of them!" she shouted, anger suddenly clouding her thoughts, like the swirling haze enveloping her, choking her. "You left Brandon to die!"

"Miss Donaldson! Stop! Don't shoot!" came a faint cry. *"We're on your side!"*

Kate hesitated when the figure lowered his weapon, a massive hang gun. Whoever this man really was, he had apparently saved her life, twice.

"We're here to protect you."

Protect me? Why?

Kate relaxed the pressure on the trigger, her confused mind struggling to put everything in perspective. This man had obviously killed that last assassin, now sprawled on the bed. But Kate had seen this man walk away from Brandon after he had been shot! This man had pretended to be a client to steal Brandon's technology. How could he *possibly* be on her side?

"No more tricks!" she shouted. "Where is Brandon? Where have you taken him?"

"We're trying to find that out ourselves. We need your help. Please, Miss Donaldson! Please!"

Kate didn't waver, once again fixing her finger on the trigger.

"Put that gun down, Kate, before you shoot the wrong person!"

She froze, the distant voice sounding very familiar. A moment later a second figure appeared in the doorway, unarmed, walking past the first. Kate closed her eyes and lowered the Sig when recognizing the face of Mike Costner, her former superior at the Central Intelligence Agency.

17

Brandon Holst woke to an ear-piercing noise. He gazed about him, not certain where he was, conscious only of the intense noise and shafts of light assaulting his eyes, which he promptly closed.

He breathed in deeply, trying to bring his mind into focus, before squinting, struggling to see in the blinding light, unable to make out anything but a blur, which spun around him, making him dizzy.

Where am I? was all his mind could stitch together in the form of a cohesive thought before flashbacks replaced it. He saw Kate, smiling, before hooded figures replaced her, clutching weapons, one of them holding the hard disk housing his Y2K software. The slim Beretta Tomcat had fit comfortably in his hand as he saw himself firing it, before an invisible energy stabbed him in the chest, before a black cloud whirled around him, swallowing everything, shoving his thoughts to the periphery of his mind, leaving his core empty, dark, alone.

But through the murky veil shielding his sight, through the deafening noise, Brandon Holst detected upward motion. He felt as if his body was floating, rising through the air, before he once more lost consciousness.

18

Kate Donaldson slumped in one of the comfortable leather seats in the rear of the Learjet, her ears popping as the craft reached its cruising altitude following its take off from Bergstrom International Airport in Austin, heading toward Houston.

She watched a crimson sun looming behind the hills to the east, its magnificent shafts of orange and yellow-gold staining the indigo sky, swallowing the stars. But her mind could not let her enjoy the beautiful scene. She was still coping with the events that had unfolded in the past thirty minutes, since the CIA had so abruptly come back into her life.

She felt exhausted, not just from all of the physical abuse, but also mentally, having experienced pretty much the entire gamut of emotions in the past twenty-four hours, from love to despair, fear, anger, and finally the frustration that ate her alive for not having gotten the complete name of the vessel sailing out of Houston.

Costner approached her, holding two mugs of coffee. He gave one to Kate. The Chief of Counterterrorism of the Central Intelligence Agency was actually quite young, just forty-three, with a full head of dark brown hair, an aquiline nose, a strong chin, and eyes that could be blue or green, depending on the light.

"How are you holding up?" he asked, taking the seat next to her and fastening his seat belt.

"I'll survive." She kept her gaze on the violet hues of the dawning sky. "Are you ready to level with me?"

Costner nodded.

After the CIA saved her life for the second time in the past twenty-four hours—the first time just outside the warehouse on First Street—Kate had struck a deal with her old employer. She claimed she knew the location of the next link in the investigative chain and would share it with them, in return for a full explanation on their part, plus the Agency's backing to find Brandon Holst. After a ten-minute conference call between Kate, Costner, and the Director of Central Intelligence, a deal was made. The ever-paranoid Kate Donaldson, however, would not release her information until the CIA first explained its actions and its current understanding of the situation.

Mike Costner tilted his head in the direction of the silver-haired man who had posed as a businessman.

"That's Gam Davidson. He's a CIA officer, one of hundreds of our guys working in conjunction with the FBI to protect key American industries like software, computer chips, communications, automotive, energy, and aerospace from foreign agencies."

Kate shrugged. The CIA and the FBI had been protecting American industries for as long as she could remember.

"Keep going."

"As you might remember from your last two years with the Agency, much effort was expended by the U.S. intel-

ligence community to protect American industries as they
struggled to get themselves ready for the Year 2000. That
effort led us to keep tabs on all American software companies that, according to their IRS records, claimed to have
spent research and development capital on the development of Y2K solutions. What we found was that over
eighty percent of software companies and consulting firms
who claimed to have solutions or plans to get their clients
Y2K-compliant were not really developing anything new.
They were simply charging their clients a small fortune for
advice of the kind of dumping all Windows 3.1 systems
and replacing them with new systems capable of using
Windows 95 or 98. But some companies, like Holst Enterprises, were actually creating algorithms to attack certain aspects of the Y2K problem. Holst's solution was
particularly revolutionary, not because of the way it fixed
two-digit years, but because of the way it *found them*.''

Kate was now listening intently, remembering her conversations with Brandon, who never really told her how it
was that his software found the non-compliant dates before
fixing them with one of many industry-accepted solutions,
which he had explained in fair detail to her.

"So you tried to purchase the technology from him by
having two of your men pose as businessmen?"

Costner nodded. "You can imagine our surprise when
you entered the picture. At first I was suspicious of your
presence and had you followed. But then it became evident
that you were sticking to your agreement with us and were
simply working on enhancing your security business."

"So you were lying about the surveillance outside of
that steak house."

Costner nodded. "The surveillance was for Brandon
Holst. I didn't know that you were involved until you
called. You can't imagine my surprise, though I would
have found out hours later from the surveillance photos
taken that same night. Your call before the photos were proc-

essed added credibility to your claim that you had no idea what was going on. In any case, at the time that you called I couldn't afford for you to know our plan."

Kate, used to being lied to by her agency, let it go for now.

"But something obviously went wrong with your scheme," she said, taking a sip of coffee.

Costner leaned back on his chair, closing his eyes. "Brandon Holst turned out to be quite the shrewd businessman. He knew the power of his tool and refused to sell it outright to the U.S. government, even though we originally requested that he develop it for us."

"Did he violate a contract?"

Costner shook his head. "No, we didn't pay him any fees up front or sign any agreements. We only put in an informal request with him and hundreds of other software companies across the country to consider developing Y2K software. Like I've said, we figured that if any of them came up with something interesting, we would then negotiate for a contract based on the expected impact of the software fix."

"I see," Kate said. "So Uncle Sam wouldn't commit up front, but he expected the software companies to honor his non-commitment later on if they came up with a worthy product? Doesn't quite seem fair to the corporations, does it?"

"This was viewed in Washington as one of many contingency plans for dealing with the Y2K dilemma. The problem was that we barely had the capital to research the problems in our own government agencies—let alone those of the nation as a whole. The IRS alone, for example, has spent hundreds of millions of dollars trying to get its own systems compliant. To commission projects to address *all* of the nation's Y2K problems was fiscally impossible."

"All right," she said, not wanting to argue the point. "What happened next?"

"Holst essentially followed Bill Gates's number-one rule of marketing software: Don't sell it, *license* it. Holst wanted to license his software to anyone willing to pay his price, which varied according to the size of the corporation."

Kate grinned briefly. "How much did he stick it to you for?"

"One million, plus a hundred thousand per year for the next ten years in consulting fees for upgrades and tweaks."

"Good for him."

Costner frowned. "His price wasn't that unusual for a software license. They're very expensive. He actually gave us a break on the price because we came to him with a verbal proposal. But then we realized that given Sweeper's power to penetrate systems, it could have enormous destructive potential if it fell into the wrong hands. So we tried to convince him to sell it to us. We offered him a hundred times the amount of our licensing fee, but he wouldn't budge, claiming that he wanted the world to benefit from his software. He was about to offer licenses to corporations worldwide—again, based on their annual sales, making it affordable to virtually anyone. From his perspective, it was a good business move, the kind that allows a small company to gain market share and open doors for future products. But from our perspective, it was like a government subcontractor retailing cruise missiles on the open market."

Kate leaned forward and set the coffee mug on the tray in between the seats, turning sideways. "You're saying that someone could turn his Y2K software into a weapon."

"The key to Holst's software is its ability to *seek out* two-digit years, even in the most cryptic and complicated of programs. The rest of his code is good, but fairly generic, using standard methods, and a few good twists to those techniques, which patches non-compliant code."

Kate nodded, remembering the examples that Brandon

had given her during their dinner conversation at Sullivan's a few weeks back. His software did not transform two-digit years into four or more digit years. It merely enhanced a computer system's understanding of the two-digit years to buy programmers more time to fix them. In fact, most of his fixes—whether through windowing, sliding windows, or encapsulation—left the two-digit years unchanged. *Elegant patches,* Brandon had called his fixes. Kate also recalled how evasive the software entrepreneur had been about sharing the concept of the two-digit-year recognition software, the heart of Sweeper.

"I still don't see how . . . Uh-oh. I think I've just figured it out."

Costner smiled. "Amuse me."

"A hacker—armed with a tool that seeks out two-digit year—could use that tool to find these two-digit years and then, instead of fixing them like the rest of Brandon's software, could *alter* the two-digit years in Y2K-compliant systems to *revert* them back to non-compliance, to reverse the process, to lower a country's level of compliance."

"It's a shame you left the business, Kate."

"Don't go there."

"Sorry."

"Anyway," she continued, "someone could turn loose such a program on the Internet with devastating results."

"Exactly," said Costner. "Imagine what it could do. The software patches are already delicate enough. Let me give you just one example: A mortgage company may patch its software by shifting the window thirty years ahead, the limit of most of its mortgages, so that any number higher than thirty would be interpreted to belong in the current century and any number lower than or equal to thirty would be interpreted to belong in the next century. That way a thirty-year mortgage that began in 75, properly interpreted as 1975, and scheduled to be paid off by 05, properly interpreted as 2005, would go through the Y2K

transition without a hitch. The same would apply to a new loan started in 1998 and finished in 2028, thirty years later. But a hacker could come in, seek out the two-digit years and alter them by adding a new offset—for example, shifting the window by an additional sixty years, so that now any number higher than ninety would be in this century and numbers equal or lower than ninety in the next century. In the original example, the loan that began in 75, now incorrectly interpreted as 2075, would end in 05, also incorrectly interpreted as 2005, creating an error because it would yield a negative number.''

"That would certainly explain why the Serbs want the Y2K software," she said. "To use it as a weapon against the West.''

"You're the one who planted that seed in my mind right before you resigned. Since then we've been tracking Y2K-related activities around the world, and our Serbian friends have shown up in quite a few places, either purchasing the software outright or, in cases like this one, stealing it. Our guess is that they have a place somewhere in Yugoslavia where they're creating this monster program, which we believe they're planning to unleash very soon, certainly before the turn of the century.''

"What's their motive? Money?"

Costner nodded. "That's our current guess. It's no secret that Slobodan Milosevic has become the world's latest plunderer, following the tradition of Fernando Marcos, Anastasio Somoza, Manuel Noriega, and even Leonid Brezhnev. Milosevic has looted his country blind, devastating Yugoslavia's industrial output to the point that it is now just under twenty-five percent of what it was in 1989. By empowering his top ministers to also run state-owned companies and banks, Milosevic's government has turned into a dictator's police state, run by an exclusive group of money-hungry ministers. They've channeled billions of dollars in state funds out of Yugoslavia and into their

Swiss bank accounts. Just last month, for example, one of our men tracked a shipment of Russian oil to Yugoslavia. The official order from the government of Yugoslavia was for one million tons of gas. Jugopetrol, Yugoslavia's giant oil company, placed the order with Russia, but for one million five hundred tons, charging the Yugoslav government a slightly higher price to cover the additional five hundred tons. Jugopetrol delivered the one-million-ton order to its government and funneled the balance to companies controlled by Milosevic's politicians, who would in turn resell it for a profit. In another incident, Yugoslav Vice Premier Nedeljko Sipovac, who ran a grocery chain, was accused last year of skimming over three hundred million dollars from the state-owned company.

"And the examples go on and on. Those who protest simply disappear in the middle of the night, victims of Milosevic's dreaded state police. But Milosevic can only rape his country so much. If you keep taking out of the well without putting anything back in, the well dries up. That's exactly what's happening to Yugoslavia. After years of racketeering, manipulation, and looting to benefit a selected few, combined with NATO-imposed sanctions and restricted trading, *plus* the bombing, the Yugoslav well is finally drying up. Milosevic is coming to the realization that he's squeezed just about everything he could possibly squeeze out of his ravished nation, and has now turned to other money-making schemes to keep his army and state police from revolting against him."

"Like using the Y2K software to hold the world hostage."

"Exactly."

"So," she said, beginning to grasp the entire picture, "when Brandon refused to agree to your terms, you decided to simply take his product, right?"

"It wasn't that simple, Kate."

She exhaled. "It never is. Go on."

"We knew that Milosevic had launched a worldwide campaign to get his hands on as much Y2K software as he possibly could. He sent his people everywhere, and when he ran out of people he went after independent contractors. For the past several months we've worked very closely with other intelligence services to track down this industrial espionage ring, but have had very little luck. By the way, the event that ended in your resignation was just another attempt by Milosevic to gain access to Y2K technology."

"Hold on," she said. "How? The bastards just blew the place up, killing every Y2K specialist inside, along with their demo hardware and software."

Costner shook his head. "The bombing was just a smoke screen, Kate, to cover their tracks. They bombed the place to make us all think it was just a terrorist strike in reprisal for a NATO air strike. In reality, Milosevic's cronies had stolen much of the Y2K technology to be disclosed at the conference, thanks in part to the CIA unknowingly assisting them. Then they blew it all up to hide their high-tech theft, which not only benefited them, but also hurt the world's Y2K efforts. Many software specialists died that day, in addition to many techniques that were to be disclosed for the first time. When their creators were killed, their high-tech secrets died with them. We eventually figured out the Yugoslavs' scheme—again, thanks to your planting a seed in my head prior to your resignation."

Kate kept her gaze on the layer of clouds extending to the horizon, finally beginning to comprehend the international scope of this problem.

"Anyway, since we have had little luck infiltrating Milosevic's network, we decided to use Holst's software as bait. Through a ring of informants, we got word into Belgrade that an independent network had found a very unique and capable Y2K program, which could be turned into a powerful weapon. It didn't take long before the word got back to us that Drljaca Ltd., a import-export conglomerate in Nicosia, Cyprus, that also runs air and sea cargo vessels, was interested in acquiring the software. Through our connections in Europe, we tracked this company and found it to be a wholly owned subsidiary of the Makario Investment Group, a Greek firm operating out of Athens. The MIG, as it turned out, has strong affiliations with Beogradska Banka, Milosevic's state-run bank, which just happens to have branches in Athens, Moscow, Istanbul, *and* Nicosia, Cyprus. That told us that the fish had bitten, so we moved to the next phase: reeling it in. We began to work closely with some of their low-level agents; most of them, unfortunately, were independent contractors sent to test the waters. After a short period, we gained their confidence enough to make initial contact with their key operative in this country, Mirko Todorovic.''

Kate remained silent, her stomach knotting in anger at finding herself so very deep in the middle of an operation of such magnitude, and what it meant for Brandon and her. She would definitely need some time alone to analyze this carefully.

''We got CIA Officer Davidson, working undercover as an independent contractor, to work closely with Todorovic to set up the operation at Holst Enterprises, orchestrating a strategy that would get us full control of Holst's technology, as well as a peek into Milosevic's international espionage ring.''

''But something went wrong,'' Kate said, remembering the video she had seen of the botched operation. However, she abided by her own rules, holding on to that knowledge until she could use it as a bargaining chip. Information was yet another weapon in her arsenal. She also chose to keep her feelings from surfacing. These bastards had essentially *brought* the terrorists to Holst Enterprises. They had used Brandon as bait, as a stepping stone to achieve a larger goal, in the process causing so much pain to Brandon Holst, his family, and also Kate Donaldson. Her operative mind told her to shove that aside for now; in time she would find the right way to get even for this.

Costner nodded. "The operation was proceeding normally, until Brandon Holst pulled out a gun and began shooting Todorovic's men. Davidson never saw Todorovic after that moment. The Yugoslav terrorists left the scene in a different vehicle and never showed up at the rendezvous point."

"You didn't pin a tail on them?"

"We did, but lost them in the commotion of trying to avoid the incoming cruisers from the Austin Police Department."

"Tell me *everything* that happened at Holst Enterprises."

Costner cleared his throat and went on to relate an incident that Kate Donaldson was all too familiar with. The tale, which Kate let Costner relate in full, told her that her old boss was being truthful, especially since he shouldn't have knowledge of the hidden surveillance cameras, or did he? Kate remembered how Gam Davidson had looked straight into one of her cameras the first night she had seen him meeting with Brandon. Davidson also may have spotted Kate's subcontractor installing any of the cameras that day, even though they had looked like smoke detectors.

"Now we must find that code, Kate. We can't allow the Yugoslavs to have that software. It's too powerful."

She looked away, the old familiar pain stabbing her abdomen. She opted not to disclose the fact that access to Sweeper was at least temporarily protected by her software password. "Is that everything?"

"As much as we know," Costner replied.

Questions peppered her mind. Was Costner being truthful, or was he fabricating this whole story, adding the incident inside Brandon's company at the end to help add credibility to his story because he knew that Kate may have seen the whole incident through the cleverly disguised surveillance cameras? If these bastards had gone to the extreme of putting an American and his company at risk to capture the terrorists, they would not hesitate to create a whole new story just to get her to tell them what she had learned from her short interrogation of the late Mirko Todorovic.

She took a deep breath and did what she had done for nearly twenty years: She stored her concerns away for later retrieval, keeping them in the back of her mind, choosing to pretend to trust Costner for now, since she needed him as much as the CIA needed her assistance.

"If you knew that the terrorists wanted Brandon Holst so badly, why didn't you post some of your own men with him at the hospital?"

"I did," Costner replied.

"The APD officers?" According to Jones, the APD officers were ex-Marines, but that could have been part of their cover.

"No. Those were real. My people were the orderly and the nurse who were also killed outside the X-ray room. They were working undercover. They were also two of my best."

Kate shook her head, wondering if Milosevic's men were that good or if the CIA was slipping, hiring too many people like Hollis Carter, the London station chief who had also been tricked by the Yugoslavs.

"Now," Costner said. "Do you mind telling us what you expect to find in this list of sea vessels that you requested from the officials at the Houston Port Authority?"

"Have you gotten it yet?"

"We should get a fax any moment now."

"Good," she said, leaning back on her chair and closing her eyes, pretending to want to go to sleep in order to have time to think. "Wake me up when you do."

19

The lists were quite long. Kate Donaldson never realized just how many merchant ships moved through the Port of Houston in any given day. There were literally dozens of them. They received two lists, one for yesterday, Monday, November 15th, and one for today.

Costner read over her shoulder as she checked the names on Tuesday's list, focusing her search on the ships starting with the letter J. The list was arranged in alphabetical order.

TUESDAY, 11-16-99 PORT OF HOUSTON, TEXAS			
VESSEL	FLAG	DEPARTURE	PIER
JACEGUAY	BRAZIL	11-20 07: 35	17
JARESUAN	THAILAND	11-16 11:25	9
JARRETT	USA	11-16 11:05	29

JEAN MOULIN	FRANCE	11-16 20:15	31
JEANNE D'ARC	FRANCE	11-18 13:00	32
JIAN	CHINA	11-19 21:14	25
JIANGHU	CHINA	11-23 11:30	8
JIUJANG	CHINA	11-16 06:45	10
JUEL NIELS	DENMARK	11-19 17:50	22

"I don't recognize any of the names," she said, frowning, switching to Monday's list.

MONDAY, 11-15-99 PORT OF HOUSTON, TEXAS

VESSEL	FLAG	DEPARTURE	PIER
JAAUCHKA	RUSSIA	11-15 09:21	4
JAKARTTA	CYPRUS	11-15 19:00	20
JARESUAN	THAILAND	11-16 11:25	9
JARRETT	USA	11-16 11:05	29
JEAN MOULIN	FRANCE	11-16 20:15	31
JEANNE D'ARC	FRANCE	11-18 13:00	32
JIAN	CHINA	11-19 21:14	25
JIUJANG	CHINA	11-16 06:45	10
JSARA	GREECE	11-15 09:20	27
JUTHAR	INDIA	11-15 10:35	13

Kate stared at the second entry from Monday's log, the name *Jakartta* catching her attention. She remembered Todorovic's final words: "Jakar . . . Jakart . . ."

Her eyes moved from the name to the vessel's flag, Cyprus.

Cyprus? Of course! If Costner had been truthful about his briefing, then it all made sense. The *Jakartta* could belong to Drljaca Ltd., the import-export conglomerate that operated out of Cyprus.

Kate pointed to this vessel. "I think that's ours." Then she realized the departure date and her heart sank. "Damn. It has already left port."

Costner nodded. "Roughly twelve hours ago."

Kate swallowed the lump in her throat, remembering the time when Brandon had been kidnapped, roughly around 3:30 P.M., meaning that the kidnappers only had three and a half hours to get Brandon down to Houston and make the departure date. There was a reasonable chance that they could have gotten him on board before sailing away. "How far can they be?" she asked.

"Not very far," replied Costner, unfolding a map of Houston and running a finger over the southeast section, where the long and winding Houston Ship Channel connected the piers to Galveston Bay and the Gulf of Mexico. "Here," he added. "I doubt that in twelve hours it could have gotten too far." He reached for the phone.

"Who are you calling?"

"The Coast Guard. The *Jakartta* will not make it to international waters."

20

Forty-five minutes later, the Learjet touched down at Scholes Field in Galveston, Texas. A Coast Guard helicopter already waited across the tarmac, it main rotor beginning to spin.

Kate was blinded by the sun reflecting off the concrete as she climbed down the jet and followed Costner and his team toward the transport that would take them to the USS *Nicholas,* a Navy frigate assisting the Coast Guard patrolling the Gulf of Mexico in the fight against drug trafficking. The Navy ship was already sailing an intercept course with the merchant vessel twenty miles off shore.

They were airborne a minute later. She sat in the rear of the craft, the vibrations of the rotor reverberating through her as they left the Galveston Island behind and ventured over the gulf, its crystalline waters gleaming below. Kate spotted the shadow of the helicopter following the rippled surface; it raced by a few sailboats, catching up with several fishing boats farther out. Oil-drilling rigs broke up the vast expanse of water as the coast disappeared in the distance.

"We should get there in five minutes! We have them on radar!" shouted Costner over the noise of the rotor after a brief chat with the navigator, who was working the radio and other instruments while the pilot kept his right hand on the center stick and the left on the collective, the bar on the left side of the seat that resembled a parking brake. Kate remembered that much from the missions where she had been flown in by helicopter.

The craft flew in from the northeast, just a hundred feet over the waters, its noise thundering inside the small cabin. The federal agents sat on the floor, their automatic weapons resting on their laps. Costner and two other men checked their sidearms. One leaned his head against the side door and had his eyes closed. The silver-haired Davidson stared into the distance, before shifting his gaze to Kate, who frowned and looked away.

She hated being here, among people who had used Brandon Holst, who had dared put his life at risk, only to let the terrorists shoot him and then kidnap him after his surgery. And Gam Davidson had been one of them, leaving Brandon bleeding, dying. Had it not been for Brandon using his panic button and alerting the police, he would have certainly died from the gunshot wound.

How could the bastards leave him like that?

Kate's anger swelled inside of her. Then the realization struck her hard. She had once been as cold as Davidson and the rest of Costner's operatives, focusing only on the mission, without regard for the collateral damage, for the pain inflicted on innocent civilians who happened to be at the wrong place at the wrong time.

Wars have casualties, but those casualties are acceptable as long as the war is won.

Wasn't that what she had been taught at CIA? Wasn't

that one of the ground rules in the world of field operations?

Kate remembered that rule well, just as she recalled another ground rule, one which she had been warned time and again about violating, for it would make her vulnerable. She was never, *ever,* to get personally involved in a mission. She was never to develop feelings for someone else, because the other side could then turn those feelings into a weapon against the her.

But I was already out! I had quit the Agency! I had a right to a normal life!

Kate remembered Costner's words the day she had told him she was leaving the Agency.

You can quit the CIA, but you can never stop being who we trained you to be. You are an operative, a trained spy. You can't deny who you are.

She stared out the window, her eyes gazing at the waves, at the eternal pattern of crests and valleys, like a perpetual roller coaster, never settling, always changing.

Just like my life.

"Over there!" Costner shouted over the noise of the main rotor, pointing out of the side window. "That's the *Nicholas!*"

Kate stopped daydreaming and spotted the Navy ship, its bluish-gray color blending it nicely with the waters of the Gulf of Mexico. The helicopter approached the vessel from the rear, toward the aft flight deck, at the end of the runway-like wake created by its screws, white in color with a tinge of green. It trailed the ship until disappearing in the horizon.

The landing was smooth, considering the fact that the *Nicholas* was currently doing twenty knots, according to what Costner relayed after a brief discussion with the co-pilot.

A seaman in a khaki uniform greeted them on the flight deck. He introduced himself as Lieutenant Commander

Moore, the ship's executive officer. Kate shook hands with him. Moore ushered them inside, through an open hatch that led to a narrow corridor with very low ceilings and exposed pipes and wires, then up a steep set of stairs that looked more like a ladder, which Moore climbed up with incredible agility. Kate had to duck as she went up to avoid bumping her forehead on the ceiling of the upper deck.

They reached the vessel's bridge, where another officer in khakis welcomed them to the *Nicholas*. His name was Commander Gino Vatarelli, a husky, tanned man in his early forties, with brown hair and brown eyes. He shook hands firmly with Costner and then with Kate.

"Our target's just ten nautical miles south of our position," Vatarelli said in a commanding voice, leaning over a table in a room behind the bridge, pointing at a navigation map of the Gulf of Mexico. "The radar shows that they're stationary."

"Stationary?" asked Kate, standing across the table from Vatarelli.

"That's right, Ma'am."

"That doesn't make any sense," said Costner, standing next to Kate.

The sailor shrugged. "The radar officer reported that the *Jakartta* has been just drifting in the gulf's current since we first picked it up on radar after we got the call from the Coast Guard. We tried to raise it on the radio but no one's answering. Very strange."

Kate didn't like the sound of that. "How close can you get to it?" she asked.

"As close as you need. What do you have in mind?"

21

Commander Gino Vatarelli got his vessel right next to the stationary *Jakartta* before a pair of sailors extended a gangway down to the deck of the merchant vessel, which on the surface appeared deserted. Costner crossed first, followed by Davidson and then Kate. The ship resembled an oil tanker, only much smaller, with a long upper deck and a bridge at one end.

A misty breeze swept across the ship, swirling her hair as she rushed past Costner and Davidson, racing toward the stern, where the only visible structure on the vessel looked down at the main deck.

She drew the Sig, concern filling her. Why wasn't anybody here? Kate feared that the terrorists could have gotten word that Mirko Todorovic may have been compromised, along with his knowledge of the *Jakartta*.

Her sneakers thudded loudly over the wooden deck as a hundred thoughts crossed her mind. If they weren't on the ship, where did they go? And how? The ship was miles from shore.

She reached a set of stairs connecting the main deck to a platform below the bridge. She climbed it two steps at a time, reaching the next level, scanning the platform with the pistol, finding no sign of life, except for the clattering below as Costner and his cronies rushed up.

Kate went up the next set of stairs, dropping to a crouch as she tiptoed over the landing, keeping her head below the round porthole on the door to the bridge, counting to five before yanking it open and rolling in.

The spring-loaded door slammed shut behind her with the sound of a gunshot as Kate finished a second roll and rose to a deep crouch, the coppery smell of blood mixed with that of cordite, knotting her stomach.

She spotted two men hunched over an instrument panel, both shot in the back of the head. A third man lay next to the ship's wheel, in front of the large window panes facing the bow, through which Kate watched several sailors from the *Nicholas* already aboard the merchant vessel.

Costner came in, followed by three of his men and Commander Vatarelli, who briefly inspected the control room before grabbing his radio.

"Looks like the crew's been shot. Check the decks below," Vatarelli spoke into his handheld unit.

"Where in the heck are they?" asked Costner, his face tight with apprehension.

Kate looked about her, spotting a door at the other side of the bridge, beyond the bullet-riddled bodies and panels of navigation hardware. She headed toward it, opening it, facing a narrow passageway that ended in a set of stairs heading down. She peered at the murky landing below, her gun still cocked, finger resting on the side of the trigger casing as she held it over her right shoulder, the muzzle pointed at the array of pipes lining the low ceiling.

Blocking out her emotions, considering the possibility that the terrorists were still aboard, perhaps holding Brandon hostage, the former CIA officer rushed down, hearing someone behind her, not caring who, making it to the bottom, where the stairs made a U-turn before going down another level. Again she followed them, this time keeping the Sig in front of her, the finger caressing the trigger, the white dot on the gun's forward sight aligned with the yellowish floor below.

A wide passageway projected beyond her, probably as long as the vessel's length. Flickering fluorescents, spaced by a dozen feet or more, cast an eerie glow in the heart of the silent ship. She could hear her own breathing, amplified by the enclosing structure of steel and wood.

Move and search.

Kate obeyed her instincts, stepping away from the stairs, checking each of the compartments connecting to the main hallway by large sliding doors. Costner, his guns, and several sailors assisted in the search, finding rooms filled with machinery, others with stacked crates, and yet others housing bags of cement, or grain, or an assortment of other products. But no sign of the terrorists or Brandon Holst. For the next hour the team scrutinized every cubic inch of the *Jakartta*, finding a dozen other crew members, all shot dead, but no one else.

"He's not here," said Costner, standing next to Kate on the main deck, by the stairs leading up to the bridge.

"No kidding," she mumbled, arms crossed, a new plan already taking place in her operative mind.

"What do we do now?"

Kate regarded her old superior with contempt, before handing him a folded piece of paper, where she had jotted down a list of items she would need.

Costner read it once, glanced up to her, and read it again before saying, "Kate . . . this is—"

"Exactly what you will ask the director to get for me,

right away, while there's still time to do something about it.''

"We're not allowed to go there. The place is off limits to all Americans.''

"I'm not asking for any of you to go. Just me.''

"Besides," Costner said. "This is well beyond our operational budget. I don't have the authorization to—''

"Then *get it,*" she hissed. "*You* started this. *You* burst into my personal life and drew those terrorists to Brandon and me. *You* handed Milosevic the Y2K software on a silver platter. Now *I'm* going to finish what you started.''

"I don't think you under—''

"Wrong. I don't think *you* understand. I'm doing this with or without your help. However, if the CIA does not assist me, I promise you that by tomorrow morning every major newspaper in the United States will know what took place in the past twenty-four hours, how the mighty CIA used a law-abiding citizen and software entrepreneur as bait to draw in international terrorists, and how they botched the whole plan, which resulted in losing valuable technology to a foreign state *plus* the abduction of Brandon Holst.''

"*Kate,*" said Costner, lowering his voice a few decibels. "You can't threaten the CIA. They will *bury* you.''

"It's not a threat, Mike. Call it a . . . *business deal.* You gain control of the technology and I get Brandon Holst back.''

Costner looked into the distance, apparently considering her proposal. "How do I know that Holst will abide by this deal? How do I know that he will not attempt to license his technology, like he promised he would do?''

"You do *your* job," she said, stabbing the paper in Costner's hand, "and I'll do mine.''

Kate left him there and strolled alone onto the main deck, stopping by the railing on the port side, gazing at the expanse of bluish-green water blending with the clear skies in the distance. She had spent nineteen years developing the skills to serve her country, to protect it, to keep it safe from a myriad of enemies. And she had been quite successful, earning a reputation at the Agency, becoming a legend in her field. But all of her training, all of her instincts, all of her experience had not prevented the shooting and later abduction of Brandon Holst, the most important person in her life. And now it seemed as if the terrorists were always a step ahead of her, always anticipating her moves, as if they could read her mind. They had escaped by unknown means and gone somewhere else.

Taking Brandon with them!

Bastards!

Her wet eyes stared east, into the far reaches of the Gulf of Mexico, her mind going farther, beyond Florida, past the Atlantic Ocean, traversing the European continent, crossing the Adriatic Sea, reaching a land torn by a war of ethnic and religious hatred, ruled by a monster.

A monster.

Kate Donaldson knew at that moment that if she wanted to see Brandon Holst alive again, that if she wanted to prevent the Yugoslav terrorists from accessing a computer program that could empower them to lower a country's Y2K compliance, spreading chaos at the turn of the millennium, she herself would have to become not just a monster, but something *worse* than a monster. She would have to apply every skill she had learned in almost two decades of espionage to become something beyond the very evil that she had fought.

The waves slapped the hull of the weathered vessel with a rhythm that matched her heartbeat, that matched the resolution in her mind, in her very soul.

She watched them through tears.

Book Four

■

Monsters

■

"Men loved darkness rather than light, because their deeds were evil."

—John 3:19

1

Belgrade, Yugoslavia.

The Sava River twisted its way across the war-hardened city, overlooked to the west by the sleek lines of office buildings and luxurious apartments of the New Belgrade—among the twisted ruins of buildings destroyed by NATO—and to the east by the rundown façades of the gritty old city. The rich and connected headed home after another day of making deals, of government payoffs, of robbing their country blind. Ministers and other connected officials, who also controlled the state-owned companies used to launder their money into foreign bank accounts, sat in the rear seats of Mercedes Benz and BMW sedans chatting on their cellular phones, oblivious to the stares of the crowd at one of many flea markets, where the middle-class, devastated by their country's ruined economy (compounded by the NATO strikes), either shopped for bargains or ran stalls to supplement their decimated incomes.

Many were engineers, lawyers, doctors, machinists, bankers, teachers, businessmen, who once enjoyed the relative comfort of their education, of their efforts. But now, in the Yugoslavia of Slobodan Milosevic, a professional without *veze,* connections, might just as well have no education at all. Most were forced to work for slave wages, raped blind by Belgrade's underworld, the closed circle of Milosevic and his political and business allies.

The luxury cars rushed by Karadord and Brankova Prizre Boulevards, their chauffeurs accelerating when passing through a middle-class neighborhood, sometimes followed by one of more vehicles, packed with bodyguards ordered to shoot anyone coming near their motorcades. Lately, a handful of "serious guys," as members of Milosevic's circle were referred to by the local population, had been shot dead by a rising wave of resistance against the strong arm of the president and his corrupt government.

A run-down bar, receding into the shadows of a dilapidated apartment building, its windows boarded up after NATO bombs pulverized the government building next door, stood across from a flea market near Central Station. Several motorcycles and a few Skodas—Czechoslovakian-made automobiles—crowded a small gravel field in front of the local bar. A steady rock bass streamed across the dusty parking lot as a breeze from the Sava River swept the impoverish east side of town.

Dressed in a pair of local black jeans, old boots, and a white T-shirt beneath a stained leather jacket, her hair greased back, Kate Donaldson stepped out of an old delivery truck, walked past Central Station, and crossed Penezica-Krouna Avenue, reaching the bar's parking lot and striding by the Skodas. She glanced at the truck as it disappeared around the corner, headed to a prearranged location outside the city. She had ridden in it since crossing the border into Serbia. The vehicle, driven by two Bosnian nationals working for the CIA, carried the hardware she would need to execute a plan which had taken her almost two days to work through in fine detail, mostly on her way over to this part of the world.

Kate took in the misery, the economic and social despair on this side of the river, in sharp contrast with the modern architecture of the Sava Congress Center across the river. She remembered the last time she had visited Belgrade, during the Cold War years, back when the iron fist of the Communist rule of Marshall Tito had at least maintained a sense of order in the streets. Now Milosevic had transformed that government, which was far from perfect, into something even worse: a system of patronage, of rackets, of payoffs, all protected by Milosevic's powerful army and state police.

Four long days had gone by since she had boarded the *Jakartta* with hopes of finding Brandon Holst and the missing Y2K software.

Kate frowned, tired, jetlagged. Much had happened since then, including the expected agreement of the CIA to support her calculating plan, up to the point when they had to enter Yugoslavia. Kate had been on her own then, hoping that the CIA would stick to its end of the deal and send a rescue helicopter to extract her and Brandon Holst when Kate requested it using a long-range radio.

She slowed her pace near a red Skoda, its license plate matching the one given to her the day before. She took a quick glance inside, recognizing a white handkerchief on the front seat, telling her that the meeting had not been compromised. A red handkerchief meant trouble, telling her to stay away and try again tomorrow. A black cloth meant imminent danger, and would have prompted Kate to unzip her jacket and reach for the 9mm Beretta 92FS shoved in her jeans by her left kidney, easily concealed beneath the jacket yet quite accessible to her right hand.

She continued walking, reaching the front of the aging

wooden structure, studying the desolate scene behind her before going inside.

The smell of whiskey, body odor, and cheap perfume struck her like a moist breeze. The hazy cloud of cigarette smoke stung her eyes. The music blared, the powerful bass resonating in her chest.

A man came up to greet her even before she closed the door, saying something that sounded obscene. He smiled, exposing two missing front teeth and blackened gums. She waved him off in disgust, marching past him. Her eyes, adorned with a dreadful lavender hue from a locally made eye shadow, focused on two men sitting in the rear, both dressed in gray overcoats. One was very thin, his bony face framed by black hair, a few strands falling across his long forehead. His dark eyes flashed recognition. The Yugoslav, a half-smoked cigarette hanging off the corner of his mouth, tapped a mug filled with beer next to the pack of cigarettes, a further sign that the meeting would continue as planned. An empty mug would have signaled trouble.

Kate knew this man from her old days with the Agency. Vladimir Vucic, locally known as Tref, had been one of the CIA's best agents in Yugoslavia, now one of the few independent smugglers in the region who had managed to avoid the obscene payoffs required by Milosevic's police for "protection."

The second man, with closely cropped blond hair and a stolid face, kept his gaze on his own mug, which he sipped casually in between drags from a cigarette. He was solidly built, his bulging muscles pressing the fabric of his overcoat.

She approached them, sitting in the chair across from Tref.

"It has been a long time," the Yugoslav said in heavily accented English. Kate spoke very little Serbo-Croatian.

"Hello, Tref."

The gaunt man took a drag from his cigarette, regarding Kate through the smoke spewing out of his nostrils.

"This is Zoran. He's agreed to assist us. He doesn't speak English."

The blond Yugoslav kept sipping his beer.

Kate nodded. "What's his motivation to help us?"

Tref grinned. "As cautious as ever, I see. He used to be one of Marko Milosevic's bodyguards, until the spoiled son of the president raped Zoran's young sister, quite a beautiful girl she was."

"Was?"

"Our friend was out buying whiskey while Marko and his close associates held a private party with several local girls at one of their clubs. One of the girls turned out to be Zoran's nineteen-year-old sister, Mirna. Apparently one thing led to another and the drunk Marko and his friends went after the girls, tearing off their clothes, using the bodyguards to keep the girls from running away. Zoran returned with the whiskey and joined the bodyguards in controlling the sobbing girls, until he realized that Mirna was among them, already raped by Marko himself. The poor bastard went nuts, pulling out his gun and trying to shoot Marko. His sister, three other girls, a bodyguard, and a couple of Marko's influential friends were killed in the shooting. Our friend managed to escape with his life but he is now a hunted man in all of Yugoslavia. He could have used his money to escape to Italy, but instead he headed south to Kosovo.

"Zoran is a quarter Albanian, sympathizer of the Kosovo Liberation Army. He offered his services there to the KLA. Because of his insight into Milosevic's operation in Belgrade, he was assigned by KLA commanders the position of district head of this region. He helps me get my merchandise across the border. I help him wage his local guerrilla war against Milosevic. He has plenty of volunteers but not that many weapons, which makes it difficult to fight openly against the state police, who are armed with the latest hardware.''

Kate glanced at Zoran, who set the heavy mug on the table and turned his indifferent stare to her. She locked eyes with the Slav for several seconds, before returning her gaze to Tref. ''All right.''

''What information do you have?'' asked Tref.

''Two names. One belonging to a vessel. The second belonging to one of Milosevic's agents.''

Tref Vucic motioned her to keep going.

''The *Jakartta* is the name of the sea vessel, the last known location of Brandon Holst and the Y2K software.''

''And the agent?''

''Dragan Kundat.''

Zoran's eyes locked on Kate's, glimmering with anger, before looking away.

Tref swallowed hard. ''Dragan was one of Zoran's comrades-in-arms during his years with the Serbian army in Bosnia. Zoran requested a transfer to Belgrade when the army stopped fighting soldiers and started killing civilians. His courage in the battlefield is what got him the transfer to become a personal bodyguard of the Milosevic family, assigned to protect the life of Marko Milosevic for a lucrative salary.''

Kate nodded, warming up to the large Zoran, a man with a reason deeper than money to assist her.

''Did you bring the merchandise?'' Tref asked.

She nodded. ''Here's a sample.'' She reached into her jacket pocket, producing a tiny envelope which she slid over to the smuggler.

Zoran's eyes flashed interest for the first time as Tref's hairy fingers opened the brown envelope, unveiling a one-carat emerald-cut diamond, one of hundreds of gems confiscated by the Federal Bureau of Investigations after cracking a criminal ring in Los Angeles the month before. The ever-practical Tref Vucic had insisted on precious stones, particularly diamonds, commodities effortlessly sold or traded in any market, relatively immune to currency fluctuations, and easily concealed.

Tref stood. "Wait here," he said.

Walking away, he disappeared in the crowd, leaving Kate with the muscular Zoran, who grabbed the pack of cigarettes and tilted it in Kate's direction. She shook her head. The former officer and bodyguard then pulled one from the pack with his lips. Producing a lighter, he clicked and cupped a flame. Leaning into it, he took a few drags.

Tref Vucic returned five minutes later, taking his seat across from Kate. "Top quality."

"Did you expect anything less?"

He shrugged. "I can't afford not to be cautious. Where is the balance?"

"You get half when we execute the first phase of the plan, and the other half after we rescue Holst, recover the Y2K software, and are airlifted to safety by my people."

"How? Are you bringing helicopters?"

"You'll know the details when it's necessary that you do. For now let's focus on the first phase of my plan."

"What about the weapons?"

"I'll be also providing the weapons, as agreed. The first installment now. The second, and largest, installment when we're airlifted to safety. In return for his assistance, your friend will get plenty of guns to fight his war. As you said, the KLA has many volunteers but not enough weapons."

Tref nodded before whispering to Zoran, who closed his eyes before mumbling something back.

"Zoran wants to know how is it that you plan to find your friend and the software, while also helping Zoran achieve his personal vendetta against the Milosevics, including the supply of weapons you've just mentioned."

Kate told him, watching Tref's expression. The smuggler's face tightened with concern. He lit up a cigarette, took a drag, shifted his gaze between Kate and the table, and then translated for Zoran, who gazed at Kate first with surprise, then with admiration, and finally with respect. Then he said something back to Tref.

The former agent of the CIA smiled at Kate, revealing his crooked teeth. "He likes your plan very much."

"Good. You do this right and you get richer and your friend gets weapons, ammunition, *and* also gets even."

Tref translated to Zoran, who pressed his lips, nodded, and said, "I help you," in a heavily-accented English that reminded Kate of Arnold Schwarzenegger. In fact, the large KLA guerrilla even had a vague resemblance to the famous actor.

Five minutes later, Kate rode in the rear of the old Skoda while Tref drove and Zoran sat in front. She was mesmerized at the way Belgrade had changed for the worse since she had last been here, over a decade ago. Compared to what Milosevic had done to this nation, the regime of Marshall Tito had been heaven. At least back then those with an education had had a shot at making a reasonable living, though still not anywhere near Western standards. Now only *veze* mattered. An education was literally useless without *veze*. Of course, NATO bombing had also taken its toll on the city, turning a number of buildings to rubble.

Kate stared at what seemed like one continuous ghetto. Boarded-up buildings. Mothers in rags surrounded by half-naked children. People gathered around barrels of burning trash to keep warm while trading anything from cigarettes, candles, and old clothes to homemade liquor and even sexual favors to put food on the table. And with such poverty always came a wave of crime. It had always amazed Kate how quickly hunger turned law-abiding citizens into criminals.

They continued up Takovska Avenue, which dead-ended at 29 November Boulevard, behind the Botanical Gardens. The streets in this section of Belgrade were nearly deserted at this time of the evening. Crime, plus a police force too busy assisting Milosevic's kleptocracy rather than protecting the general public, kept many people home after hours.

Kate got out, inspecting the brick structures around her. One of them had a gaping hole on its third and fourth floors, exposing rubble, pipes, and the twisted steel beams of reinforced concrete columns. A pile of debris covered the sidewalk beneath the damaged section of the building.

"What happened here. A NATO strike?"

"Misolevic's police," said Tref Vucic, resting his forearms on the top of the door frame as he stood by his car. "They tried to break up one of my operations two months ago. But, thanks to Zoran, we got a tip and had left the building the day before. Come. Let's go up."

Kate remained by the car. "Why would you go back in this building when the police already know of its existence?"

Tref grinned. "A trick I learned from you. Always do the unexpected. This is the last place the police will expect me to be. Now come. There is much planning to be done."

Kate gazed about her, alarms going off in her head. "Are you *sure* this place is safe?"

Tref shrugged. "As safe as a place can be in Milosevic's Yugoslavia."

2

Feeling a bit light-headed, Brandon Holst paced the windowless room, his prison for what seemed like a couple of days now, ever since the terrorists had him locked him here.

Or was it longer than that? Or shorter?

It was hard to tell, especially because of the medication that the terrorists had administered.

And where am I? He asked himself, trying to clear his head.

Based on the plush carpeting, matching wallpaper, and fluorescent light fixture, he guessed that this place had been used as an office not long ago. He could still see the indentations in the carpet where a desk must have rested. The room was now devoid of any furniture, save for the mattress in the corner.

But his concern went beyond the room he was in. Brandon Holst wasn't certain if he was even in the United States anymore, at least based on the electrical outlets on the wall, which had the three-prong shape of most European countries. That clue, plus the terrorists' heavily accented English, suggested to him that he might be quite a ways from home.

And Kate, he thought. *Where is she?*

The terrorists had indicated that they had kidnapped her as well. But no one had granted his request to see her. During his last confrontation, with a man called Dragan, Holst had refused to yield the security password of his Y2K software unless he would be assured that he and Kate would be set free.

Amazingly enough, no one had attempted to torture him, probably because they needed him to break into the Y2K software, as well as interpret it afterwards. As long as he held the technology card, he felt that the terrorists would likely leave him alone.

"And they can kill me for all I care," he mumbled, far angrier at the fact that Kate may have been harmed than the injuries he had sustained or the stolen Y2K software, which meant little to him in comparison to Kate's well-being. He felt he could take their physical punishment and then some. During his ranch days, in addition to having been shot by his stupid little brother, Brandon Holst had fallen off horses a dozen times, and twice had gotten stomped by them, on one occasion fracturing a few ribs. His body was used to some level of physical pain, but he could not bear the thought of someone hurting Kate.

During this time of isolation, with no one to talk to and literally nothing to do but wait for something to happen, Brandon Holst thought about his life, and about his short but quite meaningful relationship with Kate Donaldson. As he paced the small room, Brandon took a deep breath, wincing with the now-familiar pain as his expanding chest pulled on the stitches traversing his sternum. The wound was healing quite nicely, thanks to the better-than-expected care he had received from his captors. In addition to his short conversations with Dragan, a pair of doctors had been visiting him twice a day to change the dressing and administer painkillers and antibiotics. There was also the hooded terrorist who brought him his meals, but he was in and out in seconds, dropping off a new tray and picking up the old one from the previous meal. He relieved himself in the small bathroom beyond the door by the mattress.

The food was another clue that he was in a foreign place, consisting mostly of a variety of soups, some with lamb and vegetables, others with potatoes, and others yet with seafood. He had also been fed meals that bordered on Italian, making him wonder if that was where he was being held. Their accents, however, had not been Italian, but Slavic, suggesting perhaps—

The door opened. The man who called himself Dragan stepped in. He wore a pair of slacks and a black silk shirt. His long hair was pulled back and tied in a ponytail. Brandon's eyes shifted from the man's intense eyes to the gun shoved in his pants, and back to his face.

"I have just left our scientists upstairs. They will be breaking into your code soon. It would make things much easier for you if you told us the access password now."

"We have gone over this before. The answer is still no."

"In that case . . . there is something I want to show you," he said, grinning. "Perhaps it will change your mind about releasing the password."

Brandon frowned. "I've already given you my answer." He had to hold on. The password was his only ace. In fact, he assumed it was the only thing keeping him alive. If and when he gave it up, it had to be at the most opportune moment. "Where is Kate Donaldson?"

The man's grin broadened. "Have you ever heard of an ancient Chinese torture called the death of a thousand cuts?"

He had never heard of such thing but could picture it.

It also sounded as if the terrorists were fed up with his lack of cooperation.

He stared back at Dragan without expression.

"This way," the terrorist said, waving an open palm toward the hallway. "Let's go pay your lady friend a visit."

His heart began to race the moment he made the connection. *They couldn't . . . they wouldn't—*

"Now, Mr. Holst."

Dragan walked in front, followed by Brandon and two terrorists. They continued down the hallway, at which end a large window exposed the night skyline of a city he did not recognize.

"Where am I?" he asked, just as he had done for the past few days, since arriving here.

"Not in Kansas anymore, Mr. Holst," replied Dragan without turning around, the ponytail swinging behind him.

The terrorist stopped in front of the last door to his right, blurting something in a Slavic language, which prompted the two men flanking Brandon Holst to seize his wrists and cuff them behind his back.

He cringed in pain as the stretched skin on his chest tugged at the stitches.

"For your own protection, Mr. Holst," explained Dragan, before opening the door.

Brandon didn't understand at first what the terrorist had meant by that. But a moment later, as he stared in frozen horror at the interior of the large office, he realized that the terrorists had won, that he would not be able to keep the secret password from them any longer.

"You . . . *bastards!*" he hissed, his heart aching at the sight of Kate Donaldson hanging naked by her hands from a hook on the ceiling. She was struggling to free herself, moaning as her contorted features, further distorted by a black stocking over her face, turned to him.

Brandon eyes filled with rage, with anguish, with the

desire to help her, to do anything in his power to stop this abuse. He tried to move forward, to get to her, roughly thirty feet away, suffering, crying, sobbing, her slim body hanging in the murky room.

"The death of a thousand cuts, Mr. Holst," said Dragan, producing a small utility knife as he walked up to her, patting her on the buttocks, kissing one of them before slashing the knife down her skin, making a tiny incision.

Kate tensed, then jerked, then tugged at the rope, then tensed again, her cries muffled by a gag in her mouth. Brandon's knees weakened.

The terrorist struck again, cutting her in the left thigh, a trickle of blood running down her knee, followed by her writhing body swinging beneath the hook, like a farm animal about to be slaughtered.

"Stop! Oh, God! Please, stop!" he shouted. "For the love of God! *Stop this!*"

Dragan slashed again on her back and a second time, beneath her left breast. The sobs intensified. Her fingers tensed as they clutched the rope securing her to the hook, as she jerked her head from side to side, moaning, shouting, begging for this madness to end.

The room became surreal, dreamlike, as he stared at this monster, at this creature slowly shredding Kate's silky skin.

"Stop, man! I'll do anything! Anything! But, please, stop this! Now!"

This time the terrorist stopped, turning toward the software entrepreneur, dark eyes flashing triumph.

"The password, Mr. Holst. Give it to us and I'll stop."

His eyes blinking as he shifted his wet stare between this medieval torturer and Kate Donaldson, Brandon Holst blurted out a sequence of numbers and letters.

One of the terrorists next to him jotted the sequence down and rushed off, returning moments later, giving Dragan a single nod.

The terrorist walked up to Brandon, who struggled to control his breathing, hope filling him at the thought of being with Kate soon, of freeing her from that dreaded torture, of—

"Go, Mr. Holst," Dragan said, walking past him, grabbing a small bag from one of the terrorists. It was a first-aid kit. "Go and help your whore!"

One of the terrorists holding him back released the handcuffs, pushing him forward. Dragan shoved the kit in his hands while giving him another push.

Ignoring his burning chest, Brandon moved away from them, reaching Kate, dropping the small kit on the carpet, lifting her by the thighs as the terrorists broke into a laughter.

"Hold on, Kate!" he shouted, his chest ablaze from the strain as he moved her body up, giving her enough slack to free the rope from the hook. Her arms dropped over his shoulders as Brandon lowered her, gently setting her on the carpet while Dragan and his goons shut and locked the door behind them.

"You're with me now. You're going to be—" he began to say while, lifting the pantyhose, staring at the face of a stranger, of someone who bore a strong resemblance to Kate Donaldson, but who was *not* Kate, was *not* the woman with who he had fallen in love, was not . . .

It . . . it can't be!

The stranger coughed in between sobs after he removed the gag, dried blood crusting the skin between her nose and upper lip, which was swollen at one end. Brandon forced control into his confused mind. The bastards had tricked him. They had found a look-alike, someone who could pass for Kate from a distance, and tortured her to get him to release the access password. Now he had nothing! *Nothing!*

Insanity!

Madness!

Kneeling next to her as she rested on her back, her small breasts rising and falling as she breathed heavily, her sobbing filling the sudden silence in the room, Brandon Holst prayed for control, fought the overwhelming desire to . . .

Keep your head.

He exhaled, a mix of emotions sweeping through him as he turned his focus to the wounded woman, still naked, looking so much like Kate Donaldson on their last night together. This woman, however, was much younger, probably in her late twenties.

She cried again, forcing his mind back to his current situation.

"Shhh . . ." he whispered, reaching for the first-aid kit, recognizing only the red cross on the top, the rest of the instruction written in a Slavic language.

He unfastened the side latch and opened it, spotting a plastic bottle labeled ALKOHOL. He opened it, also ripping a plastic bag filled with cotton balls labeled PAMUK.

"This is going to sting a little," he said, doubting that she could understand him. She had her eyes closed, still crying, her hands beneath her chin, finger interlaced, as if she were praying. He eyed the cuts, superficial, inflicted to cause pain, not death. But they needed tending to stop the bleeding, to disinfect. In his years at the ranch, he had learned much about first aid from his older brothers, curing everything from cuts and scrapes to broken bones.

"*Upomoc,*" she whispered between sobs, turning on her side, facing him. "*Bole . . . me leda.*"

"I don't understand," Brandon said, holding her hand, "But I'm going to disinfect the cuts, all right?" he held up the alcohol and the cotton balls.

She nodded, her eyes flashing gratitude. "*Molim.*"

3

"Did you gain access?" asked Dragan Kundat, standing behind Erik Haas in a massive room two floors above the office where he had left Brandon Holst and the young courtesan. Dragan had selected her from dozens of women walking the streets of Belgrade this evening. Once students at the local university or workers at any one of many manufacturing shops, a lot of girls like that one had turned to prostitution when the economy shattered during the early nineties. Dragan had selected her because of her uncanny resemblance to Kate Donaldson, a trick that had yielded expected results.

Over thirty workstations hummed to the rhythm of several servers and disk drives mixed with the light whisper of a nearby laser printer. This antiseptic room, its temperature controlled to keep the machinery in working order, formed the core of Slobodan Milosevic's attempt at creating cyber-havoc on his enemies with the end result of holding them hostage for ransom. Around the room sat half a dozen high-tech mercenaries like Haas, their services bought by the Yugoslav president to digest the stolen software and hardware from countless Y2K sources around the globe for the sole purpose of creating the ultimate retaliatory weapon against NATO countries.

The German programmer, the head of this secret software division, nodded, drawing his bony finger down the screen, pointing at lines of computer code. "This is the source code." He glanced over his left shoulder. "*Exactly* what we needed."

"Can you modify it to reverse the effect?"

Another nod. "This is straight C++ code. Give me a day and it will be ready for a trial run."

"I hope you don't need the services of its creator."

"Why?"

"Let's just say that it will take quite a bit to get him to tell us anything else." After what he had just done to Brandon Holst, Dragan felt quite certain that the software entrepreneur would rather *die* than reveal anything of value to him.

Haas inspected the screen for a few additional moments, before saying. "It looks fairly well documented. I do not believe that his assistance will be needed."

Dragan Kundat crossed his arms while walking to the windows behind the workstation, watching a caravan of cars head out of the parking lot. The second vehicle from the front, a gold Jeep Cherokee, belonged to Marko Milosevic, the president's son, who was leaving quite late this evening, followed by his usual mob of heavily armed bodyguards in dark Mercedes Benz sedans. When Marko left late it usually meant that he had been detained at his office—which resembled more a luxurious penthouse than a place of work—by one or more of his young female assistants.

"I'm glad you won't be needing Holst's assistance, my friend," Dragan said, his eyes following the cars as they reached the street and turned north. "Because I'm planning to kill him before dawn."

4

The caravan left the Sava Congress Center at exactly 10:30 P.M, just as Zoran had predicted. A black Mercedes Benz led the procession, followed by Marko Milosevic's bulletproof Jeep Cherokee and two more black Mercedes sedans. According to Zoran's sources, fifteen well-armed men escorted the president's son everywhere he went.

Kate Donaldson, Vladimir "Tref" Vucic, and two members of the Kosovo Liberation Army hid behind the knee-high bushes of Friendship Park, flanking the west side of Lenjinov Boulevard, halfway between the modern Sava Center and the Museum of Contemporary Art, where Marko was hosting a private viewing of dozens of stolen works of art from London, Paris, and Rome. His visitors were mostly gray-market art dealers. According to Zoran, who had escorted Marko Milosevic to many such showings, Yugoslav agents periodically stole artwork from around the world and smuggled it into Belgrade, where the proceeds from the gray-market sales fattened the coffers of Slobodan Milosevic.

Kate peered across the quiet boulevard, roughly two hundred feet down to where a second team silently waited, also armed with the weapons smuggled into Belgrade by Kate Donaldson and her Bosnian agents, who had returned to their country early this afternoon after making their delivery.

"Three minutes," whispered Tref Vucic, tapping his watch, before whispering Serbo-Croatian into his handheld radio.

Kate screwed the metal cylinder containing rocket propellant into the warhead section of an RPG anti-tank rocket system. Kneeling on the soft grass, she inserted the round into the muzzle of the launcher unit, just as she had been taught years ago, uncovering the nosecap of the warhead and extracting the safety pin, before reassembling the explosive cone.

"Sixty seconds," Tref said, listening to his radio as distant headlights stabbed the dark street.

Glancing over her right shoulder to make sure no one was behind her, Kate shouldered the RPG, balancing it as she aimed it at the windshield of the lead vehicle of the incoming caravan. This version of the Russian-made weapon, customized for urban guerrilla warfare, had a range of five hundred feet without a crosswind. Tonight, a light breeze swirled her hair. She estimated it was no more than five miles per hour, and it was coming more or less from the direction that she intended to fire, which made it a headwind.

The caravan got within two hundred feet. Kate shifted the crosshairs of the aiming unit to a spot in space a foot in front of the lead Mercedes's windshield to compensate for the headwind and the forward movement of the vehicle.

As a delivery truck appeared to her far left, followed by

two vans—all moving in the opposite direction of the caravan—Kate took a deep breath, exhaling through her
mouth, pulling on the trigger just as she had finished
breathing out.

The solid-propellant rocket came to life, shooting the
5.4 lb HE-shaped charge toward the incoming vehicle, the
rocket's exhaust blasting through the back of the unit and
into the trees behind her in a flicker of fire that lasted but
a second or two, the same amount of time that it took the
warhead to cover the short distance to its intended target.

The lead Mercedes disappeared behind a sheet of orange
and yellow flames an instant before the roof and doors
separated from the car, the blast hurling them into the night
sky. The Cherokee steered around the burning vehicle, its
driver attempting to escape the ambush. The delivery truck
and the vans came in fast from the opposite direction,
blocking the street, cutting off the Jeep and leaving it no
way out but back in the direction it had just come from.

Making a last-ditch effort, the driver put the Jeep in
reverse, wheels spinning furiously, rushing the vehicle past
the charred Mercedes once more. Gunfire erupted as KLA
guerrillas used their new Heckler & Koch MP5 submachine guns to blow the Jeep's tires. In the same moment,
the trailing Mercedes also blew up in a billowing column
of fire, glass, and smoke, victim to an RPG round fired by
Zoran, leading a second KLA team across the street.

The Jeep stopped by the single surviving Mercedes, the
doors of which were flung open, and men clutching Uzis
rolled onto the asphalt, aiming their submachine guns at
the surrounding bushes.

Multiple reports whipped the night. Two of Marko's
bodyguards clutched their chests, dropping their guns before firing a single round, succumbing to Zoran and his
recently armed urban warriors. The other three tried to run
for the protection of the bushes, but never made it, getting
caught in a deadly crossfire, collapsing on the pavement.

Feeling the heat radiating from the burning vehicles, the smoke reminding her of the botched operation in London, Kate Donaldson focused on the Jeep. It had stalled, steam hissing from half a dozen bullet holes punched across the hood.

She approached the Cherokee from the side, flanked by two KLA warriors, their dark clothing blending them with the night. Three more KLA guerrillas—Zoran included—scrambled up from the opposite side of the street, surrounding the Jeep, its tinted windows preventing anyone from looking in, the screams of women from within the vehicle mixing with the whining starter as the driver attempted to crank the engine back to life.

In a single, swift motion, Kate flipped the MP5 around and drove the weapon's metal stock into the windshield, creating a gaping hole, before flipping it around and aiming it at the stunned driver, who took his hands off the wheel.

"Van kuce, Marko! Sada! Sada!" shouted Zoran, standing next to Kate, his weapon trained on the front passenger, who lowered his pistol at the sight of submachine guns pointed in his direction.

The rear door swung open. Two women came out, hands on their faces, crying, their tight evening dresses slowing their movements.

"Van kuce! Svako! Van kuce, Marko! Sada!"

Slowly, hands over his head, a handsome Slav in his early thirties with dark hair and a neatly-trimmed beard stepped out of the car, peppering Serbo-Croatian with haste at Zoran, who replied with matching intensity in his words, before poking him in the chest with the muzzle of his MP5, motioning him toward the waiting delivery truck, whose rear door lifted, revealing two more men bearing automatic weapons. Several KLA guerrillas forced the two women, the Jeep's driver, and Marko into the truck, which sped away.

"Let's go," Tref Vucic said, his gaunt features alive in the flickering light of the nearby fires. His eyes displayed a fear absent until now. It was clear to Kate that this attack would create a wave of reprisals. "Milosevic's *policija* will be here soon."

"I'm counting on it," she replied, grinning, dropping one of her business cards on the Jeep's rear seat. Earlier in the evening she had scribbled a warning on the back. "And this should make it easy for them to understand why this happened."

5

Slobodan Milosevic had always been a calm, serene individual, a cold operator, seldom losing control, always remaining focused, even in the worst of moments. He had remained calm when learning of his father's suicide. He had remained calm after his mother hung herself. He had remained calm as NATO planes razed his nation, setting it ablaze with nonstop bombings. And he had remained calm as the world criticized his actions against the barbarian Muslims, invaders of his land, of the cradle of the Serbian people.

But tonight, as he sat behind his desk in one of his safe houses, deep beneath the streets of Belgrade, Slobodan Milosevic sensed control escaping him, giving way to a tidal wave of raw anger. In his hands he held a business card, one small piece of paper that had offset his controlled disposition.

His aides remained silent, staring at the lush carpet of

his superior's luxurious quarters. None of them dared say a word.

Milosevic continued to read the business card in his trembling fingers, his jaw clenched, his heartbeat rocketing, a single word flashing in his mind.

Marko.

Milosevic could tolerate NATO planes, could tolerate economic sanctions, could endure the state of siege that the world had imposed on his nation while he unflaggingly fought for his beliefs, for his people, following a tradition started many centuries before, and which was likely to continue for centuries to come. Milosevic could bear that and much more.

But not this.

Not Marko.

Standing, an action that made his aides step back, away from his desk, Milosevic crossed his arms and began to shout orders. A moment later his aides had vanished, leaving him alone with his anger, with a rage he would have to control in order to rescue his son. But in order to achieve the serenity required to focus on the problem, Milosevic first needed to vent, to let out the steam building up in him, and the only way he knew how to do that was by punishing those responsible for his son's security.

6

Dragan Kundat remained quiet as he followed President Slobodan Milosevic down a flight of stairs leading to the basement of the *policijski okrug,* the main police precinct in Belgrade. Its chief, Ivan Goseliv, shouldered the responsibility for the security of Belgrade's elite class, including the members of Milosevic's immediate family. Milosevic now held Goseliv responsible for his son's kidnapping.

The situation carried a difficult personal aspect for Dragan, who had fought side by side with Goseliv in Bosnia. And to make matters worse, Goseliv had even saved Dragan's life once. Now he would have to witness the slow execution of his friend and former comrade-in-arms. Goseliv was the man with whom Dragan had planned to discuss a possible coup against Milosevic.

Milosevic, a finely pressed Italian suit hanging from his broad shoulders, wore the crestfallen expression that always warned his close advisors to keep their distance, par-

ticularly when heading to the place where his *policija* used
to interrogate and torture his enemies using methods
largely unchanged over a thousand years—but still as effective.

Dragan, although not directly associated with this fiasco,
could very easily become the target of this man's wrath.
There was something about getting in the way of one of the
most feared and wanted men in the world that tended to
humble even a seasoned warrior and terrorist like himself.

They reached the bottom of the stairs. The assistant chief
of police entered a security code on the keypad next to the
door, unlocking it and pushing it open for his president, who
rushed by without acknowledging him, followed by his
usual entourage of bodyguards and aides, and Dragan in the
rear, trying to keep a low profile even though Milosevic had
personally called him an hour ago, after news of the kidnapping of his son reached the presidential palace.

Dragan remembered quite well the fate of so many colo-
nels and generals who had disappointed Milosevic in Bosnia and Croatia. His body shivered at the thought of their
terrible fates, of their gruesome deaths.

They continued down a long hallway, flanked by doors
leading to interrogation cells. The group went inside the
last one on the left hand side. Dragan followed them.

The large room, illuminated by an array of fluorescent
lights hanging from a high concrete ceiling, was damp; the
coppery smell of blood tingled in Dragan's nostrils. A naked man also hung from that ceiling on this night, his feet
just a few inches from the stained floor.

One of Milosevic's aides approached Dragan, handing
him a business card, before motioning him to step to the
front of the small crowd and stand beside President Milosevic, just an arm's length from Goseliv.

Dragan inspected the card in his hands, feeling something
stir inside, not just at the sight of his friend Goseliv, and the
torture he was about to endure, but also at the sudden reali-

zation of why he had been summoned here, away from his primary mission, which was proceeding ahead of his committed schedule. In the few hours since obtaining the code, Erik Haas had managed to crank out the first version of *Cekic*, or Hammer, as the German programmer had baptized the altered version of Holst's Sweeper program. Cekic did exactly that, find a compliant Y2K program and "hammer" it back into noncompliance.

Under normal circumstances, Dragan Kundat would not be concerned, but this was anything but a normal circumstance. Milosevic's son had been kidnapped, and Dragan just now realized who had done it, and how he had been unfortunately linked to this disaster.

The legendary terrorist remained calm, resolved to face whatever fate threw in his direction, just as he had endured the mutilation of his parents at the hands of the Albanians, just as he had beaten overwhelming odds on multiple occasions in the battlefields of Bosnia, of Croatia.

Dragan Kundat walked steadily, refusing to let anyone know how he felt, how adrenaline now seared his veins, augmenting every movement, every thought, every emotion.

He stopped next to Milosevic, who regarded the naked Goseliv with a stern face.

"*Moj predsennik!*" Goseliv shouted, his voice filled with the strain reflected on his lined face. "I promise to find him . . . immediately! I shall—"

Milosevic kicked him in the groin, hard.

Goseliv's cry echoed hollowly inside the large room, injecting it with a sense of raw fear that now swept through Dragan, though no one could tell, for externally he didn't even flinch. Instead, he maintained his stolid expression while staring at the swinging chief of police, whose testicles were certain to be severed from his body before this night was over.

Milosevic looked at Dragan for the first time, his dark eyes consuming, admonishing. The terrorist's heartbeat intensified, pounding his ears, his chest, drilling his temples. The Yugoslav president's piercing gaze shifted to a table next to Goseliv, filled with medieval-looking metal and wooden tools, a few of them red-hot from resting on a fire pan next to the table, the smell of sizzling metal mixing with the stale air. Dragan Kundat had used these on countless Muslims and Catholics across the war-razed Balkans over the past decade.

"One hour," Milosevic said, checking his watch before crossing his arms.

The terrorist stepped forward, understanding the silent order as well as its powerful hidden message. If Dragan failed to inflict enough pain on Goseliv in the next hour, quenching Milosevic's anger before the man died from his wounds, Dragan Kundat would follow Goseliv on the rope. It was now obvious to Dragan that Milosevic held the terrorist somewhat accountable for the kidnapping because it had been at Kate Donaldson's hand, the woman that Dragan should have killed by now. Forcing him to torture his old friend was Milosevic's way of punishing Dragan, who could only redeem himself—and avoid a similar fate—by showing no mercy during the torture phase.

"Dragan, *moj muz,*" mumbled Goseliv, also understanding his fate, as well as Dragan's if he failed to satisfy Milosevic. "Do what you must."

Dragan exhaled, grabbing a tool that resembled an ice pick, only longer and with a hooked end. He looked in the distance, spending a few seconds to get into the correct frame of mind, disconnecting any emotions as he stood in front of Goseliv.

"Dragan, my friend—" Goseliv began to say.

In a single swift motion, Dragan Kundat plunged the end of the instrument into Goseliv's left eye, jerking it back out, quickly, along with his eyeball, still attached to a string of nerves and tissue. Gel spurted, followed by blood.

The ear-piercing scream echoed inside the room, like a shriek from hell, tearing at the terrorist's sanity as he held the tool at eye level, still connected to the pulsating web of tissue, grayish fluid mixed with blood staining his hand. Then slowly, he pulled it away, completely severing it.

Goseliv jerked and screamed, also urinating as he lost control of his bladder muscles. He twisted and turned for another minute, before settling down in a soft cry, his head down, blood tricking down his face.

This shock treatment, which Dragan had used on so many captured Bosnians and Croats, set the base level of pain for the torture. From here he would launch his first offensive.

Setting the bloody tool down on the table, he picked up one resembling a spring-loaded garden clipper, its blades red-hot from being in the fire.

Without hesitation, he stood on a stepladder behind Goseliv, directing the instrument toward Goseliv's right hand—the same hand which had pulled Dragan Kundat out of a burning tank in Bosnia eight years ago—placing a finger between the sizzling blades. As expected, Goseliv flinched when his skin came in contact with the hot steel, but he could not move his hands, secured by the rope while hanging from a rusted chain. Dragan applied pressure to the clipper's handles, closing the blade across the first joint.

Another scream, followed by a cry, and more sobs. Dragan forced himself to ignore it, inspecting the damage. As expected, the red-hot blades had cauterized the cut while slicing off the section of Goseliv's finger, preventing any blood loss.

The smell of burnt skin and singed hair mixed with the stench from the small pool of urine and other bodily fluids oozing from Goseliv's maimed body.

Dragan continued, systematically amputating Goseliv's fingers, one joint at a time, pausing in between strikes to let the pain level settle down, to prevent him from passing out, and also to reheat the instrument. In the twenty minutes that it took him to slice off his fingers, Goseliv had lost a mere trickle of blood, remaining very much awake but in intense pain.

Next came the toes, which the seasoned terrorist clipped one joint at a time, without vacillating, without remorse, never once gazing at either Goseliv's face or Milosevic's, whom Dragan knew was scrutinizing his every move, testing his loyalty, his ruthlessness, his right to belong to the inner circle of loyal subjects, capable of torturing and killing *anyone* without objecting, without showing the smallest hint of uncertainty. The tortured warrior shouted for mercy, for a bullet in the head.

Not today, old friend, Dragan thought, forcing savage control in his mind, indifference in his stare, his movements reflecting the triviality which contrasted sharply with the turbulence of emotions sweeping through him as he reached for the *donje rublje,* a little-known instrument found by one of Milosevic's assistants during a research of obscure medieval torture devices.

The tool looked like steel underpants split in two, connected at the rear by a heavy-duty hinge and in the front by an adjustable latch. Dragan set the latch to its widest setting, so that as he secured the *donje rublje* around Goseliv's waist, the sharp needles lining the inside of the *donje rublje* would merely rest against him, tickling his skin. The needles, also adjustable, varied in length according to its position on the instrument, following the body's contour. They could be driven farther into the victim by twisting the butterfly keys on both sides of the *donje rublje* after the latch had been fully closed. Two smaller keys controlled larger spikes, one aimed at the groin and another at the rectum.

Goseliv cringed the moment Dragan secured the heavy instrument, covering him from his waist to his upper thighs. Then he adjusted the latch to its first of five settings, watching his old comrade-in-arms wrench away with a blood-curling howl as hundreds of prongs pierced his skin.

The cries, echoing in the room, mixed with the slow laughter from Milosevic as he patted Dragan on the shoulder.

The seasoned terrorist felt like vomiting, but controlled the urge. Instead he focused on the *donje rublje's* lock, adjusting it one setting at a time, closing it around Goseliv's waist, pausing until his victim had settled down before readjusting, driving the steel needles into him, slowly, very slowly. The blood running down Goseliv's legs began to puddle beneath him. Dragan glanced at his watch while turning the rear key, driving a six-inch-long spike up Goseliv's rectum. His back bent like a bow as he shouted something incomprehensible.

Dragan heard Milosevic's laughter, mixing with the cries of his friend, of his colleague. He wanted to vomit, to shout in anger, to turn around at that very moment and strike at Milosevic himself.

But he controlled such thoughts, focusing on the job at hand, on the *donje rublje*'s front key, driving it into Goseliv's groin.

More shouts and cries mixed with laughter from behind him.

He finished his old comrade-in-arms by gouging his right eye, removing the *donje rublje,* castrating him, and shoving the testicles into his mouth.

Goseliv still breathing, Dragan Kundat turned around, sprayed with blood, his crimson hands falling to his sides, his eyes locking with the Yugoslav president.

Milosevic nodded. "I see you have not lost your old touch, my friend. You are now my new chief of police.

You have twenty-four hours to find my son. If a single hair on his head is harmed, I will hold you personally responsible, so *do not* take any chances.''

The president turned to leave but stopped, adding, ''And you must also get the Y2K software ready to be launched against the world. I want all the NATO countries to pay dearly for their atrocities against our people.''

Milosevic stomped away, followed by his entourage of bodyguards and aides, leaving the terrorist alone with the scourged Goseliv.

Using his own knife, Dragan slit Goseliv's throat, putting him out of his misery. Then he walked away without looking back, determined to do everything within his power to avoid such a terrible fate.

7

The forested mountains near the border with Kosovo—remote, isolated, inaccessible to armored transport, to tanks, to missile launchers, to the heavy weaponry that made the Kosovo Liberation Army an easy target for Milosevic's paramilitary units—provided the ideal hiding place for Kate Donaldson and her rogue warriors. It was also just under two miles away from the recovery point where a pair of Navy helicopters would come to pick her up in another twenty-four hours, per her agreement with Mike Costner during their last radio conversation.

Kate sighed, wondering how Costner would feel if he knew that she still didn't have Brandon Holst or the Y2K software.

A cold wind whistled down from the snow-covered peaks. Kate zipped up her heavy jacket while standing alone on a boulder overlooking the log cabin monopolizing a small clearing, dotted with patches of snow, where Tref Vucic had set up the simple exchange: Brandon Holst for

Marko Milosevic. Nothing else, contrary to what Kate had promised Mike Costner in return for the arms and diamonds that had allowed her to buy herself the temporary loyalty of the Kosovar guerrillas.

The hell with it. She would deal with the CIA later. Right now her first priority was rescuing Brandon from the deadly clutches of Milosevic and getting him airlifted to safety. After that she would figure out a way to make good on her promise to her former employer.

Using her binoculars, the seasoned operative inspected the woods surrounding the clearing, spotting Zoran across from where she stood, roughly a thousand feet away, small clouds of condensed air curling skyward as he breathed.

The local KLA chief, dressed in camouflage fatigues beneath a thick dark-olive coat, had deployed his forces efficiently, covering all angles of that clearing, at the center of which stood the empty cabin. A wispy column of dark smoke curled upward from its chimney, giving the impression that someone was there, namely Marko Milosevic.

Illusion. Deception. Kate had mastered those arts long ago, and she used those skills now, keeping her hostage secured by the tree line with the burly Zoran close by. Kate wanted to check her opponent's talent, his willingness to carry out the exchange without trying to turn the tables on her. Zoran and Tref had selected this location, which allowed them multiple escape routes should Milosevic attempt to deploy paramilitary units with helicopters. The dense woods would protect them, preventing the Serbs from using their heavy equipment, leveling the playing field. And if all else failed, Kate Donaldson had already prepared a diversion, a way to distract Serbian troops and give herself and her team of mercenaries time to escape.

Everything was proceeding just as she had devised it. Even Zoran had reluctantly agreed to keep Marko Milosevic alive until Brandon Holst was safe. After that, Kate didn't want to even see how the rugged KLA guerrilla disposed of his sister's rapist.

The distant *wop-wop* sound of helicopters mixed with the light wailing of the wind. Kate hid behind a towering pine next to the boulder, a gloved hand clutching a branch as she pressed the rubber ends of the binoculars against her eyes, making out three glistening spots against the pale-blue sky.

She lowered the binoculars, letting them hang loose from her neck while snatching the radio on her utility belt.

"Keep low. Let's see what they're here to offer."

The helicopters came in from the west, dropping to tree-top level as they neared the clearing. One of them continued toward them while the other two began to circle overhead, surveying the grounds. The single helicopter approached the clearing, the downwash from its main rotor swirling the smoke from the cabin as it flew over it before hovering on the field of snow and frozen shrubs adjacent to the old wooden structure.

Kate now followed it with the scope of her sniper rifle, a silenced Heckler & Koch PSG-1. She recognized the transport helicopter, Russian-made, sporting the markings of the Yugoslav government on its sides over olive-green camouflage paint.

The helicopter touched down gently, just as the side doors slid open. A large man in civilian clothes stepped outside, flanked by two soldiers clutching automatic weapons.

She adjusted the scope, zeroing in on the civilian, recognizing the familiar features, the dark hair framing a square face, the tanned skin, the high cheekbones.

Her mouth went dry at the sight of Brandon Holst, her throat aching with affection, her mind perplexed that the Serbs would give him up so easily, without any apparent attempt at deceiving her. She had fully expected a fake, someone who looked like Brandon.

But it's him!

Concentrate.

"Awaiting instructions," came the muffled voice of Tref Vucic, who covered the northern side of the clearing with two of Zoran's men. The KLA force waited for Kate to execute the plan she had so carefully laid out for them on the outside chance than Milosevic's people showed up with Brandon Holst.

"Proceed," she replied, and a moment later Zoran and one of his subordinates flanked Marko Milosevic as he stepped away from the trees just enough for the Serbs to recognize him.

8

Brandon Holst shivered from the cold, bracing himself, squinting as he stepped away from the helicopter and into bright sunlight. The frosty wind from the main rotor chilled him, swirling his hair, the noise thundering in his ears, rattling him. He felt the vibrations in the stitches still holding his chest together.

The flight had been sudden. One moment he had been sleeping, after the terrorists had taken Kate's look-alike away. The next he had been escorted out of the Sava Congress Center building—information he had learned from the young woman—and into a waiting car, which sped him through the streets of Belgrade directly to the airport, where he'd boarded this craft just twenty minutes ago.

Now here he was, in the middle of nowhere for reasons he did not understand.

God, it's cold.

And he was freezing. In their haste, the terrorists had not given him a coat, leaving him with the same pair of slacks and woolen shirt that he had worn for the past few days.

He stared at the men by the tree line, what looked like two soldiers flanking a civilian . . . *just like me!*

One of the Serbs pushed him toward the distant trio as the other soldiers did likewise to their civilian.

A trade?

Brandon Holst was now utterly confused, and concerned. *Who am I being traded for? And who are those soldiers at the edge of the clearing? What do they want with me?*

One of the Serbs poked him in the back with his rifle, motioning him to start walking.

Brandon complied, moving toward the distant figures as the civilian at the end began to walk toward him.

Halfway to the forest, the helicopter and the Serbs roughly thirty feet behind him, a single report echoed in the mountain range.

The civilian fell on the snow clutching his leg, screaming. Then one of the soldiers by the tree line ran toward the fallen man, slashing at his face with a knife.

What in the hell's going—

The ground erupted by Brandon's feet. He turned around, watching one of the Serbs clutching his coat before falling to his knees, blood spurting from his mouth, a patch of blood forming in the middle of his chest. A second soldier swung his weapon in Brandon's direction, but an invisible force lifted him off the ground, shoving him back against the craft. In the same instant, gunfire sparked from several locations at once, the multiple reports overpowering the rattling of the chopper's main rotor. Rounds punched holes in the helicopter's Plexiglas canopy, speckled a instant later by a crimson mist as the pilot and copilot doubled over their controls.

Everything was happening too fast. Brandon Holst's mind struggled to catch up to the reality of the moment, to the sudden intensity of his situation. The Serbs were under attack by someone in the surrounding forest, and he was about to get caught in a deadly crossfire. A single word flashed in his mind.

Run.

Despite his medical condition, he kicked his shoes against the frozen soil, filling his lungs with cold air as he raced away from his captors, from the guerrillas by the tree line, from the incoming helicopters, their muzzles alive as they flew right over the treetops, sweeping the surrounding woods.

Brandon Holst ignored it all, his eyes focusing on an empty patch of forest, on the tree line, not knowing what he would do after reaching it, but knowing he *had* to reach it, had to seek shelter, had to lose the nearing enemy.

The helicopter noise intensified, but Brandon did not look back, did not stop running, even as the ground exploded to his left, to his right, even as his ribcage protested the abuse, stinging him, raking his chest like a hot claw. Ignoring the pain, racing past tiny clouds of dirt and snow closing in on him, Brandon reached the tree line, the beating of his heart pummeling his ears and temples, nearly drowning out the fusillade of rounds tearing into the clearing.

He kept up the pace, the forest swallowing him as he lost himself in a sea of green, the pine resin fragrance overpowering the smell of cordite staining the clearing.

For a moment it seemed as if he were back home, deer hunting in the pine-forested hills east of Austin, near Bastrop State Park, twisting his body to correspond to the heavy foliage, to the frozen vegetation, to the evergreens pelted with snow.

The cold stung him now as hard as the stitches, burning his nostrils, chilling his core as he took in lungfuls of frosty air, as he bumped into a low-hanging branch, the accumulated snow falling on him, bathing him.

He brushed it off, beginning to tremble, hypothermia quickly setting in as the extreme cold assaulted his unprotected body.

A hooded figure loomed from behind the trunk of a pine, motioning him to stay down, to seek shelter. Brandon Holst saw it just as the forest began to spin around him, as his mind grew cloudy, as he became light-headed—a mix of his weakened condition, the stress, and the temperature shock.

He dropped to his knees, sinking into the frozen shrubs lining the forest floor, the blaring noise of the helicopters and the thundering gunfire suddenly fading as his vision tunneled, as he collapsed, as he heard his name spoken by a familiar voice.

Kate?

His mind had to be playing tricks on him now, making him hear what he so desperately *wished* to hear, the voice of the woman he loved, the—

''Brandon!''

That voice again. *Was it real?* Nothing seemed real anymore as he felt himself falling, deep beyond the vast expanse of this alien world, of this foreign land, far away from home, from his life, from Kate Donaldson.

Kate.

As his thoughts vanished, as his vision failed him, Brandon's mind rewarded him with a final vision, a mirage in this forgotten land. He saw Kate Donaldson reaching down for him, embracing him, before all went dark.

9

"I've got him!" she shouted into her radio, enraged that someone had opened fire before Brandon was out of harm's way. "Get me some help! He's freezing! I need a large coat!"

All she could hear in reply was hastily spoken Serbo-Croatian mixed with static and the echoing noise of the helicopters and gunfire.

At that moment Kate spotted two figures entering the forest clutching large weapons, their dark silhouettes back-lit by the bright clearing. The soldiers swept the jungle with their guns, obviously not seeing Kate Donaldson as she knelt by Brandon's shivering body even though she was less than forty feet away and could see them clearly.

Then she realized why. The bright sunlight had dilated the Serb's pupils, making it difficult for them to see in the murky woods, where the dense canopy formed by a sea of stately pines let little sunlight through.

That realization also told her that she had only seconds

before the Serbs adjusted their vision, spotting them, cutting them to pieces with their machine guns.

But she couldn't hide and wait for the Serbs to search the area. Brandon's temperature was dropping rapidly. If she couldn't cover his body soon, he risked the chance of falling into hypothermia and dying of prolonged exposure.

It was at that moment that the operative in Kate Donaldson regained control, eyes narrowing at the pair of Serbs, at their thick coats, at their mountain boots, at their gloves, at the items Brandon Holst needed to survive.

But she couldn't reach for the sniper rifle strapped to her back without excessive movement, which could telegraph her presence to the enemy. Instead, she opted for her sidearm, the Sig Sauer .45 caliber pistol which, though it was not silenced, Kate Donaldson easily aimed at the incoming figures, breathing out slowly before squeezing the trigger four times in rapid succession, firing two rounds into each Serb, both in the face, assuring instant death while preserving their clothes.

Her eyes surveyed the tree line, ears ringing from the multiple reports of the weapon she still clutched. She checked for reinforcements and saw none, feeling confident that the gunfire on the clearing had masked her shots.

She scrambled toward the nearest Serb, a large man, like Brandon. The rounds had torn off most of his face below the eyes, which seemed to float in a pool of blood and tissue.

The professional ignored it, concentrating on the heavy-duty snaps running the length of the heavy coat, olive in color, removing it from the dead Serb, along with his boots, winter pants, and gloves. The helicopters continued to fly overhead, occasionally firing back at KLA positions on the ground.

She returned to Brandon's side two minutes later, giving the clearing another glance before slipping the winter pants over his trousers. She ran his arms into the sleeves of the coat, turning his body from side to side to get him inside the coat, closing the metal snaps before protecting his hands with the gloves, removing his shoes and slipping his bare feet into the wool-lined boots.

As she finished, Kate spotted two figures coming toward her from the forest. She automatically swung the Sig toward them.

"Hold your fire," Tref Vucic said over the noise of the choppers and the sporadic gunfire, stretching a gloved hand at Kate. Zoran marched right behind him, his olive coat sprayed with blood, as well as his face and pants.

"What in hell happened out there?" she hissed. "I thought we had an agreement!"

"He didn't want to let Marko stray too far from him," Tref replied, tilting his head toward Zoran.

"Tell him that I didn't appreciate him putting Brandon's life at risk. Remind him of our agreement."

Tref exchanged Serbo-Croatian with Zoran before turning back to Kate. "He says that Brandon was already out of reach when he decided to attack Marko."

Kate sighed. "Is Zoran all right?"

"Marko Milosevic's blood," Tref replied.

Zoran opened the palm of his left hand and dropped a pair of human eyeballs by Kate's feet.

"He also castrated him and now wears the blood with pride," added the smuggler.

"Terrific. Brandon almost got killed because of this man's personal vendetta." She shook her head, not understanding these people, and not *caring* to understand them. She just wanted to get Brandon to safety as soon as possible, certainly before Slobodan Milosevic leveled the region in retaliation for the slaughter of his son.

"Is your friend alive?" Tref asked.

She nodded. "I just need to get him out of here. Find some shelter."

Tref turned to Zoran, exchanging more Serbo-Croatian

for several seconds before looking back at Kate.

"There used to be a small village up this mountain, in the direction of your recovery point. We can reach it by nightfall if we hurry. Maybe you can contact your friends and change the recovery location."

She nodded. "Good. Now it's time for our diversion." She stretched a thumb toward the clearing, where the helicopters hovered just feet off the ground near the cabin, apparently clearing the area before offloading more troops.

Tref got on the radio, spoke briefly, and then put it away, whipping both hands to his ears. Kate and Zoran did the same.

A moment later the clearing rumbled as a hundred pounds of C4 explosives turned the area into an inferno, forcing the helicopters temporarily out of the area.

Kate watched the fireworks, grinning, but also realizing that she had just kicked the bear. Slobodan Milosevic would not let this attack go unpunished. She had to get out of the area fast, before a new wave of airborne troops arrived and razed the forest.

Five minutes later, the group headed uphill. Two KLA warriors carried Brandon Holst in a stretcher.

10

Eric Haas had a new boss, someone whose name he didn't know and didn't *care* to know. The less he knew about the workings of this operation the better off he felt he would be. Since arriving from Dresden two years ago to head up this rogue group of programmers, the software engineer had had over a dozen superiors, all of whom had mysteriously disappeared after a short while. Haas had known better than to ask about them. Dragan Kundat had been the last in the series of vanishing men. The terrorist had left the building in a hurry over two hours ago, taking Brandon Holst along, and never returned.

Instead, a new person had shown up just ten minutes ago inside the computer room, this one clean-cut and impeccably dressed in a business suit—in sharp contrast with the rugged Dragan. The businessman had informed Haas that Slobodan Milosevic had just had another reorganization of his technical division.

Haas, quite used to those sudden changes in the reporting structure, simply nodded and welcomed his new boss, who told him to continue the development of the Y2K software. As long as his paychecks kept getting deposited into his Dresden bank account, the lanky German couldn't care less who he reported to or what happened to those around him. He was making more money than he knew how to spend, and in another six months he planned to return home and live like a king for the rest of his life, perhaps writing Internet software on a contractual basis from the mansion he planned to buy for himself.

But first you must prove yourself worthy in their eyes, he thought, also well aware of the stiff penalties under-performers paid in the unforgiving government of Slo-bodan Milosevic.

Haas's software torpedo, which he planned to fire at the Pentagon both as a test case and also in retaliation for NATO strikes—following direct orders from Milosevic himself—represented the culmination of months of work, patching together dozens of Y2K techniques, the most re-cent of which had been developed by Brandon Holst. The head of the torpedo housed the software password he had stolen a week ago, after lurking around the computer-system entryways of the American military establishment, waiting for legal users to log in, tagging their systems' physical addresses on the Internet, and then waiting until they logged out. Haas had then forced a snippet of bad code into one of the user's systems, forcing it to crash and activating the core dump that all Unix systems generate during a system crash. The core dump, designed to provide software engineers with a post-mortem file of the system's vital statistics prior to the crash, also included all key-strokes entered by the user from the moment he or she logged in until the time they logged out. Haas had captured and decoded those initial keystrokes, containing the user's password, which he now loaded into the torpedo to gain access to the first level of security of the Pentagon.

The rest of the torpedo housed Eric Haas's Cekic: a combination of Brandon Holst's Sweeper, the best work of several others Y2K programmers, and Haas's own ingenious twist. Holst's program identified for Haas the two-digit year segments in the target software. If the two-digit year had already been adjusted to be Y2K-compliant through any one of several methods commercially available, like windowing or encapsulation, then Haas would alter that fix by providing a new offset to the two-digit code, turning any compliant two-digit year into a non-compliant two-digit year. If the two-digit year was still not compliant, then Haas's offset would make it even less compliant.

The purpose of this initial setup became evident when the second section of his software struck. Haas's program would find the local clock of the target network and advance it to January 1, 2000, bringing down the entire network—or, even worse, keeping it running but generating incorrect results, just as it would have at the turn of the millennium.

With a final click of the mouse, the highly paid hacker released his potion to the Internet, which carried it across Europe and the Atlantic Ocean, delivering it just a minute later to its intended target inside the Pentagon.

The software torpedo reached the network of Army Intelligence within the Pentagon. Armed with the correct password, the illegal software received instant access, penetrating the firewall, entering the outer shell like an armor-piercing missile before spilling its virulent code into the network. At once, elements of Sweeper kicked into high gear, multiplying, attaching themselves to every file in the target system, just as a virus would, before scrubbing the files, flagging every two-digit year, and dumping the information into a log. It was at this point that Sweeper ended and Cekic began.

While Sweeper would take that log and use it to adjust

the dates and bring the files into Y2K compliance, Cekic did the exact opposite, altering the offsets, creating a chaotic brew of mixed years. And just as Cekic finished altering dates, just as the files in the network reached their highest level of Y2K non-compliance, Haas's software torpedo released its third and final virus, which attacked the system clock, advancing it to the new millennium, beyond the Y2K deadline.

In an instant, dozens of Army intelligence analysts stared at their screens as their Unix workstations either crashed or began to corrupt their files when conflicting dates triggered the operating system to interpret the billions of instructions it normally processed every second in a radically different way, writing over files when it should not, deleting others instead of archiving them, and saving those intended to be deleted, creating a software engineer's ultimate nightmare. It took just over a minute of this destructive cycle before someone from the systems administration department reacted, catching on to the cyber-attack, shutting down the entire network to prevent further data loss.

Eric Haas grinned behind his terminal. Although an average systems administrator could easily pinpoint the attack to the Balkans, and a *really good* one might even identify Belgrade as the origin of the attack, Eric Haas had nothing to worry while operating under Milosevic's umbrella. He was untouchable, yet he could launch attacks of this nature as he saw fit, even before the real Y2K arrived. In a way, his weapon, which he could deliver with surgical precision, had a similar effect to that of a Tomahawk missile. One missile alone would not win a war because it was too localized, but it would terrify the population because more could be on the way. And once Y2K struck, Cekic could spread chaos throughout the world.

Eric Haas could just hear Slobodan Milosevic the moment news of the successful cyber-attack against the Pentagon reached his office. He had just provided the Yugoslav president with a powerful weapon against the West, and he knew that Milosevic would demand more strikes against America, probably a minimum of one for each cruise missile and laser-guided bomb fired at him by the NATO strike force.

And that's just the beginning, Haas thought, already at work on the next phase of his Y2K strategy: creating the world's ultimate virus, one which would overshadow previous attempts by other viruses released into the Internet, like *Melissa,* which had achieved limited results at best.

But that was because he hadn't allowed the virus to expand deep enough before striking. Haas's Y2K virus—which was already over eighty percent complete, thanks to the handiwork of Brandon Holst and others—would pierce the world's networks and replicate at an exponential rate without doing anything at all, without causing any harm, biding its time until midnight on December 31st. Then it would attack all compliant Y2K software in the same fashion as it had ravaged through the localized network at the Pentagon, only on a global scale, causing havoc, spreading chaos, achieving the ultimate retaliation of President Slobodan Milosevic while at the same time making Eric Haas one of the richest men in the industry. The Y2K virus would provide Milosevic with the ultimate hammer to hold the world hostage, to demand the cash and weapons that his regime would need to remain in power for a long time to come.

11

Kate Donaldson continued moving uphill after a short but
stressful radio conversation with Mike Costner, who was
aboard the USS *Fletcher*, a Spruance-class destroyer patrolling the Adriatic Sea. Apparently a snowstorm was
heading her way, forcing all aircraft out of the area for at
least the next twelve hours.

Terrific, she thought, not cherishing the idea of having
to remain in the region that much longer, especially with
Brandon unconscious and the patience of her hired army
wearing thin after the episode down in the—

She detected the powerful stench coming from beyond
a bend in the trail they had been following for the past
half hour.

She turned to Tref Vucic, walking behind her amidst
snow layered pines and frozen vegetation as the group
headed single file to the top of the mountain, where the
CIA was due to extract them.

"Smells like the carcass of an animal," he offered, his

gaunt features veiled by the obscure woods.

Kate followed Zoran, the point man in this little expedition, feeling certain that only the promised balance of weapons, to be delivered by the rescue helicopter, plus the final installment of diamonds, kept her mercenary group from disbanding in light of Milosevic's likely reprisal in this region *very soon*. She knew that was also the compelling reason the KLA guerrillas continued to haul Brandon Holst's large bulk uphill without protest. The hardened warriors were in desperate need of weapons.

Kate breathed the frigid air, praying that *very soon* meant *after* she had left the area with Brandon, and also *after* the KLA team vanished.

Zoran abruptly halted, whispering something in Serbo-Croatian, which Tref passed down the line before translating for Kate.

"He wants us to hold here while he inspects the source of the smell."

The Yugoslav opportunist draped a handkerchief around his face, like a *bandido* from the Old West.

Zoran disappeared into the thick bush, returning a moment later, his usually stolid face ashen, as if he had just seen a ghost. He closed his eyes, took a deep breath, and opened them, motioning the team to follow him.

The clearing was quite small and dark, shadowed by the merging canopies of the surrounding pines. On it the ruthlessness of the Serbian paramilitary units finally struck Kate Donaldson with full force, beyond the sanitized images broadcast by CNN and other networks, far cruder than any photograph published in a Western newspaper or magazine.

Kate's knees quivered as she walked with faltering steps into a nightmare that belonged in a scene from Dante's *Inferno*.

Hell.

That was the word flashing in Kate's mind, describing

the slaughter on that clearing, in the middle of nowhere, invisible to high-altitude surveillance planes and satellites. She stared at the partially decayed bodies of women and children piled in the middle, now preserved by the extreme cold, frozen in time, overlooked by two dozen naked men, still standing upright, like wax statues in a horror show, impaled through their rectums by spear-like rods driven into the ground, causing the slow and painful death painted on their contorted faces, frozen in silent testimony to the medieval horror they had endured before dying.

Her mouth opened but nothing came out, except for a sobbing gasp at the sight. All the men had been castrated, their members hanging out of their mouths. Within the pile of bodies in the middle of this circle of death lay dozens of naked woman, their spread-eagled legs another silent account of the war of ethnic hatred created by a monster, by something *worse* than a monster, perhaps the devil himself. Several of the women, some still just girls, had sharpened sticks or other objects shoved up their vaginas, from which signs in Serbo-Croatian marked them as Muslim whores.

Her eyes stared at one of them, a woman probably around Kate's age, slim with short brown hair, her wide-eyed stare piercing, her lips parted in silent scream, her arms stretched out, conveying the unimaginable pain she had endured before succumbing to that metal rod.

Kate felt light headed. For a moment visions of those gang members in San Antonio came back with appalling clarity. She shivered when remembering how close she had come to suffering a similar fate to that of these women, raped in front of their children and husbands before being brutally murdered.

But nothing, absolutely nothing could have prepared her for what she saw next, for among the raped and maimed women were also children, ranging from infants to early teens, the boys missing their testicles, the girls spread-eagled like their mothers, sporting signs labeling them as future Muslim whores.

The seasoned operative dropped to her knees, eyes closed in prayer, fighting the desire to vomit, to purge, to somehow clean herself of this terrifying vision, somehow wishing they would have avoided this clearing altogether, perhaps have missed this whole nightmarish experience.

"Now you finally understand the meaning of ethnic cleansing," said Tref Vucic, squatting by Kate as she sat on her ankles, hands cupping her face. "It's one thing reading about it in *The New York Times*. It's a whole different experience seeing it, smelling it, *tasting* it in the back of your throat."

"But . . . but the children. *Why?*"

"Like the signs say, to prevent them from growing up to become Muslim men and women. To kill off their race, to pull their roots. I'm sure that the Serbs let some of them witness the carnage before cutting them loose, using them as messengers to spread the word of the impending fate of any ethnic Albanian caught inside of Yugoslavia. That is the true meaning of this war. Milosevic, as well as the entire Serbian population, regards the southern province of Kosovo as the cradle of their civilization and want to purge it of every last Muslim, to return it to whom they consider its rightful owners even though the Muslims were here first, before the Serbs arrived during the early Middle Ages."

Kate listened to the explanation, her eyes absorbing the incredible images, the visions she knew she would take with her to her grave.

Control.

Priorities.

Standing, forcing discipline into her voice, into her movements, the former CIA operative gave the dreaded clearing one final glance before motioning Zoran to move on. They still had another mile and a half to go before reaching the extraction point. Besides, witnessing a scene like this made Kate want to put as much distance from the place where Marko Milosevic had died as possible. If Milosevic's genocide-happy troops did this to strangers just to force them out of Yugoslavia, Kate Donaldson didn't want to consider what that monster would do to the people responsible for the death of his son. And the fact that Zoran had gouged his eyes and emasculated him in plain view of the circling helicopters would only kindle the flames of retribution certainly burning inside Slobodan Milosevic at this moment.

After briefly checking on Brandon Holst, still unconscious, Kate Donaldson followed Zoran into the forest.

12

Dragan Kundat stepped out of the Olympic Airlines plane at Leonardo da Vinci International Airport in Rome, Italy. Short blond hair had replaced his dark, unkempt hair. His dark eyes, now blue-green in color thanks to corrective lenses, surveyed the crowd, looking for any sign of recognition.

Detecting none, the terrorist followed the passengers down the concourse leading to customs, which would present no problem to the former Yugoslav strongman. In his possession were passports from three different European countries, all under different names.

"Buon giorno, Signore Tomasino," said a customs official, an Italian woman in her late fifties, her salt-and-pepper hair pulled back and secured in a bun, making her eyes look a bit Asian. "How was your business trip to Greece?"

"I'll know in a week," he replied in a language he had learned to master long ago, and which, unlike English, he spoke without an accent. "The Greeks never make a decision on our proposals without much discussion."

The customs official smiled, stamped his passport, and waved him through.

A minute later he flagged a taxi by the arrivals ramp. As he eased himself into the rear seat, the driver turned around, pointing a gun at him. Two men in business suits also stormed in, one in the rear and one in the front. Both pointed weapons at the surprised terrorist.

"You have much to answer for, Dragan," said the driver in Serbo-Croatian, turning around and putting the Fiat in gear.

The seasoned terrorist closed his eyes, a wave of surprise swept through him at the realization that Milosevic, somehow, had caught up with him so soon.

Then he steeled himself for what lay ahead.

13

The only standing structure in the village was an old school, somehow spared by Serbian paramilitary units three months ago when cleansing these mountains of ethnic Albanians. In it Kate Donaldson and her team had found shelter from the cold. Temperatures had already fallen into the teens, and the thick cloud coverage that swept over the region brought along heavy snow and a strong wind.

Kate gazed out of the window. Zoran and Tref had seen the storm as a blessing, covering their tracks and maybe even discouraging the Serbs from searching the entire mountain until the weather cleared.

She frowned, having just finished another short radio conversation with Mike Costner, who was aboard *Fletcher*. Costner had indicated that because of the storm, not only was Kate's urgent request to pull in the extraction to an hour from now impossible, but the scheduled extraction at dawn ran the risk of getting postponed if the storm didn't move out of the area soon.

A light moan by her feet made her look down. Brandon Holst, still resting in the stretcher, was coming around. The software entrepreneur had been out of commission since she had found him, sleeping through their entire climb, much to the displeasure of the KLA warriors, who had taken turns hauling him uphill.

She knelt by his side, wetting a small rag in a bucket of melted snow, washing his face without wetting his hair. She didn't want him to catch a cold. Even inside the one-story stone building the temperature was only around forty degrees, and Zoran had opted not to build a fire to avoid tipping off Serbs to their position. Although a rising column of dark smoke could not be seen from a distance in this weather, the ever cautious KLA commander didn't want to take chances when it came to jeopardizing the delivery of their new weapons by the American helicopters.

Brandon Holst opened his eyes, gazing about him, before closing them again and reopening them several seconds later, this time blinking rapidly, trying to clear his sight.

"Hey, stranger," she said, wiping his cheeks. "How goes it?"

"Ka—Kate? You're . . . all right. . . . I thought that . . ." he tried to sit up but could not, closing his eyes and leaning back down on the stretcher.

"Easy, now," she said, caressing his cheek the way a mother would a sick infant. "I'm all right, but you're *definitely* not. You pushed yourself down in that clearing, honey. You're still recovering from surgery."

"Where . . . where am I?" he asked, taking a deep breath, gazing about him. "What are you doing here?"

"You're in a safe place," she replied, keeping her palm on the side of his face. "For now."

"I thought I'd lost you." He placed a hand over hers.

She grinned. "It's going to take a lot more than that to get rid of me." She kissed him lightly on the lips. "I sure missed you."

Brandon hugged her, slowly coming around, gaining focus. "Not as much as I missed you, little lady." Then he held her at arm's distance. "But I think you owe me an explanation."

"All in good time."

He tried to sit up, succeeding this time, grimacing in obvious pain as he yawned. "Damned stitches," he mumbled.

"You're lucky you didn't rip them off during that little sprint."

"Why don't I feel lucky?" He put a hand to his chest, gazing down at the fresh bandages.

"One of Zoran's men changed the dressing while you were out."

He made a face. "Who's Zoran?"

"One of our friends. They're in the front room."

"The last time I checked I was in Yugoslavia. Americans *don't have* friends in Yugoslavia."

"They're KLA, Kosovo Lib—"

"I know who the KLA is," he said. "Why are they helping us? And you still haven't told me what you're doing here."

"I came here to find you and take you home."

He gave her a puzzled glance. *"Find me? Take me home?"*

Just then the door to the room opened. It was Zoran, a submachine gun in his hands.

Brandon crawled back at the sight of the burly warrior, who looked even more intimidating with snow and dried blood covering his thick coat. Behind him walked Tref Vucic.

"It's okay," she told Brandon. "They're here to protect us."

"Not for long," said Tref. "Zoran's men are getting restless. They think that if they wait until the storm clears Milosevic's men might catch up with them. They want to leave now."

Kate extended a thumb toward the window behind her. "In *that* storm?"

"They are used to traveling in worse weather than this. They want to use the storm to put more distance from this mountain."

"What about the weapons? Don't they want them?"

Tref tilted his head toward Zoran. "He said to tell your CIA friends to hide them in the woods. He will come looking for them in a few weeks."

"CIA friends?" asked Brandon. "*What* CIA friends?"

"Hold on," she told him, an index finger pointed at the ceiling, keeping her gaze locked with Tref's. "What if they come in the morning?"

Skepticism in his stare, Tref asked, "A helicopter in this weather?"

"My people are aboard the USS *Fletcher*. It carries all-weather helicopters which can fly in worse weather than this." Kate actually didn't think they could, but she had no other options. Brandon Holst couldn't possibly survive outside in this weather and she felt she might need the protection of Zoran's dozen KLA warriors until their scheduled rescue.

Tref translated for the KLA commander, who looked at Kate, then at Brandon, before replying.

"Zoran will check with his troops. He can only promise one volunteer."

"Who?"

"Himself. I'll also stay."

The Yugoslavs left Kate with as many concerns as Brandon Holst now had questions, which he started asking the moment the door closed behind her hired hands.

"Who *are* you, Kate Donaldson?" he asked. "Assuming that's your real name."

Kate exhaled, closing her eyes. It was time for a little heart-to-heart with the man she loved.

14

The software torpedo cruised at the speed of light down a fiber-optic cable in central Texas, reaching the Dallas–Fort Worth International Airport. Using a stolen password, the illegal program made it past the first firewall of that airport's scheduling and reservations software, spraying the network with the Cekic virus and waiting a full hour while the virulent code replicated itself, contaminating the entire database, creating a log of all two-digit years. Then an internal timer in Cekic triggered a full frontal assault, first altering all two-digit years, then striking the system clock, advancing it beyond Y2K. The scheduling and reservation code, which airport officials had gotten to a ninety-eight percent compliance level in recent months, turned into havoc.

The first sign of trouble appeared on the airport monitors, whose screens flashed twice before going blank, returning moments later with flashing 00:00 for the times of arrivals and departures. Nationwide, thousands of travelers were unable to make reservations or get information on flights into and out of DFW. At the airport everything came to a halt as the systems administrator tracked down the problem, bringing down the entire system before the virus could do more harm, and switching the system to a redundant network normally operating in backup mode, restoring the flight information just thirty minutes after the strike. In a conversation with FAA officials an hour later, the airport administrator stated that they had been lucky on two counts. First, since it was not yet Y2K, another system could be brought on line right away. And second, the attack had been launched against the reservation and scheduling system and not something more vital, like the air traffic control software, where the thirty minutes it had taken to bring the backup system on line could have caused a major disaster.

15

By midnight the snow had stopped falling, but a dense fog had descended over the region. Temperatures continued to drop. The wind whistled across the mountain peak, rattling the old structure of the school.

Brandon and Kate sat next to each other, his arm around her, her head resting on his shoulder. The former CIA officer had chosen the honest path, telling him everything she could without revealing government secrets. She picked up where she had left off the last time she had opened up to him, talking about life after college, discussing her association with the Agency, the countries in which she had operated, the reason for the early retirement, and everything else that had happened until this night, including the involvement of the CIA in this mess and the help that she had demanded and received afterwards. Brandon had listened intently, never once interrupting her.

He exhaled heavily. ''And I thought *my* kidnapping

story was exciting. This is . . ." he commented, his face awash with incredulity.

"I'm sorry I didn't tell you my whole story from the beginning," she said, eyes closed, fearing that her past would make him feel too uncomfortable to continue his relationship with her. "All I wanted was a normal life. I never wanted to return to the field, but I had no choice."

"The people that you've killed . . ." He looked into the distance, obviously troubled by the harsh revelation.

"I was a spy, Brandon. I was trained to defend, to kill if threatened. But I was not an assassin. I gathered intelligence for my country."

"I'm sorry if I sound a bit shocked. This is all just a little hard to swallow all at once."

"I never meant to deceive you."

"Why didn't you tell me before? You were already out, right?"

"I was bound—still am—by my contract with the CIA. They suggested a number of acceptable career paths. I chose the security business because it fit to some degree with my previous line of work. The rest just sort of fell into place."

"When did you learn that the CIA had targeted my company?"

She looked at him. "I began to suspect soon after we met. I noticed troubling patterns, like the men you called your business associates. They fit the operative type too well. I also thought I had spotted a surveillance team outside of Sullivan's during one of our first dates. But I chose to ignore it, thinking that I was just being paranoid. I should have listened to my instincts. Maybe I could have prevented this from happening."

"So you didn't know about the CIA's interest in my company before you got involved with me."

Kate knew where this was headed. "I swear to you that

I had absolutely *no idea*. What the Agency did to you was beyond reproach."

Brandon looked into the distance. "Bastards. They didn't want me licensing Sweeper, and when I refused to agree to their terms, they set me up to be attacked by these animals."

"They wanted to accomplish two objectives at once: keep you from licensing Sweeper and nail the terrorists by using the Y2K software—and you—as bait."

"And they screwed up on both fronts," he said. "They lost the fish *and* the bait. No wonder your agency gets so much bad press."

"*Former* agency. And yes, this wasn't one of its finest moments." Kate could think of a few other such moments.

"Well," he said. "For what it's worth, the only reason why I'm still alive's because of the little stunt that you pulled. Kidnapping the son of Slobodan Milosevic? I have to grant it to you, you're a tough cookie." He grinned.

She shrugged. "It's the first rule when dealing with someone who has taken something or someone you hold very dear. You retaliate by taking something they hold dear and then set up an exchange—while trying to stay alive in the process."

He looked at her long and hard with a mix of admiration and respect. "You're . . . *amazing.*"

"Save it for *after* we're out of here. I got you back, but Milosevic's son died. There's going to be hell to pay."

"Anything I can do to help?"

"You can start by telling me everything that's happened to you, everything that you know." As she said this she realized that she had violated her own rules with Brandon. She had released information *to* him first instead of collecting it *from* him. The realization further confirmed her feelings for him.

Brandon covered everything he remembered, from the moment he'd awakened inside his room-cell to his near-death encounter in that clearing halfway down the mountain. He also told Kate the way Dragan had tricked him into releasing the code, including his detailed recollection of the modern building where he had been held.

"There's one thing that doesn't make sense, though," he said. "Why are the Yugoslavs so damned interested in Y2K software?"

Kate related what Costner had said.

"*Of course,*" Brandon said, almost to himself. "Sweeper can be used to find any two-digit code, compliant *or* non-compliant."

"Did you actually see this computer center?"

Brandon shook his head. "But it was located in the same building, one floor above where I was being held, according to Dragan. Although after the way he tricked me I'm not really sure what to believe."

"Deception is a weapon that works both ways. I used it to get you back. Dragan Kundat used it to get you to release the code, capitalizing on the knowledge that you cared for me."

He grimaced. "Let's just say that it wasn't one of *my* finest moments. I can't believe I fell for it."

She cupped his face. "I'd say it was your *finest* moment. It shows me how much you care about me. And then helping that poor woman, a total stranger. You are indeed the man I knew you were."

"Is the CIA *really* coming to get us out of here in the morning?"

She sat up and turned to face him. "I was on the radio with them a little while ago. There's a chance we might have to postpone. The clouds are too low and it's very windy. I'll check with them again in a couple of hours."

The rugged cowboy, his hair messy, a stubble covering his cheeks and chin, gave her a puzzled look. "But I thought you said that. . . ." he stopped, realizing that she had lied to the Yugoslavs. He pulled her to him and gave her a kiss. "I'm going to have to keep an eye on you when we get back, little lady. You're too good at this."

Kate Donaldson smiled ever so slightly, before looking away, praying to be good enough to get Brandon and herself off this mountain alive.

16

Dawn.

The early morning sun pierced through breaks in the cloud coverage, striking the snow-covered cliffs with yellow and red-gold shafts of light. A strong wind swept through the mountains, its trilling sound mixing with the distant drone of helicopters echoing off of the snowy peaks.

Kate gazed at the sky with her powerful binoculars, fingering the adjusting wheel in between the lenses to bring the shapes into focus.

"I see three of them."

"Are they ours?" asked Brandon Holst. He was holding an MP5 submachine gun while they covered the southern edge of the small village, hiding behind the rubble of what had once been a house, based on the broken clay jars and remnants of clothing by their feet. They had left the school twenty minutes ago, shortly after Kate had gotten word from the *Fletcher* about the rescue helicopters en route.

"They're not supposed to be here for twenty minutes," she replied, shifting her binoculars to a waist-high rock wall, all that remained of another house. She could see Tref Vucic and Zoran peeking over the edge, looking at the sky. Zoran had a pair of binoculars.

Kate reached for the radio strapped to the utility belt hugging her waist. She dialed in the access password and was about to contact the rescue party when a bright flash preceded a missile, arcing down toward the clearing, its exhaust whooshing. A moment later the schoolhouse exploded, the blast thundering across the mountain range. A column of flames billowed up to the sky, like an erupting volcano, spewing rocks and dust across the clearing.

Her throat felt tight as the helicopters, Russian-made, hovered closer, machine guns blasting, strafing the clearing. She squinted, her ears ringing from the reports.

"We're under attack!" she shouted into her handheld radio. "Three helicopters. Repeat, three Yugoslav helicopters are firing on us! We need help. Fast!"

Static, followed by the cracking sound of Costner's voice coming through. "Read you loud and clear! We're on the way. Hang on!"

The helicopters stopped firing, hovering near the flaming wreckage, their rotors reflecting the orange and yellow flames. The smell of cordite assaulted her nostrils as a dozen ropes flipped out of the sides of the hovering craft, followed by men in camouflage gear rappelling toward the ground.

"Bad news," she said. "Time to hide in the fore—"

She froze when she spotted Zoran, an RPG launcher on his shoulder. The KLA guerrilla fired. From such close distance, the warhead covered the hundred feet separating it from the closest helicopter in two seconds.

The craft shook on impact, vanishing behind a sheet of flames, its main rotor severing from the fuselage, streaking across the sky like rotating scalpels, striking a second chopper, slicing through its fuselage and tangling with its rotor. The second helicopter also blew apart, dropping to the ground like a rock, the rappelling men beneath it screaming as the smoldering wreckage swallowed them.

Both helicopters crashed with an ear-piercing blast, the explosions dwarfing the flames and swirling smoke of the schoolhouse.

The third craft swiftly moved out of the way, dragging along the rappelling men, swatting them against the forest canopy. Many screamed, letting go, plummeting to the ground.

Zoran and Tref opened fire on the half a dozen Serbs who had made it safely to the clearing, all of whom sought shelter behind the rubble of fallen houses and began to return the fire. Two figures in flames screamed across the snowy clearing. Zoran and Tref ignored them, obviously wanting them to burn alive.

As Kate selected her targets, the surviving helicopter launched a missile toward the Yugoslav guerrillas, who disappeared behind a fist of flames and flying rocks.

"Your friends!" Brandon shouted over the noise, ducking beneath the wall as dust and debris fell over them.

Kate clutched her submachine gun, pointing the muzzle not at the surviving Serbs and their helicopter, scanning the clearing for surviving rebels, but toward the forest, the trees.

"This is not a battle we can win with this," she said, slapping the side of her weapon. "Come! Follow me!"

They crawled back in the snow, away from the wrecked house, caked with dust and pulverized rock, reaching the trees as shouts in Serbo-Croatian preceded bullets crashing into a pine to their left.

Running, they raced deeper into the forest, the helicopter's roar growing louder, the wind from its rotor rustling the trees, bathing them with snow just as its grotesque silhouette whooshed by like a bird of prey.

"This way," Kate said, cutting sharp left, doing the unexpected, running not *away* from the clearing but *parallel* to it, keeping it up for a couple of minutes, following the twists and turns of a frozen game trail, splashing into a narrow stream.

Her wet jeans clung to the bottom of her legs, numbing them as they followed the icy stream for fifty feet, until it disappeared beyond a cluster of trees. Crossing it, continuing down the snowy trail, they made another sharp left, heading back to the village, crossing the stream once more beyond the thick pines.

Kate knew she couldn't outrun the Serbs, not only because of Brandon Holst's condition but also because the fresh snow left a clear trail for their pursuers. Sooner or later the better-equipped and -rested troops would catch up with them. She had to find a way to reverse the trap, to go beyond her delay tactic of altering the point of crossing a stream. That would only slow down the enemy, not lose it. Sooner or later the Serbs, reaching the stream, would realize the trick and search up and down the banks for the point where their footprints picked back up again, then continue the search.

Tired, shivering from the cold, their pants freezing below their knees from getting wet in the stream, Kate and Brandon reached the tree line almost two hundred feet from where they had started, hiding behind a fallen log, her weapon searching for a target, finding three soldiers inspecting the area. The rest had already gone after them, probably spotting their trail by now, following it. It was just a matter of time before they came upon them from behind, encircling them.

She glanced at Brandon, noticing the strain on his face from their short sprint through the woods.

"Stay with me, honey."

He nodded with obvious effort, swallowing hard,

breathing deeply, blinking, trying to focus. "I'm . . . with you," he finally said, swallowing again.

"All right. I need you to get the one on the right. I'll take care of the two on the left," she told Brandon, pointing at the Serbs, just under a hundred feet away, their dark-olive uniforms contrasting sharply with the snow shrouding the ground and trees. "Just like at the rifle range. Can you do it?"

He nodded.

Kate lined up the forward sight of her MP5 with the leftmost figure, a bulky man in camouflage gear and a crew cut, his frozen breath curling upward like a steam engine as he walked, weapon held in front as he searched the snow-capped woods.

"Got your target?"

"Yes," he replied.

"On my count, three, two, one, now!"

Kate and Brandon fired in unison, the reports thundering, drowning the rattling of the helicopter circling the clearing.

The outer Serbs fell to the ground, both dropping their weapons, collapsing. Kate already had the middle figure lined up, firing two additional rounds. One struck him flat in the chest. The second missed, but a third round, fired by Brandon Holst, scored a perfect shot in the face, which turned crimson as the soldier fell.

While the helicopter hovered back above the clearing, Kate and Brandon doubled back carefully stepping in their original footsteps, listening to incomprehensible shouts of anger mixed with splashing sounds.

"Hurry," she said, slightly ahead of him as they retraced their path for thirty feet. Brandon stumbled once, nearly losing his footing. Kate jumped back, steadying him.

"I . . . I can't go any further. Light-headed . . . I'm feeling dizzy."

"All right," she said. "See these bushes?" She pointed at the shrubs flanking the game trail.

He nodded.

"Good. Then do as I do." Kate jumped over the frozen shrubbery to their right, knees buckling, rolling down into a ravine on the other side. Brandon followed her, grunting as he landed on his side, sliding a dozen feet down to her.

"Are you all right?" she whispered.

Half-buried in the knee-high snow that had accumulated at the bottom of the V-shaped ravine, Brandon Holst winced in pain, his lips turning purple, shivering. "Never been . . . better," he mumbled, puffs of condensed air forming around him as he breathed in short sobbing gasps.

"I can see that," she replied. "Can you walk?"

"I can try." He managed to stand with help but collapsed back onto the snow after a few steps.

"I'm . . . sorry," he mumbled, eyes closed. "Leave me here."

"No. I'm not getting separated from you again."

"Don't be silly . . . you're the professional. I'll slow you . . . you down."

"No."

"Alone . . . you have a chance . . . to save us both."

Kate heard noises from above but couldn't see the game trail, which also meant that the soldiers on top could not see them. Their hastily spoken words mixed with the constant drone from the helicopter, which continued to fly over the area.

Leaning down, she whispered in his ear, "Do not make a noise, but shoot anyone who comes near."

Brandon Holst nodded, wiggling his index finger. "I may not be able to walk . . . but I can still shoot."

She moved quickly, propping him up, resting his back against the dry wall of the ravine, removing her waterproof coat, draping it over him before shoveling snow on his feet and legs, making it impossible for anyone glancing down from the game trail to see Brandon.

"Don't . . ." he said. "Keep your . . . coat. You will need it."

"Too bulky," she said. "It'll slow me down. You need it more. Now don't argue."

He nodded.

Wearing only a thick sweater and a flannel shirt underneath, already unable to feel her legs from the knees down, Kate shivered, hoping that keeping her body in motion would prevent her core temperature from dropping.

She kissed him, his lips trembling, dry. "I'll be right back."

"I'm . . . I'm not going anywhere."

Hating to leave him behind but out of choices, Kate rushed up the ravine, losing sight of Brandon as the dry creek curved away from the village. She forced control into her thoughts, convincing herself that Brandon was safe, that the Serbs would not be able to spot him, that—

A bullet ricocheted off a rock with a high pitched trill. Kate dove for the cover of a fallen log, one end of which dipped halfway into the ravine, a layer of snow covering its upper side.

Her chest heaving, she scrambled beneath it as another bullet hit it, chunks of wood and bark exploding.

Reaching the opposite side, she squinted over the snow caking the log, scanning both sides of the ravine, flinching when a second bullet struck a large boulder to her right, where the end of the log rested. A splinter of rock cut the side of her neck.

Ignoring the warm liquid running down her shoulder, she focused on the origin of that last shot. It had come from behind her, meaning that there were Serbs on both sides of the log. Her only chance for survival rested in the hope that the Serbs were only on the village side of the ravine, on the frozen game trail.

She charged toward the side of the ravine where the shots had come from to force the enemy to lean over the edge in order to get a clear line of sight down the ravine. As she did this, she also huddled by the boulder supporting the log, covering at least one of her flanks, using the MP5's muzzle to protect her other flank, aiming it anxiously above her, then to the side, then back over her, realizing the futility of her situation. She couldn't stay here. The enemy knew where she was and would flush her out with smoke, or worse, with a grenade. Besides, without a coat she couldn't stay put for long. Her strategy for survival depended on mobility, avoiding hypothermia through exercise.

Taking her chances while in motion, Kate lunged away from the log, keeping her upper body leaning toward the wall of the ravine, making herself a difficult target for anyone firing down into the icy gorge.

Glancing upward, searching for a target, her peripheral vision distinguished the blur of a man in camouflage gear rushing toward her around the next bend in the ravine. Someone had already jumped into the snowy creek and was clearing it out from this end.

Reflexes overtook deliberation, commanding her muscles as she dove behind a mound, bullets stabbing the rocky walls where she had been just a moment ago, spraying shards of rock and pebbles over her. She fired back on instinct, before her mind could really focus on the target.

A male scream told her at least one of her rounds had found its mark.

Instinctively, she rolled over, facing the top of the ravine, her MP5 nearly empty. The trees above her were alive from the downwash of the helicopter, its moving shadow visible through small breaks in the rustling canopy.

Kate charged forward once more, her boots kicking snow as she reached the man she had shot, blood spurting from his neck. He was still alive, choking on his own blood, angered eyes fixated on Kate, who slung her MP5 around her back and grabbed the man's weapon, a Kalashnikov AK-74. She knew the weapon well, having become proficient with its predecessor, the venerable AK-47.

Powdery snow exploded to her right, a second bullet striking the soldier in the chest, blood jetting like a fountain, spraying her legs, staining the pristine frost. Both shots had come from behind, from the game trail side of the ravine.

Again she jumped to the same rocky wall, getting herself out of the immediate line of sight, moving farther away, relief sweeping through her when spotting a sharp bend in the ravine.

Cautiously, she followed it, finding no one lurking around the corner, racing away from the village, reaching for her radio to contact Costner.

Her gloved hand slapped an empty case strapped to her belt. She had lost it, somewhere, maybe when she had jumped into the—

A bullet nipped the collar of her sweater, forcing her to dive once more, landing behind a boulder, peering around it. Another round splintered a chunk of rock before it ricocheted into the opposite wall of the ravine.

Kate jerked back, spotting the silhouettes of two men peeking around the bend in the ravine, both clutching weapons pointed at her. Her instincts once again took command of her movements.

Dropping back down behind the boulder, Kate let loose three short bursts with the AK-74, forcing the Serbs to sneak behind the corner, her gunfire pummeling the rocky wall, creating multiple explosions.

In the same motion, she jumped onto the boulder, using the precious seconds that her fire had bought her wisely, taking another leap from the top of the boulder to the edge of the ravine, rolling out of sight, by a row of frozen sagebrush, shattering hundreds of tiny icicles layering the dormant vegetation. Her woolen sweater, without the insulating layer of the waterproof coat, grew damper, chilling her.

Her forehead aching with tension, Kate clenched her teeth, ignoring the cold. She rose to a deep crouch and dashed into the forest, drawing the threat away from Brandon, moving from tree to tree. She stopped after a minute, her chest heaving, the Kalashnikov in her hands.

Gazing back, struggling to see in the murky woods, she finally spotted three figures roughly a hundred feet away, their silhouettes backlit by shafts of sunshine from the clearing.

The men abruptly split. One raced to her right, disappearing in the dense forest. Another cut left. The third came straight toward her.

She scrambled away from them, taking in the chilled air through her nostrils, her lungs burning, her thighs protesting the extreme effort as she reached a trail that angled up toward the snow-capped peak overlooking the deserted village.

The helicopter made a noisy pass overhead, rustling the canopy, bathing her with snow from the tangled boughs, unable to see her through the dense foliage. Kate kicked her boots against the icy rocks, slipping, trying again, sliding, persisting, clambering up the slope, struggling to reach a vantage point that would even out the playing field.

The terrain leveled off. Her instincts forced her to go left, away from the trap the Serbs were springing for her. She needed to attack the enemy one at a time, from a single flank.

Divide and conquer.

The snowy woods blended into a tunnel of brown and green and white as she raced past countless trees, beyond moss-slick slabs, the frozen jeans clinging to her skin and making her legs feel like logs, dragging her down, slowing her progress.

Mustering strength, Kate reached a gap between two large boulders, peering at the half-light beyond the pine boughs, desperately trying to spot the shape of her quarry. She waited, shivering, her body temperature dropping, the damp sweater stripping her of heat.

A shadow detached itself from the trunk of a wide pine, dashing across the snow like an apparition, vanishing once more behind another tree, then repeated the process, moving toward a spot a dozen feet to her right, obviously not realizing she hid here.

An edge.

Kate had gotten an advantage over the well-armed Serbs. They had lost her in the woods and were now sweeping the area, hoping that she would make a mistake and somehow telegraph her presence.

Breathing deeply, she lowered the Kalashnikov. The AK-74 would accomplish precisely what her hunters hoped for, drawing them like ships to a beacon in the middle of a storm. Her right hand—aching from the cold slipping through the glove—reached for her knife.

Crawling around the boulders, Kate dragged herself across the snow-shrouded hill, silently, with purpose, burying herself in the knee-deep snow like an Arctic predator, furtive eyes following the silhouette dashing between trees.

She waited, letting the figure creep closer, within her reach, his camouflage fatigues just half a dozen feet from her. She could see his face, his expression, his hard-edged Slavic features, a rifle she could not recognize firmly clutched in front of him, the muzzle pointed away from her.

Kate considered her options, wondering if her legs would allow her to move fast enough to close the gap before he could react.

Out of choices, hindered by the cold, realizing that the

longer she waited the less elasticity her body would have, Kate lunged, rising from the snow like a winter ghost, jolting the man, shoving him against the trunk of a pine. Her knife found its target, the soft skin between his Adam's apple and the top of the sternum, slicing through the larynx, blood and foam exploding.

He dropped his weapon, drowning in his own blood, unable to scream, to shout, to warn. She pulled out the knife, the sound of ripping cartilage and tissue mixing with the constant drone of the helicopter, still searching the area, still looking for her.

The Serb collapsed. Kate stripped him of his thick coat. She removed her wet sweater, tossing it aside, cringing from the extreme cold, wrapping herself with the coat, concerned that her body temperature might have fallen so much that she might not be able to warm herself back up.

No time to analyze.

Shivering, the former CIA operative doubled back, going after the man in the middle, her joints aching with every step, the knife once more secured to her belt, the Kalashnikov in her hands. She reconsidered her strategy, realizing her lack of choices with the second figure, her vanishing energy altering her original plan. She lacked the strength for a second stealth attack. The coat shielded her from the cold but did little to regain lost heat, to stop her lips from quivering. Her face grew numb. Her vision grew cloudier. Soon she would lose her ability to—

A powerful explosion startled her, the shock wave dislodging snow from overhead branches, caking her. She heard a rumble in the trees, heard a second blast.

Kate ignored it, moving across the hill in a crouch, slower now, praying to spot the second Serb before he spotted her.

A gun cracked, the sound muffled, distant. Another report whispered across the woods. The sounds originated from different locations, confusing her. Who was firing?

And why wasn't Kate seeing the round impacting a nearby object? Why didn't she see it strike a tree or ricochet off of a boulder?

Puzzled, disoriented, she stopped to listen, to appraise. Someone had changed the rules, and before she could proceed she needed time to reevaluate her—

Kate slipped on an icy slab, dropping the weapon, bumping the crown of her head against a rock. The blow disoriented her, tunneling her vision, blurring it, but not to the point that she couldn't see an incoming shadow.

She blinked, crawling back, pawing through the snow, away from the threat, away from the hands that lifted her with incredible ease and slammed her against a tree with barbarian strength, shouting words she could not understand.

Her weakened body tried to fight back, her right knee rising on instinct, trying to reach the man's groin, her kneecap colliding with a solid thigh instead.

Kate kicked again, and again, frustrated at her inability to stop the attack, at the—

A blow to the side of her face stunned her. More foreign words followed as he shoved her on the ground, as she felt his hands on her jeans, yanking them down, as snow stung her bare buttocks.

The nightmare returned with ghostly clarity, the hands spreading her legs, the dark alley in San Antonio, the visions of the Muslim women, ravaged, violated, slaughtered.

Kate heard the cracking of wood, watched the blurry figure clearing the leaves off a long branch, sharpening one end.

No! They weren't—They weren't going to—

She tried to scream, to protest, to shout in anger, but the cold had constricted her throat, letting nothing but short sobbing gasps escape in the form of puffs of white veiling the animal on top of her. The man tried to violate her with the pole. Kate used every ounce of strength left to jerk sideways, cringing in pain as the pole stabbed her inner thigh, missing its intended target by inches.

She kicked her legs, feeling the sharp object turn inside her leg, grinding against her femur, as she twitched in pain, before the brute pulled it out.

The sound of multiple shots mixed with her own screams. The reports sounded far away, detached, followed by a grunt from the Serb, who collapsed over her.

She kicked again, banging her fists against his limp bulk, pushing him aside, crawling back, the forest spinning, growing murkier, her lower body numb from the cold.

Then another figure emerged, followed by others. One of them whispered her name, reaching her side, unseen hands pulling up her jeans, covering her, lifting her.

Kate Donaldson let it all go, surrendering herself to the cold, succumbing to exhaustion, letting these men with unseen faces carry her away.

17

Brandon Holst sat at the head of the table in the officers' lounge of the Spruance-class destroyer. The software entrepreneur, tired and cranky, regarded the group sitting around him with resentment. Brandon and Kate had arrived at the vessel via helicopter, following a last-minute rescue by the CIA. NATO jets from a base in Italy had cleared the area for a pair of Navy helicopters from the *Fletcher* and another American destroyer in the area. Kate, unconscious, had been taken to the ship's infirmary, where the surgeon was able to restore her body temperature and close the wounds on her neck and thigh. Brandon had checked on her just ten minutes ago. She was still sleeping, resting from one hell of a battle against the Serbs. Brandon knew he should also be sleeping, recovering his strength, but he couldn't bring himself to do so until after he had settled his business with the CIA.

He reached for the steaming mug of coffee in front of him, taking a sip, setting it back down.

"I realize that you've been through a lot, Mr. Holst," began the man who had introduced himself as Mike Costner, Chief of Counterterrorism of the CIA. He was in his mid-forties, the stereotypical spy, brown hair, average height and build, nondescript face, eyes that seemed green but could also pass as blue. "But I'm afraid this is not over yet."

"Really?"

"The Y2K software," Costner continued. "It's still in the hands of Milosevic."

"Why is that my fault?"

Costner exchanged glances with his poker-faced colleagues, one of whom leaned over and whispered something into Costner's ear.

"Exactly what kind of information did Ms. Donaldson disclose to you regarding this case?"

"Nothing I didn't already know ... or strongly suspect."

Brandon shifted his gaze toward the man he knew as Astor Kendell, the silver-haired CIA man who had posed as a businessman back in Austin. Kendell looked away.

"We made a mistake," Costner conceded. "But right now we need your help to keep them from using this code against us."

"They have already started using it," said Kendell, speaking for the first time.

Brandon Holst turned to the silver-haired operative. "I don't think I want to hear *anything* that comes out of your mouth, whoever you are. You're lucky I'm not carrying a gun right now."

"Mr. Holst, please. Don't let your animosity against our agency punish the American public. The Yugoslavs have already launched three cyber-attacks against us. One against the Pentagon. The second against a New York bank. The third against the Dallas–Fort Worth International Airport, right in your own backyard. Fortunately, all of the attacks were quite localized.''

Costner went on to explain the nifty trick that Milosevic's rogue scientists were using, firing their code in the form of a virus, which altered two-digit code while also advancing the local system clock beyond Y2K.

''Our scientists can mitigate the attacks now,'' added Costner, ''because of their localized nature. But when January 1st comes along, they can essentially carpet bomb us, and we have very little to fight back with.''

''How do you know that the cyber-attacks came from them?''

''We were able to trace them back to Belgrade. We need to find a way to pinpoint their origin better than that. We obviously can't just bomb the entire place.''

''If I help you do that,'' Brandon Holst, the businessman, asked. ''What are you willing to do in return?''

Costner exchanged more glances with his men, this time receiving whispers from two of them before replying to Brandon, ''What do you have in mind?''

Brandon told them, taking just under a minute to do so. ''I want it in writing, and then I need access to a telephone to call Austin and confirm the transaction.''

Costner and his entourage stood and left the room. The Chief of Counterterrorism returned alone five minutes later.

''Do we have a deal?'' asked Brandon Holst.

Costner nodded, handing him a cellular phone.

18

Erik Haas strolled around the computer room, listening to the incessant clicking of his subordinates as they refined his creation.

Haas walked with pride, having been commended by Slobodan Milosevic himself for the three successful cyberstrikes against the United States. The German scientist had given the Yugoslav president a weapon unlike any other in his arsenal. Now he could retaliate for every bombing strike ever launched against his country, against his people, against his race. No longer was his country isolated, at the mercy of NATO, unable to fight back. Haas's Cekic had changed all of that, giving Milosevic a power that the Yugoslav president considered so priceless, that he had personally not only congratulated Haas, but had also provided him with a luxurious apartment, a private Mercedes limousine, and unlimited access to every club and restaurant in town—in addition to a healthy injection of Eurodollars into his private account in Dresden.

Haas had committed to strike the United States a minimum of once per day. So far he had done so thrice in less than two days, exceeding expectations in the way that brought out the best in Slobodan Milosevic. The attacks, in addition to punishing the Americans, also served another purpose: they established that Milosevic's Cekic would spell chaos at the turn of the millennium unless NATO countries agreed to a list of twenty concessions, carefully drafted by Slobodan Milosevic and his closest advisers.

And here Erik Haas was, in the middle of this global event. He was now the best-paid programmer in the Balkans, probably in most of Europe for that matter, being chauffeured around in the company of beautiful women, all courtesy of a grateful president.

Haas had finally gotten it all, the money, the respect, the fame. He breathed deeply, enjoying his success, stopping by one of the windows overlooking the Sava River.

That's when he first saw it, a glint on the horizon, like a speckle of crimson light, but also pulsating, and with a dark center. The distant halo-like figure grew in size in the few seconds that it took the German programmer to realize what it was, memories of old CNN footage suddenly flooding his mind, also filling it with the realization of his imminent fate.

Before he could react, to run, to scream for help, the missile filled the window. His last thought was the regret that he had not been successful in convincing Milosevic to archive a copy of the virus off-site, at another location, in case the computer room was compromised. But the paranoid Milosevic wouldn't hear of it, concerned about security leaks, about the off-site copy getting stolen. Inside the Sava Center, with its many guards and multiple access codes, the Y2K software was well protected, isolated from other hackers—but an easy target for a well-placed Tomahawk.

The missile was black and red, and large, very large.

19

Kate Donaldson saw herself racing through a dark alley, figures in black pursuing her, closing in. She tried to go faster, to move away from them, kicking her sneakers against the asphalt, ignoring her burning legs, her throbbing temples, her constricting throat as she swallowed a lump of fear, as she filled her lungs with the frigid air, as her feet sank in the snow, slowing her.

She tripped on an exposed root and fell head first into the frosty powder layering the forest. The snow stung her face, chilling her as she staggered to her feet, slipping on an icy slab, falling again, bumping her head on a fallen log, her vision blurring from the impact, her mind losing focus.

The shadows converged on her, gloved hands pinning her to the snow, unbuckling her pants, lowering them . . .

Kate Donaldson screamed, soaked in perspiration, sitting up in bed. She saw a large figure entering the room, racing toward her.

She jerked back, bracing herself, pulling the white sheets up to her chest.

"Kate! Are you all right?"

She blinked, clearing her vision, recognizing the voice, welcoming the arms that embraced her.

She buried her face in his shoulder, closing her eyes, surrendering herself to the comfort of his nearness.

"You're safe with me."

"Where . . . where am I?" she asked, putting a hand to his face, blinking, swallowing.

"Aboard the USS *Fletcher,* in the Adriatic."

"All I remember was this Serb . . . this . . . *animal,* he was going to . . ." The soldier had tried to impale her, just like those Muslim women.

"The CIA," he said, still hugging her, stroking the back of her head. "They got there in time. They found me first and I sent them your way." He spent another five minutes relating how they had gotten her on board the helicopter, their flight back to the ship, the emergency surgery, the deal he'd made with the CIA, the Tomahawk strike, the satellite confirmation of the kill. "So it's all over," he added.

She frowned. "Why do I feel that it's not quite over yet?"

"You're too paranoid," he replied, kissing her forehead. "I saw the satellite pictures. We blasted their little high-tech operation into hell. There've been no cyber-attacks from Belgrade since."

Kate stood, grimacing from the pain shooting up her left leg. She lifted the white gown she was wearing, exposing her upper thigh, sighing at a pink seam on the inside of her leg, traversed by dark stitches. "The first rule about this business, dear," she said, lowering the gown, "is that nothing, absolutely *nothing,* is ever quite over. As far as being too paranoid, living in a state of constant paranoia is the *only* thing that kept me alive for almost two decades, and that will also keep *us* alive in the future. I call that operating in Yellow Mode, always keeping a close watch on everything that's going on around you, never letting your guard down. I thought I was out and forced myself to let my guard down. It almost cost us our lives.''

"Who should we be afraid of? Do you think that Milosevic might send a retaliatory strike against us?''

She shrugged. "I know he holds me responsible for the death of his son. We also took away a very powerful weapon. Based on everything that I've read about him, he will not be forgetting about this little incident any time soon. You're looking at someone who has been marked for termination. At this moment I'm quite certain that the word is out about me in the independent contractor community. The offered price will be high. There will be many takers. For the rest of my life, at least while Milosevic is around, I will be a target, and a threat to those around me. The kind of people that I'm talking about will not hesitate to kill bystanders to get me.''

"In that case I'm a target as well, because like it or not,'' he hugged her tight, "you're not getting rid of me that easily.''

Kate Donaldson pushed him back. "I don't think you understand the level of the problem. I'm going to have to vanish, to disappear, to assume a new identity, known to no one, including my former employer.''

Brandon grinned, embracing her again. She tried to resist but in her current state, he easily overpowered her, even with his chest wound. "I don't think *you* understand,'' he said, his face inches from her. The bulky cowboy kissed the tip of her nose. "When I told Costner that I still had a copy of Sweeper, he offered us lifetime protection in exchange for the code.''

"That's not good enough. Every network can be penetrated, even the CIA and the FBI. The witness protection program works fine for protecting people against normal crooks, but not against an international assassin.''

His grin broadened. ''You're not giving me enough credit. While you were out I had a little more coaching on the art of vanishing from our old friend Rich Jones, who, by the way, vanished into Texas ten years ago, after someone from the Middle East put a contract on his head during his days with the Defense Intelligence Agency.''

Kate was confused now. ''So, what did you do?''

''I sold Costner not only the location of Milosevic's computer center, but also Sweeper *and* Holst Enterprises.''

She was stunned. ''You sold him . . . but *why?*''

''Because,'' he said, pressing her against him, ''nothing, absolutely *nothing,* matters if you're not there to share it with me.''

''How much did you get?''

He told her, and the amount stunned her even more. ''They gave you *that* much?''

''It's already in a numbered bank account in the Cayman Islands . . . *our* bank account. We just need to figure out two things, honey.'' He ran a hand beneath her gown.

''What's that?'' she said, her eyes narrowing as he caressed her torso.

''First we need a new place to live.''

''I have a few opinions on that,'' she replied, enjoying his touch.

He kissed her on the lips. ''I figured you would.''

''And what's the second thing?''

''A good knife.''

''What on earth for?''

''To carve your name next to mine on the family tree at the ranch,'' Brandon said, and he took her in his arms.